THE FLAVOUR OF OUR DEEDS

THE GOLDEN REDEPENNINGS

BOOK FIVE

JUDE KNIGHT

THE FLAVOUR OF OUR DEEDS

When Luke finally admits to loving Kitty, she thinks their troubles are over. They are just beginning.

"It is a bitter thought to an avaricious spirit that, by and by, all these accumulations must be left behind. We can only carry away from this world the flavour of our good or evil deeds."
Henry Ward Beecher

Kitty Stocke loves her brother-in-law's gamekeeper—has done for six years. Luke keeps her at arms length. Social class, wealth, an age gap, and the secrets he hides stand between them.

But then his secrets catch up with him. When murderers come for him and Paul, the boy everyone believes to be his son, he goes on the run. Kitty follows. He might need the help of her powerful relatives and friends.

The villain has Luke arrested on a false charge of murder, but Luke's allies turn the tables. With the villain behind bars and Luke's secrets all disclosed, the way is clear for Luke and Kitty to marry and settle at the estate that is Paul's by right, in the far north of England.

However, the villain escapes prison and is determined to destroy their happiness. In Northumberland, he is the one with the allies. Soon, Luke and Kitty are fighting for their future and their lives, hindered by hidden enemies and helped by unexpected friends.

Only courage and an abiding trust in one another will win them the day.

If you love stories where adventure, romance and history combine, join Luke and Kitty in this fifth novel of the Golden Redepenning series.

PART 1: AN UNUSUAL COURTSHIP

CHAPTER 1

"Killing a boy? I don't like it."

The gravelly voice came from the other side of the stone wall in the shade of which Kitty Stocke was picking violets.

"Devil take it, talk French," ordered another voice, in that language. This voice was that of a gentleman, light and refined. "Can't have a villager warning them."

Kitty lowered herself to the soil, the violets forgotten. Her little dog Pierrot hurried up, ready to play now that she was down at his level. She lifted him into her lap, and put a hand over his muzzle in a signal to be silent. He was a continental dwarf spaniel, and very smart.

The speakers were on horseback. She'd heard the clopping of the hooves in the little lane beyond the garden wall and glimpsed them approaching. They could, perhaps, see over the wall into the garden, but if she stayed in the shadow of the wall, she would be invisible to them.

"I don't kill children," gravelly voice insisted, his French stilted and uncertain.

"You do what I tell you," the gentleman insisted. "But, if it makes you feel better, I will take care of the brat while you deal with my bastard relative."

"We go in tonight?" That was gravelly voice.

"Tonight," the gentleman confirmed. "The earl and his family are away, except for the two spinster sisters, and they are unlikely to go visiting the gamekeeper and his son. We take our runaways out tonight, and no one will know, perhaps for days."

Kitty stopped breathing rather than gasp. A general concern for an anonymous victim had suddenly become very personal.

"There's a school," said gravelly voice, diffidently. "The teacher might check if the boy does not turn up."

"Why should he care?" The gentleman sneered. "But let us be safe. Today is Thursday. I shall meet you here tomorrow at sundown. Now go. Best if we are not seen together."

The clopping of hooves resumed, one horse going west towards the church, the other in the opposite direction, turning north towards the village at the end of the lane.

To the inn, perhaps? And if so, was it gravelly voice or the gentleman?

Kitty suppressed the urge to stand up and peer after them. She could not afford to be caught. She had to warn Luke, the gamekeeper, though why anyone should want to kill him and his son Paul, she had no idea. *His bastard relative.* The gentleman was related to Luke. What made no sense to her would probably be quite clear to Luke.

She waited until she could no longer hear the horses. She had intended to leave the way she had come in, through the gate at the bottom of the garden. But if the rider who had gone west had paused within sight of that gate, she would be exposed and stopped before she could reach Luke.

Instead, she gathered the violets she had dropped while she listened, picked Pierrot up in the other hand, and knocked on the back door of the cottage.

"Mrs Deeken, I thought I'd just let you know that I found the violets and picked a few of them."

The cottager, a tenant of her brother-in-law, greeted her with a smile. "You are welcome to them, Lady Catherine. Is that all you want? That little bunch?" She wiped her floury hands on her apron.

Kitty managed a smile. "Just a bunch for my dressing table," she assured Mrs Deeken. "They shall scent the whole room." She suppressed her impatience. The villains would not act until tomorrow night. She had plenty of time. "Most of the buds are not open yet. I would be grateful if I might come back in a week or so to start picking what I will need to make perfume."

"Any time you wish, Lady Catherine. Pretty little things, but I've no use for them. Just come when you like." She was too polite to rush her unexpected caller away, but Kitty caught the anxious glance she cast over her shoulder at the bread dough on her table.

Kitty hated to press her, but needs must. "May I trouble you to be let out through your front door, Mrs Deeken? I have a couple of things to do in the village, and it will save me a few steps." And now she sounded like a spoiled aristocrat who never walked if she could take a carriage.

Mrs Deeken did not comment, however, but simply led the way through the kitchen and into the front room to open the door to the road that ran beside the river all the way to the village.

"Thank you. I am sorry to have troubled you," Kitty said.

"No trouble at all," Mrs Deeken assured her. "You come back for those violets any time, Lady Catherine."

Kitty made herself stroll, though her heart was insisting she break into a run. Along beside the green, past the inn and the village shops, past more cottages to the lane that led to the manor house.

She saw only villagers, but the murderous stranger could be inside the inn or in one of the shops. Not that she planned to look. She had to reach Luke.

Safely over the stile and on the grounds of the estate, she continued to walk, though slightly more quickly. She was still within sight of the cottages. Then the path turned a corner past a small group of trees, and she began running up the hill towards the wood in which the gamekeeper had his cottage.

"Bullseye!" crowed Paul. "That's all five, Dad!"

"You can barely count the third one," grouched Luke Mogg. "It was right on the line." The boy was better by far than Luke had been at twelve. Not just with a bow, but with knife, pistol, and bare-handed. Even now, Paul could hold his own against most grown men. Once he had his adult growth and strength, perhaps Luke would be able to relax a little.

"Let's try for five more," he suggested.

Paul put five more arrows into the turf in front of him, and Luke held up one hand while fixing his eyes on his watch. The exercise was not just about accuracy, but speed. Paul could count only those arrows that hit the target within sixty seconds.

As his hand came down and the first arrow flew, he heard the sound of someone running. "Stop, Paul. Someone is coming down the path."

A moment later, Lady Kitty burst into the clearing. Her face lit up when she saw him, and she didn't slow, but continued running until she was standing before him.

As always, Luke's heart ached at the sight of her. Lady Catherine Stocke, sister to his employer's wife, as far out of his reach as a star, and as tempting as a siren. Especially since he knew she thought herself in love with him.

The Earl of Chirbury, his employer, would dismiss him if he knew Luke loved her in return, and kill him if Luke ever hinted he had once stolen a kiss. A mistake, that. His birth, his age, and his lack of wealth made him an unfit match for a lady such as her, even if he was not a fugitive. Even if he was free. As it was, his self-imposed mission barred him from any personal happiness until he had seen Paul safe at last. He should regret the kiss, but he could not.

How far had she run? She had set her ridiculous little dog at her feet, and the wee thing was peering up at her as if worried. Lady

Kitty was trying to talk, but was heaving for breath. He made out the words, "Warn you."

He cast a glance the way she had come and gestured with a nod and a lift of an eyebrow to Paul. The boy nocked another arrow.

"Take your time, my lady," Luke advised. "Do you want a drink? Here, come and sit down." He offered his arm, and she let him support her to the bench by his front door, while Paul stood sentry over the path.

She shut her eyes and took several deep breaths, then opened them again. "I came to warn you, Luke. I heard two men planning your murder. Yours and Paul's."

Luke cast another anxious glance at the path.

"Tomorrow night," she assured him. "They are coming for you tomorrow night."

"You had better tell me the whole story in order." He thought about it. "Me and Paul." He called out to the boy. "Paul! Put the equipment away, would you? Then come and hear what Lady Kitty has to say. Now, my lady, how about I get you a cup of tea or a lemonade while we wait for Paul?"

She accepted a lemonade, made fresh with lemons from the earl's orangery, and he'd brought a glass each for the three of them by the time Paul joined them.

She accepted hers and started straight into her story. "I was collecting violets at our old cottage in the village when I heard two horsemen talking in the lane on the other side of the wall." She made a succinct job of her report, as he would have expected. Lady Kitty was a clever lady.

"I wonder how they found us," Paul commented.

Lady Kitty's questions were in her eyes, but she did not voice them.

"We leave tonight," Luke decided. "Start packing, Paul. You know what to take." Paul nodded and went into the cottage.

"Tonight?" Lady Kitty asked.

"If we go tomorrow, someone will see the direction we take," he explained. "Thanks to you, we can get a day's start."

Still, she asked no questions. "What can I do to help? Food? I can make up a basket."

He hesitated, then decided Uncle Baldwin was unlikely to get any information out of the kitchen staff at Longford House. "That would be a help, but please ask them not to tell anyone."

"I will pack the basket myself," she told him, "and only speak to Cook about it. The fewer people who know the better."

What a heroine she was. She deserved something of an explanation—indeed, Uncle Baldwin had given her some of the clues himself. "The man you heard, the one in charge, is my uncle, my father's brother. He tried to kill Paul eight years ago when my father died. I took the child and ran."

"And now you will run again," she said, her curiosity alive in her eyes.

"I am my father's eldest son," he told her, since she was polite enough and strong-minded enough not to ask. "Paul is his youngest and only legitimate son, and inherited his estate and his title."

Her eyes widened, but all she said was, "I take it your surname is not Mogg. Are you really called Lucas?"

That was her question? She had nothing to say about him being base-born?

"Lucius. And Paul is one of Paul's names. I had better do my own packing. Are you going to be able to make it up to the house?"

"I am quite recovered," Lady Kitty assured him. "I will bring the basket down just after dark."

Luke didn't like the idea of her out in the dark on her own, even in the park.

"I will meet you by the kitchen door an hour after sunset," he said.

CHAPTER 2

Kitty was in Cook's private sitting room, packing foodstuffs into saddle bags. She had picked them up from the tack room on her way back from making the short ride to the steward's house on the far side of the estate.

Cook had assured Kitty she would collect the items when she was unobserved and set them out in her room, but even if people saw her taking ham or bread or apples into her own quarters, no one would dare to question it. The good lady ran her kitchen with military precision.

There was enough food for several days, by which time their horses could take them far away from here. They would have to take their horses, at least as far as Chipping Longford and the public coach. If it was her, she would go the other way, straight up the Cotswold Edge and into the wild country beyond, hiding while the horses rested, sleeping rough, and never going into a village or town or even onto the more widely used roads, until far away from Longford Court.

She was counting on Luke making the same assessment.

He was illegitimate. She supposed that was another reason he refused to acknowledge his attraction to her, beyond that one searing kiss. He had stepped back and apologised, insisting he was too old for her and she would forget him once she made her debut and moved in Society.

She had done so. As the ward of the Earl of Chirbury and youngest sister of his countess, she had not been able to avoid suitors. Not only did she have a generous dowry, she had had a figure that suited the current fashions and her colouring and face were pleasant, if unremarkable. She also had relatives in a large proportion of the titled families of England, a pleasing temperament, and an attractive singing voice.

As one of her suitors informed her when she could not stop him from proposing, she would make a very ornamental wife. She had no difficulty declining that proposal and all the others.

Indeed, a suitor who refused to be discouraged was the reason she was in Longford and not in London with her sister and her sister's husband.

Mr Hardwicke-Chalmers had proposed three times, and took her repeated rejections as maidenly shyness. Her! Shy! The man was either deluded or stupid. He had decided he could overlook the flaws in her character in favour of her dowry, her aristocratic connections, and her appearance. He had assured her he did not mind her being over the age for marriage. Nor did he object overly to her being too outspoken and independent, since his mother would commit herself to correcting those faults.

His insistence on following her from event to event and trying to monopolise her attention had spoiled her usual pleasure in dancing, meeting her friends, and visiting London's museums, libraries, theatre and other entertainments. In the end, she had begged off the last two months of the Season, hoping the pest and his mother would fix their sights on some other poor female in her absence.

Kitty agreed with his assessment of what he was pleased to call her faults, and she fully intended to continue being outspoken and independent. As to her age, she was twenty-three, and she supposed she would go on being unmarried as year followed year, until she dwindled into old age.

For Luke was wrong. She had not forgotten him and no other

gentleman she had ever met had affected her in the slightest. Luke seemed determined not to have her. Kitty would have no other. Through five years of seasons and house parties and assemblies and unwanted courtships, her heart continued to belong steadfastly to Lucas Mogg. Or Lucius whateverhisnamewas.

She buckled the bags and inched the door open a sliver, to signal to Cook she was ready to leave. Most of the servants would still be in the servants hall, eating dinner. Cook had said she would take hers at the kitchen table, as she sometimes did when a sauce or a cake needed to be watched.

She heard Cook's voice, sending someone on his way. Then the door opened. "Quickly, my lady. The kitchen is clear, but you must be fast if you don't wish to be seen."

"Thank you," Kitty said. "Mr Mogg will walk me around to the side door, so do not expect to see me again tonight.

She would have crossed her fingers if both hands had not been occupied with the bags. Instead, she sent up a prayer for forgiveness for the lie, hurried across the room and let herself out of the door into the kitchen courtyard.

She looked around for Luke. He would have arrived early, not wanting her to wait in the dark. Ah, there he was. A shadow detaching itself from the wall of the laundry.

"I put the food into saddle bags," she told him as he approached. "I assume you are riding?"

Luke nodded. "Thank you, my lady." He took the saddle bags, slinging them across one shoulder.

Frustrating man, using her useless title to put distance between them even when he was leaving her. "It is the least I could do," she assured him, sincerely. And if the daft man thought she intended those saddlebags to be her only contribution to his future, he didn't know her at all.

He took two steps away. "This is goodbye, then."

"I hope not," she told him.

She could see his face well enough in the light of the lantern at the door to recognise stark fatalism in his expression. "We shall see," he said, in a grim tone with no hope at all.

What did he expect would happen? On a surge of fear and love, she held out both her hands. "May God go with you both, and keep you safe."

For a moment, he stared at her hands as if they were something alien. Then he grasped them and pulled her towards him, wrapping both arms around her and crushing her mouth under his. She opened to him, thrilling at and grieving for his desperation.

A long moment, and he pulled himself away. "Live well," he ordered sternly, then turned on his heel and slipped away around the side of the house.

Kitty returned inside, but only as far as the passage. Someone was moving around in the kitchen. Her five-minute wait for Luke to be well on his way was fraught with the fear that whoever it was would need something from one of the storerooms.

She recited a couple of prayers and a poem to time her wait, and gave a deep sigh of relief when it was time to pick up the last set of saddle bags and her bed roll, and make her way across the kitchen courtyard and up the steps to the carriage way at the front of the house.

She skirted the wall, keeping to the shadows in case someone was watching out a window.

The long line of trees that bordered the drive provided further cover. She had to hurry. She did not want to give Luke and Paul too long a lead.

Dorrie Baxter was waiting, as she had promised, half way along the carriage way. She was in the shadow of the trees with her horse and Kitty's mare, Renshaw's Star. Pierrot danced up to greet Kitty, who scooped him up. She murmured her greetings to Dorrie as she slipped the dog into the pocket of her coat before buckling the saddle bags and the bed roll onto her mare.

"Will you not change your mind?" Dorrie asked, as Kitty undid her skirt and stepped out of it.

"Would you, if Will was in danger and you could help?" Kitty retorted. The trousers she wore under the skirt were much more practical wear for a journey such as the one she intended. She picked up the discarded garment and rolled it as small as possible to tuck into the top of one of the bags.

Kitty expected Dorrie to protest that Kitty's brother-in-law, who employed Dorrie's husband as his steward, would blame Dorrie for her part in what Kitty was about to do, but Dorrie didn't bother. She and Kitty had been friends since they were girls. Many things had changed in the past twelve years, but not even Dorrie's marriage to Will Baxter had disturbed the girls' loyalty to one another.

Kitty smiled at her friend. "Thank you for helping me. I hope Will is not too angry."

Dorrie shrugged. "Will knows perfectly well that no one has ever been able to stop you once you have made up your mind about something." Her eyes twinkled. "And he will not be able to say I should have told him, for he has gone to Brighton, and will not be back until tomorrow."

"I have written him a letter, Dorrie. If he is back in time, perhaps he will be able to take some men to catch the would-be murderers? They have no business in our woods; as Rede's steward, he has the right to detain them."

She handed over a second letter, this one to her sister and brother-in-law. "This one is for Rede and Anne," she said, unnecessarily since it was addressed to Lord and Lady Chirbury at Anne's Essex estate. "I've told him what I told you. I overheard a plot to kill the Moggs, they have gone into hiding, I am going to follow them, and you tried to talk me out of it." Not the secrets Luke had told her about being base-born, Paul's brother, and hiding under a false name. Not even that the murderer was their uncle, though she had that from the villain himself. Those were not her secrets to tell.

Dorrie tucked the letters into her coat. "You will be careful, Kitty? This could be dangerous."

"The murderers are not due until tomorrow night," Kitty assured her. "We shall be far from here by that time."

Dorrie had been her friend long enough for Kitty to know what she was thinking: that the villains were not the only danger. Kitty was going into wild country to be alone with a man. If anyone in Society knew, she would be ruined.

Dorrie kept those obvious points to herself. "Do you know where Mr Mogg is going?" she asked, instead.

"Pierrot will track him," she said confidently, grateful her pet had formed a close bond with Paul's pony, Scout. "I must go, Dorrie. Thank you again."

"Stay safe and come home as soon as you can," Dorrie commanded. She flung her arms around her friend and they hugged.

"It will be an adventure," Kitty promised. She mounted Star, blessing the trousers that made it easy. Without a further word, she swiftly crossed the carriage way, pausing on the edge of the wood to turn and wave to Dorrie. Or at least in Dorrie's direction. Had her friend's horse not been a grey, she would not know that Dorrie was still there in the shadows.

She gulped back the trepidation she had been determined not to display in front of her friend. She had prepared as well as she could, was armed and capable, and would join Luke as soon as they were far enough away he would not be able to send her back. But she was not a fool. She knew much could still go wrong. And she did not like the dark.

She dismounted at Luke's cottage. Before she could set Pierrot down to find the scent, a horse and rider moved out of the shadows, giving her a jolt of shock that froze her where she stood as she peered to see who it was. Someone small. Not Paul, or Luke would be with him. Not one of the villains, either. They had both been tall men, and the rougher one had been burly.

A moment later, she recognised the face under the cap.

"Millie? What are you doing here?"

CHAPTER 3

When Millie Price came across her lady packing a saddle bag, Lady Kitty had sworn her to secrecy before explaining that Luke and Paul Mogg were in danger, and that Lady Kitty planned to go with them, wherever it was they were heading.

Millie took over the packing—it was her place, as Lady Kitty's maid, and it was her place to go with Lady Kitty, too. Not that Lady Kitty agreed, but Millie was not about to let that stop her. Once the lady's bags had been packed, Millie obediently took them and hid them where Lady Kitty would find them when it was dark.

Then she ran across the park to her father's farm and quickly made some arrangements. She had to trust her sister Agnes to have a pony ready when it was time, for she wanted to be back at the house before Lady Kitty had finished the letters she was writing. Agnes promised to prepare a pair of saddle bags, packed mostly with clothes her brothers had worn when they were boys, plus a couple of skirts. Millie took a set with her to change into.

When Lady Kitty went down to the kitchen, Millie dressed in her room, slipped down the back stairs, and dashed back to the farm. Boys' trousers were much better for running! She could see a horse waiting, not the pony she asked for but the best in the stable. Agnes waited on one side, and her father on the other.

"I have to go, Da," she insisted, before he could speak.

"Do ye?" he asked.

Kitty braced herself for an argument. "I can't be off it. She's my lady, Da."

He heaved a sigh. "Yes. Go then. Take a care to thysel', my Millie."

While they were talking, Agnes had taken the bag of things she'd brought from the house and packed them into the saddle bags.

Da wrapped Millie in his arms, let her go so she could hug Agnes, and then hoisted her onto the horse. "Old Jim be your'n now, girl," Da said. "He'll carry ye best." The horse was in his prime, but they had a younger gelding who looked to be his twin, and they'd taken to calling the pair of them Young Jim and Old Jim. Jim was trained to shaft and saddle, and would carry her well.

"I shall bring him back, Da, if I can."

"He be yours," Da repeated. "Bring thysel' back when ye can."

Milly nodded, hoping he understood how much she loved him, for her throat was thick with tears and she could not speak. She touched her heels to Old Jim, and they rode for the gamekeeper's cottage.

Lady Kitty wasn't there. Millie waited under the trees. Had she been and gone? No. Here she came, down the path from the house. She didn't notice Millie until she had dismounted by the cottage, then she caught sight of her in the trees and recognised her.

"Millie? What are you doing here?"

"I am coming with you, my lady."

Lady Kitty shook her head. "I said you could not come. It may be dangerous."

"It will be that, my lady, just you alone with two men. I am coming with you."

Lady Kitty didn't agree. "Paul is just a boy and Mr Mogg can be trusted."

"The gossiping witches cannot. If I am with you, it will help."

Lady Kitty glared. "I do not need a maid."

Millie lifted her chin. "If you will not take me, I shall follow anyway. You need another woman, and one loyal to you. We Prices are loyal."

Lady Kitty examined her with narrowed eyes. Millie met her gaze and waited.

Millie's Uncle John had followed Lord Chirbury, back when he was merely Mr Stephen Redepenning, to Canada, where the bears were, and Indians. Then he'd followed him home again, and died helping Lord Chirbury save Lady Kitty and her sister, who became Lady Chirbury.

Millie's brother Jonno had gone as valet to Lord Chirbury's cousin, Mr Alex Redepenning. He had helped his master to save the woman who became his wife, and had foiled some murderers while he was at it.

Prices were not just loyal, they were smart. And that meant knowing when to be obedient and when to be stubborn.

"Very well," Kitty said at last. "I am just putting Pierrot down to take the scent."

The dog ran, nose down, from the little stable behind the cottage to the ride that led to the river gate. Lady Kitty scooped him up again and rode down the hill. Millie followed. Lady Kitty leapt the hedge at the bottom, and Millie did, too, glad she was on Old Jim. Her ladyship turned left, which made sense. If Mr Mogg was planning to cross the Cotswolds, he must have crossed the river, either here or in Longford village.

Instead of stopping long enough for Pierrot to check the scent again, Lady Kitty crossed the bridge a few yards further up the river, then guided her horse left again, aided by the rise of the full moon. Old Jim easily kept up. Soon, they reached one of the paths that led up onto the Cotswold Edge.

There, Pierrot confirmed the Moggs had gone this way, and they made their way up into the hills.

"I would say we are, perhaps, an hour behind them," Kitty whispered at one point. That margin surely increased as the night drew on, since they had to stop whenever the path diverged to let Pierrot find the scent of Paul's pony.

Lady Kitty fretted to be away every time they stopped to rest the horses, even as she told Millie that it would not do to come upon the Moggs too soon. "We must wait until it is impossible for Luke to send us back," she said.

CHAPTER 4

Luke should not have kissed Kitty. Not just because she was above his touch and an innocent. Not even because he would very possibly never see her again. Both of those were good reasons, but the most pressing was that he should be thinking about where to go and what to do when he got there.

Instead, as he and Paul crested the road up onto the edge, he fought to turn his mind away from the taste and scent of her, the little sounds she made, the way she fitted in his arms as if born to fill that place, her tongue dancing with his.

He was still thinking about her two hours later, when they stopped to water the horses and let them rest for a bit.

"Try to sleep, if you can," he told Paul.

Paul protested he wasn't tired. He would be before the night was over. They were fortunate to have moonlight for this part of their journey, and Luke planned to make as much ground as he could before daylight.

Luke had always kept packed saddle bags ready for a quick flight in case they were discovered. When Paul turned twelve at his most recent birthday, Luke had told him the true relationship between them and why they fled. Paul had asked several questions, but the one that mattered was the last. "Can I still call you Dad? Even though you're my brother? You are the only father I can remember."

Luke felt the same way. He had been friends with Paul's mother —perhaps the only friend the young baroness had in her husband's household. Certainly, the baron was gone most of the time, pursuing one of his two major interests. Making money and bedding women.

Luke well remembered being called to her bedchamber during her final illness. "Put my son into his brother's arms," she ordered her maid. "Lucius, I am dying. I am leaving my son in your keeping. His father will care only that he has his heir. You will love him." Luke already did, from the moment he took the little mite into his arms and looked down into hazy eyes that still seemed to see more than a person could imagine.

He had argued she would recover to raise her own child, but she was right. She died before the next sunrise.

When Paul was three, their father died, and Paul became baron. Almost immediately, he became accident prone. A wheel collapsed on a gig taking him and his nursemaid to church. The driver and infant were bruised. The nursemaid broke her arm.

The gate that protected the door to the nursery was left open at the same time the second gate on the servants stairs mysteriously disappeared. The adventurous toddler was discovered scooting down the steps on his belly.

Luke came across dangerous fraying on the ropes holding up the swing he'd hung in a tree for the child, fortunately before Paul could use it.

A fire started in a clutter of papers in the corner of the nursery, and set fire to the curtains.

The little boy tossed his dinner on the floor in a tantrum, and the food was eaten by a dog who immediately went into severe cramps and died.

Lastly, after Luke had been arrested and then released, someone attempted to smother the little boy in his sleep.

It was, surely, their father's brother, who was heir after the little baron, but Luke had no way to prove it. He had staged his own death and that of his charge, and disappeared.

Successfully, until now. After all these years, Uncle Baldwin had found them again.

They had rested long enough. Luke got to his feet. Before he could wake Paul, the boy spoke. "Where are we going, Dad?"

The boy was twelve. Old enough to be part of the decision. "That depends on what we want to achieve," he said, feeling, all over again, the sweet pain of Paul's decision to still address him as Dad after he found out Luke was his brother.

"We are hiding from that villain," Paul said.

Luke nodded. "And that can be our goal, Paul. I planned to hide until you were a man grown, and then take you to London to fight for your place and your possessions. We can still follow that plan, somewhere else."

"I hate leaving Longford. My friends are there. Our friends. Can't we go back once he gives up and goes away?"

Luke shook his head. "That won't work. He clearly hasn't given up in the past nine years, Paul. I don't know how he found us, but now he has, Longford isn't safe as long as he is at liberty."

Paul sighed. "So, we have to start again somewhere else."

Yes, and it would be hard without a reference. *Will the Earl of Chirbury give me one when I left so abruptly? Unlikely.*

Also, any reference would be in the name of Mogg. Paul's enemies would be looking for the Moggs, father and son, so the name would have to change.

"I have funds in a bank in Birmingham," he told Paul. "We'll go there first, and then decide on our next step." He got to his feet. "Come on. Time to move."

The boy slept a little at the next stop, two hours later. Luke kept watch, though there was no way Uncle Baldwin could know they had been warned and had run.

He'd spent half an hour in Chirbury's library before sunset, studying maps of the routes between here and Birmingham. They would keep to the least travelled ways across the hills and valleys of the Cotswolds. They would travel all night, taking advantage of the fine weather and the near full moon. By the time the sun rose, they would be sixty miles from home, and through the hills to the far north of Gloucestershire, just south of Stratford-Upon-Avon.

After the next rest, he would have to start looking for somewhere to rest up during the day. He touched Paul's shoulder. "Time to wake, Paul, lad. Do you want a piece of cheese?"

Yawning, the boy he loved took the cheese and went to fetch his horse.

Titus Baldwin flattened himself against the overhanging bank of the stream that ran through the woods.

Damn Lucius.

The bastard had been warned. There was no other explanation. Fortunately, Titus had sent his hireling ahead to check that the gamekeeper's cottage was dark and quiet while Titus checked that no one was stirring at the manor house. Otherwise, Titus would have been caught in the ambush.

Of course, the useless idiot he had hired had betrayed him immediately, but whoever was in charge sent his men the wrong way —up to the house when Titus had only viewed it from afar and ducked immediately back into the woods.

Those men had dogs, and they would be back when they didn't find anything. He'd taken to the stream to lose the scent, wading uphill further into the woods, hoping they would assume he'd gone downhill towards the village.

He would hide until they called off the search. They would question his accomplice, of course, and the man would tell him everything he knew, but that was nothing of importance. Titus had grown a beard and taken on a false name before he'd hired the man.

Furthermore, he had stayed, somewhat uncomfortably, in an abandoned tower just outside of the nearby market town, though he'd paid his hired villain's shot at the local inn.

The dogs were back. He heard them expressing their excitement as they discovered the scent and followed it to the stream, and their disappointment at losing it.

They went silent, then. Titus strained his ears to follow the crackling and rustling as men and dogs made their way along the river banks. Which way? He let out the breath he had not known he was holding as their commitment to a downstream hunt became clear.

You are not yet out of the woods, Titus. The pun amused him. In the woods he would remain until the searchers gave up. He might as well see if he could sleep.

He couldn't. He finally arrived back at his tower long after dawn: cold, stiff, tired, and hungry. The searchers had found his horse, so he had been forced to walk, keeping to the hedgerows as much as possible to stay out of sight. He would allow himself a good wash, something to eat, and a sleep.

Lucius had evaded him. His best chance of finding his quarry, and the brat he had hidden away, was to sit in the public bar of the inn and listen to the gossip. Late afternoon and evening would be the best time, which meant Lucius and the brat had a head start of at least a day. Two, perhaps, depending on when he learned that Titus was coming.

Not for the first time in the long hours of his wait, Titus toyed with breaking into the jail and killing his faithless hireling. The man must have betrayed him to Lucius. He was the only man who knew they were here to eliminate the gamekeeper and the boy, and even he did not know why.

But Titus was not so foolish as to risk his safety and his mission by bothering with the traitor. It would be enough to leave a letter detailing the crimes for which the man was wanted in London. He deserved to hang for betraying Titus, but hanging for the other things he had done would have to be enough.

Titus shook his head in wonder. Who would have thought that such a deep-dyed villain would balk at killing a boy! Lucius was soft in the same way, and always had been, but Lucius was not a villain. Too good for his own good, as the saying went. Titus had admired and resented him in equal measure.

Years ago, when Titus spread the rumour Lucius was behind the attempts on the boy's life, he was just attempting to flick dust in the eyes of observers. He did not expect many people to believe it. They all knew Lucius could be trusted, and that he was besotted with the brat; had been since the child's birth.

But then Lucius had performed a masterly deceit of his own. Even Titus thought the man had died and taken the child with him, though he believed it an accident rather than the murder suicide that most assumed. The remains of a small child were found on a beach further up the coast after a storm some weeks later. The body was buried as the young baron, though it was too damaged to be identifiable. Lucius's body had never been recovered.

For nine years, Titus had been content, certain of the death of the only legitimate child of the former baron—the one being who could keep Titus from the title he had grown to regard as his own. Then he heard a wild story about a kidnapped boy, an English baroness who was a French spy, and a lunatic merchant captain.

What caught his attention was not the antics of the criminals, but the names of two of the rescuers, and, in particular, a couple of details. Lucas Mogg. Gamekeeper and champion archer. The attributes were right. The name nearly so. And his son, Paul Mogg, was twelve.

Titus found it hard to believe, but he checked, coming to Longford in disguise to see the pair for himself. Thank goodness he had. He didn't have to get close to Lucius to confirm who he was, and the boy Paul was clearly a Baldwin.

Titus had made a mistake nine years ago. But it was not too late to correct it. All he had to do was find Lucius, and someone must know where he had gone.

CHAPTER 5

In the first light of dawn, Luke and Paul found a ruin, perhaps the remains of a farm cottage, long since abandoned. It was set in a tiny valley—not much more than a depression in the ground—and so many trees had grown up around it, and even on and through it, that they found it by the merest chance. Paul tried to shoot a rabbit that hopped across their path then took off into the little thicket.

He missed, which was as well, as they would not be lighting a fire this day, and Luke disdained killing things except for protection or food.

Paul dismounted and walked down into the hollow to retrieve his arrow, then looked back at Luke and waved him down. "Look. Will this do?"

The roof had caved in at one end, taking part of the wall with it, but otherwise it was perfect. Luke hacked his way through a thicket of brambles and ivy to reach the door, which was wide enough to get the animals inside. Yes, as long as they stayed away from the broken end, it was sturdy enough.

While he had been exploring the ruin, Paul had ventured further down the hollow. "There's a brook, Dad. Just a bit further down the valley."

Excellent. "Let's water the horses, then settle down for the day," Luke proposed.

Before long, they were all under the remaining roof and fast asleep.

Luke dreamed he was once again the young man who took his infant brother and ran. In reality, no one had seen them go. In the dream, Uncle Baldwin was on his heels, eager to succeed in killing the little heir who stood in his way.

A horse whickered, and it was a moment before he surfaced enough from sleep to realise that the sound was not part of his dream. Scout, Paul's pony, whickered again, a soft sound of greeting. There must be other horses around. Luke unwrapped himself from his cloak and put his hand on Scout's nose, drawing its attention away from whatever had prompted the salutation.

His own horse, named Masquerade and more commonly called Mask, lifted his head and sniffed at his hand.

They stood in silence for a long moment. The pony stirred again, and Luke heard a sound. A fox yap? Not high enough. Besides, Scout would not greet a fox. Somewhere out there was a terrier or another small dog. Kitty's Pierrot had a yap just like that.

He waited, but there were no further noises. Mask had closed his eyes again, and Scout also let his head droop.

Luke returned to his place, and wrapped himself back up in his cloak. Sleep wouldn't come. That yap had sounded remarkably like Pierrot, but Kitty was more than fifty miles away, on the other side of the Cotswolds. It could not be her.

Damn his eyes. Of course, it could. This was Lady Kitty Stocke. Kitty, who had reacted to assault and kidnapping when she was a girl by demanding to learn how to fight. Kitty, who had pestered her brother-in-law's gamekeeper until he taught her woodscraft. Kitty who had partnered him in a rescue of Paul's friend Dan just a few months ago, when a crazed man tried to abduct him.

Kitty, who had not begged to come with him or offered any suggestions or plans for what he should do next.

As soon as he thought about it, he knew she was out there. Hidden somewhere, close by, when he and Paul had the best cover in miles. He rolled himself to his feet again, and slipped out of the cottage.

Kitty had found an overhanging bank large enough for both women. A thicket of holly masked them and the horses from the bridle path as well as the thicket where Luke and Paul had gone to ground.

She thought about joining the pair she pursued, but Luke would be on high alert, and she might find herself shot before she could be recognised. Better to approach in the open when he could identify her.

Pierrot was upset about not being allowed to join the friend he had followed so diligently, but settled down when she insisted, cuddled into her side. The horses relaxed enough to doze. Millie composed herself with her head resting on her saddle bag and was soon asleep.

Kitty's mind would not be still, and her body, weary though she was from the long ride, could not relax on the hard ground. She shifted and shifted again, trying to find ease, trying to let go of the teeming thoughts; the worries about the villains back at the village, her likely reception from the man she loved.

Pierrot alerted her a moment before they were invaded, rushing from their refuge to greet the invader with a single sharp yap.

She picked up the bow she had left ready and nocked an arrow, confident she knew who it was and wanting him to see she was prepared to defend herself.

He ducked around the holly and gave her a dark glower. "Lady Catherine."

She lifted her chin, refusing to let him know he hit his target with his use of her title and formal name. *So, he is angry.* She expected that, and intended to ignore it.

Millie opened her eyes, saw who it was, and sat up. Luke glowered at her, too.

Kitty waited for the explosion. Luke surprised her. "Come on."

She opened her mouth to comment. He waved her to silence, and silent she remained as she put the horse's tack and her saddlebags over Star's back and threw her blanket over her shoulder. Millie did the same with Old Jim. When they were ready, Luke scooped up Pierrot and led the way down into the hollow.

He shifted brambles to disclose a doorway, and the two women led the horses inside what proved to be the largest part of a cottage. The horses gave soft greetings, and Pierrot danced up to Scout to be acknowledged. Paul slept on, rolled in his blanket.

Luke pulled the brambles up again and came inside, closing the door behind him.

"I suppose there is no point in saying you do not belong here," he grumbled, keeping his voice to a whisper.

She could argue she belonged where he did, but as long as he rejected her love, that was merely her heart's opinion and not a fact. "I could not say goodbye," she admitted. "And I think I can help."

He cast another glare at Millie. "At least you had the sense not to come alone." Millie did not comment. Luke waved to the ground. "Sleep. We shall talk about what you can and cannot do when we wake."

Without another word, he lay down on the blanket beside Paul and pulled it over him.

Kitty looked around the tiny room, where more than half the available space was taken up by horses. Not for the first time since starting this adventure, she doubted her own wisdom. But she had spoken the truth. She could not say goodbye.

Luke was watching her. She could feel the weight of his gaze. Did he expect her to complain? To storm off to her overhang with her dignity and sense of propriety both bristling? Millie knew better, at least. She was removing her bags and the tack from Old Jim.

Kitty did the same and spread her blanket next to Millie's. She, an unmarried lady, was about to go to sleep in the same room as a man who was not a member of her family. The thought was far more appealing than it should be. *Safe. I feel safe.* She let her thoughts go and fatigue overwhelmed her.

Hours later, she emerged slowly from sleep to the sound of low voices.

"What we shall do with her now, I do not know. Two women cannot ride all that way back without escort." That was Luke, his voice harsh and uncompromising.

"She is very brave," Paul said.

"She is reckless and arrogant." Luke pitched his voice a little louder. "Would you care to join us, your ladyship? I fear the catering is not up to your usual standard. Millie Price, you too."

She hated when he went all cold and distant. Perhaps she could pretend to still be asleep, and put off meeting his eyes. She rejected the idea as soon as it crossed her mind. She was not a coward.

She shifted, and groaned at the protest of the muscles the long ride had strained. She forced herself to keep moving, untangling herself from the blanket and pushing with her hands to sit up.

A hand appeared in front of her face. She froze.

"Go on. Take it."

At the order, she put one hand in his and allowed him to pull her to her feet. He let go as soon as she was upright, and turned his back. Not before she saw the stiff mask of his face and his blazing eyes. He was furious.

Kitty was in pain. Of course, she was. She had been in the saddle all night and then slept on the cold hard ground for much of the day. She was a lady, and—for all her skill with riding and with weapons—not hardened the way he and Paul were.

Her maid was faring little better. The Prices were prosperous farmers, and the Price children, sisters and brothers alike had all been on and off horseback, racketing about the countryside since they could toddle, but Millie had been in London with Kitty until a couple of weeks ago. He did not suppose that maids had much opportunity to ride in London.

Kitty took a few stiff steps to Paul. The boy offered her a mug of water and a slice of pie.

"Shortly," she demurred. "I need to... Where can I...?" She flushed, and so did Paul when he realised what she needed.

"Around the tumbled down side of the cottage," Luke advised. "Stay within the trees and keep low."

She nodded, and limped to the door, followed by Millie. Luke caught Pierrot before the dog could go too.

It ripped at Luke's heart that Kitty had become involved in this, had been put at risk by the danger that followed him. He had not liked leaving her behind, but he hated that she had come after him.

He wanted her to be safe in her sister's home, surrounded by loyal servants, with hot chocolate to wake up to, served to her in her feather bed. Not in a ruined one-room hut, sleeping on the ground with the animals and having to relieve herself by squatting outside.

Damn her courage and her loyal heart. He could put no fervour into the curse. Her gallantry only made him love her the more. But what was he to do now?

The two women came back into the cottage. He pointed to the leather bucket of water by the door. Cold, like the food and drink. He would not risk a fire.

Kitty used a couple of scoops of the water to wash and rinse her hands and her face, then accepted the pie and the mug Paul offered. Millie did the same. All three of them were silent, sliding glances at him when they thought he was not looking.

Luke said nothing. Kitty had inserted herself and her maid into their escape. Let her be the first to speak.

CHAPTER 6

Kitty finished the pie, then said, "I am sorry you are angry, Luke, but I am not sorry I followed you. I want to be with you. I can be useful."

"My lady," he said, reminding himself as well as her of the distance between them, "Paul and I need to disappear." *Again.* "Start again under different names. You and Miss Price cannot come with us. You have family and friends who would rip England apart to find you."

At that, the lady smiled. "Not immediately. I sent a letter to Rede and Anne, telling them you were gone, and I was going after you." she said.

"Blast!" He had thought he could trust her. "Did you tell them about me and Paul?"

"I did not share anything you told me," she reassured him. "Just that I had heard a man planning to kill the pair of you, I warned you, and you escaped. I also told Dorrie Barker, and she is going to get her husband to set a trap for the villains. They may not be able to hold them for long, but they should delay them for a day or two."

Luke raised his eyebrows at Millie. "And you?"

"I told my father and sister that Lady Kitty was planning to ride cross country to join her sister and Lord Chirbury, and I could not let her go alone. If anyone asks, they are going to say that Da drove us into Chipping Longford to catch the mail coach to London, and from there to Essex to join the earl and the countess."

It was as good an alibi as any, and would at least keep Lady Kitty's reputation unsullied. Also, if Will Barker failed to catch Luke's uncle, the man was unlikely to connect his departure and hers. After all, what would a young Society beauty want with a grumpy old gamekeeper?

"We need a plan," Kitty declared, apparently seeing a softening in his expression.

Luke sighed. "Lady Catherine, I have a plan. We are going to start again with new names."

"Yes, but have you considered the alternative?" she asked.

"What," he scoffed. "Let Paul's uncle catch up with us and kill him, as he tried to do when Paul was a baby?"

She frowned. "Perhaps I should have said, have you considered other options."

"Do you have another plan, Lady Kitty?" Paul's voice was hopeful. Luke could understand his boy's point of view. Walking away from everything and everyone he knew was hard. But Luke had done it before, and kept Paul hidden and safe for nine years. The sacrifice was worth it.

Leaving Kitty is harder than all the rest.

"Ask Rede and the other peers you know for help," Kitty said. "Luke, I don't know what your circumstances were when you stole Paul away; who you had to support you. But I doubt back then you knew the likes of Rede, or Uncle Henry, or the Duchess of Haverford. Whoever this man is who wants Paul dead, and whatever title or power he has, I cannot imagine he could match the combined power of the Redepennings and their allies."

Luke was stunned into silence. It had never occurred to him to ask his employer for help, let alone to consider the man's relatives.

She took his silence for resistance, and her voice turned coaxing. "They owe you. Five years ago, you helped save me, Mia and Anne from Selby and Carrington. Just a few months ago, you helped save Dan, Mia's son."

She made an impatient gesture with her hands. "Even if they were not in such debt to you, they would help you because they trust you, as I do. You say an injustice has been done and that Paul is in danger. My family will help yours because it is the right thing to do. Don't be too proud to accept help, Luke."

Luke shook his head. How could she think he would put his pride ahead of Paul's wellbeing.

Paul misinterpreted the gesture and his face fell. "It might work, Dad," he said.

Luke nodded. "It will work," he told Paul. "You're right, Kitty. Your family connections up against mine? Our Uncle Baldwin will be well outclassed."

He thought again. "Except, why should they believe me against him? A gentleman's by-blow and an accused murderer against a peer of the realm? I cannot risk Paul falling back into his hands."

"An accused murderer, Dad?" Paul protested. "I don't believe it."

His boy's instant support softened his grim mood. He brushed his hand across Paul's head in a rough caress. "I was accused of attempting to murder you, Paul. I managed to persuade the local magistrate that someone was deliberately causing your so-called accidents, and our uncle pointed the finger at me. Convinced the magistrate I was just trying to shift the blame."

He shrugged, trying to remain nonchalant as he remembered the fear he felt when arrested—fear not just for himself but for the innocent child he loved.

"I escaped from the room I'd been locked in, stole you from the nursery, and staged a scene to convince them we'd both gone over the cliffs. So, I daresay I was convicted of your murder after we got away."

"Rede will believe you, Luke," Kitty assured him. "He knows you. Besides, you cannot be arrested for Paul's murder when here he is, evidence of your innocence."

That she believed so was evidence of her own innocence. Uncle

Baldwin would claim that Paul was his own natural son, of course, and that his baby brother had, indeed, died long ago.

When he thought about it, it didn't matter. If they arrested Luke for murder and named Paul his by-blow, the son of his heart would no longer be a threat to Uncle Baldwin. Surely Lord Chirbury would take guardianship of Paul and see him safe? It would irk not to see justice done, but Luke would die happy, knowing Paul was out of danger.

"We will try it your way," he decided. "I suggest we continue our plan to go to Birmingham and take some money from my account, then continue on to your sister's place in Essex." He gave Millie a nod. "Just as Miss Price told her father. The horses will make it if we take our time, and we can leave them there to rest before they make the return journey."

He considered that for a moment. *It should be safe enough, with all of England for Uncle Baldwin to search.* Still, they could take precautions. "First, we need to disguise ourselves and our mounts. And your rat." He cast a look of disfavour at Pierrot, whose distinctive size, flowing coat, and butterfly ears marked him as a lady's pet. "I think we shall be a wealthy merchant family. Merchant," he pointed to himself, "son," to Paul, "sister," to Kitty. The age gap was not quite enough to make her a credible daughter.

"Wife," Kitty corrected, ignoring the insult to her dog. "Second wife, that is." She grinned at Millie. "A wife would travel with a maid."

"Quite right." Paul gave a sly grin. "Everyone will remember the scandal if you call her your sister then look at her as if you want to devour her."

His answer and Kitty's were simultaneous.

"I do not."

"He does not."

Millie giggled.

When Luke slid a glance at Kitty, her face was as red as his felt, but he detected hope and desire in the look she returned. His own gaze studied all the signs of her arousal.

Paul, the cheeky brat, said, "Like that."

Luke reimposed the granite face he had perfected over the years. "That's enough, Paul. You owe Lady Catherine an apology for embarrassing her."

It was Paul's turn to colour. "I beg your pardon, my lady. I was just teasing."

"Katie," she said. "I think my name should be Katie while I am your wife, Luke."

He felt an unwilling smile tug at his lips. The woman never gave up. He surrendered the fight, for Paul was not wrong. He could not look at her without desiring her, so if she was going with him, she had better pretend to be his wife. *And you had better never forget that she isn't.*

"I can be Millicent," Millie suggested. "I like that better than Mildred, in any case."

"Or Prince?" Kitty chuckled. "I can be the kind of woman who thinks her status is improved if she calls her maid by her surname, and Prince is near to Price."

"Dresser," Millie decided. "That sort of woman has a dresser, not a maid. Millicent Prince, it is."

Luke should probably not show his amusement. It would only encourage them. "Mocham," he said. "It is near enough to Mogg that I'll answer. Mogg is a combination of my second initial and the first part of my surname. Lucius Michael Ogilvy."

"Is my name Ogilvy, too?" Paul asked.

"Your name is Baldwin," Luke told him. "Julius Paul Baldwin, Baron Baldwin of Ormswood."

Paul stared at him, his mouth moving as he tried the name on his tongue.

"Peter, for you, perhaps?" Kitty suggested to him. "Do you think you could remember to be Peter instead of Paul?"

Paul's smile was distant; his thoughts still far away. "I am a baron," he said to her. "What do I know about how to be a baron?"

"You have learned from Luke how to be a gentleman," Kitty told him, firmly. "You have learned honour and loyalty, the value of friendship. You will make an excellent baron."

If she did not already possess the whole of his heart, Luke would have lost a little more to her at that moment.

They stayed one night at Birmingham, where Luke had no difficulty at the bank.

Everyone else remained at the hotel, where they had taken two linked rooms, an inner one for the married couple, which Kitty would occupy with Pierrot and Millie, and an outer one in which Paul and Luke would both sleep.

By this time, they had been transformed with dye, hairpieces, and clothing that they had picked up from villages on the way, three of them visiting the shops and stalls while one of them took a turn at waiting outside the villages with the horses. The women were back in gowns, though they wore trousers underneath in case their skirts blew up when riding.

They had even applied dye judiciously to the horses and Pierrot. The long white blaze that had given Mask his name was now much smaller, Star no longer had a star, and Scout's four white socks had disappeared. Pierrot was now a black and white dog instead of black, tan, and white. Only Old Jim, a medium-sized chestnut horse with few distinguishing features, was not changed.

People of the class they were pretending to be would be more likely to use a carriage than to travel on horseback, but none of them wanted to leave the horses with strangers. Instead, they chose the name of a village a two-hour ride outside of the bustling city, and Luke wrote that name in the register as their place of origin—close enough to ride their own horses without resting, and far enough that the innkeeper was unlikely to know anyone there.

At first, Kitty was surprised no one questioned their account of themselves. Not in Birmingham, nor at any of the inns where they stayed on their journey across England to Fishinghame on the south coast of Essex. Or, rather, to Selby Manor just outside of Fishinghame. It was the family seat of the Earls of Selby, and Kitty's childhood home.

Luke was even more laconic than usual. Kitty, Paul, and Millie gave up addressing any remarks to him that were not necessary for the business of getting them from one place to another. He could certainly not be accused of devouring looks. He did not look at Kitty at all, though he saw to her comfort at every stop.

The one time he showed any emotion was when Kitty was attacked on her way back from an inn's privy. A couple of men leapt out at her as she took a cluttered path between a huddle of outbuildings to where the horses waited. One of them, coming from behind, trapped her arms at her side and clamped a hand over her mouth.

Kitty kicked the other, her booted foot giving an effective blow to his masculine equipment that left him writhing on the ground. At the same time, she bit the other's dirty fingers and, when he whipped his hand away, threw her head back to smash into his face while screaming as loud as she could.

Her assailant spun her around, his fist back to punch her, but Luke put paid to any such intention, beating the villain to the ground while Paul held a gun on the man she had kicked, Millie danced around them all with a large stick she had found somewhere, and Pierrot, who had been with the horses, made darting attacks at the men's boots.

In moments, the path was crowded with people attracted by Kitty's scream. One of them was the innkeeper, who sent someone for a constable, and it was all over in half an hour. Kitty gave her story. Luke spoke of his part, stoic as ever except for something turbulent in his dark eyes.

When they were free to go, he sent Paul and Millie ahead to the horses, then suddenly pulled her into an empty shed and wrapped his arms around her. It felt good. As she tucked her head against his throat, she felt the tension leave her on a shudder, and his arms tightened.

"I am so sorry," he murmured. "I should have been there. I would never forgive myself if you were hurt."

"They were hurt," she pointed out, and he stopped kissing her hair and used one hand under her chin to tilt her head back. She tried to interpret his smile. Genuine amusement and something else. Something that made her feel empty and yearning.

"You did well," he confirmed. "Two big brutes like that? You kept your head, fought well, and screamed loud enough to draw half the countryside to your rescue." He kissed her nose, but lifted his head out of the way of her questing mouth.

"I cannot," he told her, dropping his arms, his impassive mask back in place. He bowed. "I am so—"

"If you say you are sorry, I shall punch you," Kitty told him. "And if you call me 'my lady', I will punch you twice."

His stern mouth twitched at one corner and the laugh lines at the corner of his eyes crinkled, then he sobered again. "Time to leave," he said.

It had been a revealing moment. He was not as immune to her as he tried to pretend. He reverted to his silent self after that, but she had seen it for a mask and would not forget. And from that point, he did not again address her as "my lady".

CHAPTER 7

The closer she got to the estate; the more Kitty was flooded with memories, good and bad. They rode through the village where she had shopped for ribbons and sweet treats when her father had given her a penny. There was the churchyard where her mother, father, and brother were buried. Next came the gate that led to the house of her dearest childhood friend, also long dead.

Opposite was the lane that led to the beach, where their governess sometimes took them on an excursion, and where Anne had taken Kitty and Ruth the governess to plan their escape from the machinations of their aunt and uncle.

Kitty had been Paul's age. Like Luke with Paul, Anne had believed her youngest sister was old enough at twelve to understand the danger that faced them and to play a part in deciding what to do about it.

Next came the carriage way of Selby Manor. Kitty had last seen it more than a decade ago, by moonlight, as she and her sisters crept away from a place that had once been a haven.

Their father had left each of them wealthy, and the death of their only brother meant they inherited, between them, all of the remaining unentailed property. Anne had also inherited the title, in trust for a son, because the Selby earldom was one of the rare peerages that could descend in the female line.

Not that she knew that at the time. The title had passed from father to son since it was established, and none of the surviving family realised that Anne was the rightful heir. When a distant cousin turned up and claimed to be earl, they believed him. He and his family plotted to have the two older sisters committed to an asylum, and Kitty married to her cousin Simon, who was in his early twenties and a nasty rakehell. Then, when the sisters escaped, their relatives claimed they had died, and took the earldom.

Though Anne had returned several times since the estate had come back into her hands, Kitty had never wanted to see the place again.

The huge iron gates were folded back to the sides and Luke rode on through. Paul made to follow, but stopped when he realised that Kitty had. Her mare, sensing her agitation, had planted all four hooves and stood still in the gateway, twisting her neck to look back at Kitty. Millie rode up beside her, looking anxious.

Rede and Anne will be here, Kitty told herself. *Simon is dead and can no longer threaten us. His mother and her harridan sister are gone.* Pierrot yapped up at her from his saddle bag perch.

"Kitty?" Paul asked. "Is something wrong?"

Millie spoke at the same time. "My lady?"

Kitty could not answer either of them.

Then Luke was there. "Go on ahead, you two, would you? Just to the bend. Kitty requires a minute."

Paul cast her a worried look, but nudged Scout into a fast walk. Millie touched her hand and then followed behind.

"Take a deep breath and let it out," Luke advised.

The instruction cast her back into her lessons with him down through the years. Archery, tickling trout, creeping silently through undergrowth. Everything started with letting her stresses pour out of her so she could focus on her goals.

A second breath, and the panic receded. A third. A fourth.

"I am ready." Kitty patted Star's neck, and changed her weight to send the mare forward. "I am sorry to be such a coward, Luke."

"You and your sisters won in the end," Luke pointed out. "Which tends to prove you are not a coward, as does what you are doing now. Courage is not the absence of fear. Courage is doing what must be done despite the fear. You are a brave lady, Kitty Stocke, and I am proud to know you."

They were turned away at the house. Lord and Lady Chirbury were not in residence, the snooty butler declared, and the butler did not believe that the scruffy vagabonds in front of him were Lady Catherine Stocke and her maid. "A woman dressed like the pair of you and travelling alone with two men? Ridiculous."

It was, Luke thought, a fair point, and he kicked himself for not thinking of the possibility that the Chirburys might not be home.

The butler refused to let them in to write a note, or to tell them whether the earl and countess were out for the day or had left the estate.

Kitty was furious. She stalked ahead of the others down the carriageway, radiating her irritation in her glare, stiff back and furious strut. The poor footmen who had been commanded to see the four of them off the property kept a healthy distance.

"Do you think Mr Thomson is right?" one of them hissed to another.

His companion's eyes were so wide the white could be seen above the iris. "I think we'll all be in trouble when her ladyship finds out we turned away her sister," he muttered back.

"Not us," the third hoped. "We're just doing what we are told."

"I shall put in a word for you," Paul offered. "But I shall let Lady Kitty calm down, first."

Kitty cast a glare at him and kept walking.

"She's gentry, for sure," moaned the footman who had declared they were in trouble.

"Are Rede and Anne expected back soon?" Luke asked, deliberately using the names they used within the family to give the footmen even more cause to worry. "If so, can you give them a message from my lady?"

"Gone to London Town," said one of the footmen. That seemed to open the floodgates, for in short order, the three of them told Luke and Paul about the messenger from Longford Court who had arrived three days ago, and how the Chirburys had packed up and left the following morning.

"Very hush hush, it was," Luke was told. "That messenger said as how he wasn't one to gossip, and, in any case, the steward what sent him didn't tell him nowt."

Luke thanked them. "I shall let my lady know," he said. He lengthened his stride until he caught up with her.

"Rede and Anne got a message from Longford Court and left for London," he reported. "They're not expected back, but the footmen with us will pass on a message just in case they arrive unexpectedly."

"Stupid butler," she grumbled. "He would not even listen." She had tried to tell him about her childhood in this house; had asked after servants who might remember her. He had ordered her off the estate.

"Rude, I'll grant you," Luke offered. "But he's not wrong to be cautious, Kitty. He doesn't know you. If I'd thought of it, we could have turned up in a carriage, with you in a silk gown, your maid in uniform, and me and Paul as driver and tiger. He would probably have given you a fairer hearing then."

She snorted. "That is disgusting."

Luke shrugged. "That is how things are."

Another snort, but her lovely face was thoughtful. They reached the gate, and turned back to wait for Paul and Millie, who were chatting with the footmen about their time in service to the Earl of Chirbury.

Kitty addressed the footmen. "Gentlemen, a word, please."

The footmen approached, cautiously.

"My lady?" one of them said.

Kitty smiled at him. "I wish to speak with some of the servants who may remember me from when I lived here with my sisters and our governess, Miss Ruth Henwood. It was twelve years ago. Is there anyone still in service at the manor? Or perhaps retired to the village? Mrs Bolton was the housekeeper, I remember. And Mr Mexstead was the stablemaster."

"Mrs Bolton has retired to her sister's place in Kent, my lady," said the helpful footman. "You'll find Mr Mexstead at the village inn. He and his son-in-law run the stables there."

With that information, they made their way back to the village. "Mr Mexstead helped us to escape when we ran from the new earl and his family," Kitty told them.

"He hid us in his cottage for three days, and then took us to Cambridge to catch the mail coach to London." There, Anne had acquired the tenancy of a cottage in Longford, in West Gloucestershire, where they lived a retired life as a family of sisters. Until Rede moved into Longford Court and his nephew brought the false Earl of Selby visiting. Simon Stocke. Kitty's vile cousin.

Kitty preferred not to dwell on that part of her memories, except it had all ended well, with Anne married to Rede and Selby gone for good. Thanks at least in part to Luke.

The groom who came out to take their horses directed them to a cottage just behind the stables, and the girl who answered the door cautiously allowed that her grandfather was at home.

"Would you let him know he has visitors?" Kitty asked.

"Who is it, Prissy?" The elderly man approached from the back of the cottage.

"Some people to see you, Gramps." The girl stepped out of the way and the man stepped into the light in the doorway.

Kitty shifted Pierrot to her left arm and held out her hand. "Hello, Mr Mexstead." He had changed little. Perhaps more bent, and certainly his hair was white now rather than grey mixed with brown.

He took the hand in both of his, beaming. "Lady Kitty," he said. "You are the picture of your mother when your father first brought her home to Selby Manor. Come in. Come in. Prissy, darling, let your Mam know we have visitors. It's Lady Kitty Stocke! And friends. Who are these with you, my lady?"

Kitty introduced Millie, Luke, Paul and Pierrot. They followed Mexstead through to a little parlour, where they were soon joined by Mrs Mexstead and served tea and cake by the couple's daughter, introduced as Izzie.

"What happened to you after we left?" Kitty wanted to know. "Did anyone find out you helped us?"

"No one," Mexstead said, "until your Earl of Chirbury turned up a few years back and wanted to give me a reward. No need for that, I told him. Only did what any Christian would do. Pleased, I was, to hear those villains got their comeuppance. Nasty, they was. And no eye for a horse, either."

Mexstead's most egregious insult.

"I hated to leave Holly with them," Kitty commented. By the time they ran away, the manor was a place of horror instead of their beloved family home, but Kitty had been sorry to leave her pony. Holly had been one of the first inhabitants of Selby Manor she'd asked about when the estate came back into their possession, but the pony was no longer in the manor's stables. "You don't happen to know what happened to her, do you?"

"The old earl sold her, my lady," Mexstead said, with a grin that was explained when he added. "I bought her. She's an excellent little lady with my granddaughters, you see. After we've finished here, Prissie and I will take you out to the field out the back and you can see her for yourself. But you've not come to talk of old times, I'll be bound. What can we do for you, Lady Kitty?"

"We came to see my brother-in-law, Mr Mexstead, and need to follow him to London. Would you be able to look after our horses? And does the inn hire horses or vehicles? We'll need to ride to wherever we can catch a London-bound coach."

Mexstead looked over her shoulder at Luke, frowning a little. "I reckon I can help, Lady Kitty. But should you be travelling with this gent? Even with your maid, I don't know what your sister would have to say about that."

Luke's sigh was heartfelt. "That is what I have been telling her, Mexstead."

This again! Luke renewed the argument every day, and now he was trying to enlist Mexstead. "If you are so anxious to be rid of me, Luke, then you will see the sense in reaching London as quickly as possible."

"Paul and I can go," Luke told her, repeating earlier arguments. "You and Millie can stay here at Selby Manor."

Kitty snorted. "With the butler who believes I am an imposter? No. Even if I could convince him I am Lady Catherine Stocke, I am not going to be left behind. If you and Paul leave without me, I will follow."

Luke rolled his eyes at Mexstead, who gave him a grimace of commiseration. "Right, then," the stable master said. "I'll leave it to your sister to sort out. There's a coach from Southend twice a week, and the next one is tomorrow. I'll take you over to meet it in the morning. We'll have to leave at first light. Lady Kitty, you and your maid can stay here in the cottage. Ogilvy, I'll find room for you and the boy with the grooms next door."

They agreed to the arrangement, and then Mexstead took Kitty to see her old pony.

Mr Mexstead conveyed the travellers to Southend-On-Sea in the half-light before dawn, since the mail coach left at seven. Luke was able to secure only two of the inside seats, and they charged extra for Pierrot, though he would be spending the trip on Kitty's lap, securely contained by his leash.

Luke and Paul climbed to the top, but not before Luke had fixed a gimlet glare on the two men who would be sharing the space within with Lady Kitty and Millie. The two women would look out for one another, but it didn't hurt to let the other occupants know they had a man to protect them. One other passenger joined the driver, the guard, and Luke and Paul on the roof, and they were off.

The mail coaches had the advantage of speed. They were light and well-built, though for velocity not comfort. Their excellent teams of horses waited ready at each change, with capable grooms who could switch the tired team for the fresh one in as little as five minutes.

They did not stop at toll gates or even, often, at mail delivery points. The guard would blow a horn to fetch the toll keeper out to open the gate so the coach did not even have to slow down. He was also responsible for throwing down bags of mail to the postmaster of each village or town, and grabbing outgoing mail as the coach passed.

The weight and pace of the coach meant it bounded over ruts and bumps more enthusiastically than slower coaches, each sway and jerk accentuated for those on the hard wooden benches on the roof.

It was not much more comfortable inside, and at least up on the top of the carriage, they were not required to suffer the odours, grumbles, and other intrusions endured by those forced into close proximity with strangers inside a small container speeding along the turnpike.

When they clambered down in London after more than seven hours on the road, they were all stiff and tired, the two women most of all.

They walked off their muscle aches on the way to Longford House. Paul and Millie were openly yawning by the time they left the business district behind and began walking down streets lined with rows of expensive houses. Lady Kitty disguised it better, but Luke knew her well enough to be sure she would be drooping from fatigue if she was not too proud to allow herself the indulgence.

Pierrot, keen to run when they first descended from the carriage, was now drooping, but continued gamely along at Lady Kitty's heels. "That is where Rede's Uncle Henry lives," she observed, pointing to one house. "Perhaps we should ask for his help. He is a Brigadier General and works at the Horse Guard."

Luke grabbed her pointing finger with one hand and took her arm with the other. "Into the shadows," he commanded, leading—nearly pulling—her into the mouth of an alley. Paul and Millie hurried to join them.

A row of potted boxwood trees lined the pavement in front of the house beside which they sheltered. Through the gaps, Luke studied the two men coming together down the front steps of the general's town house.

"Dad?" Paul asked.

"The man with Lord Redepenning?" Luke answered. "That, my boy, is your Uncle Baldwin."

CHAPTER 8

They hurried down the back ways to Chirbury House, and were welcomed in the kitchen door, though the housekeeper looked horrified that Lady Kitty had so far lowered herself as to come in the servant's entrance. It was proper for Millie, of course. What was not proper was the attire worn by both women.

Luke and Paul had stayed at Chirbury House when they had come to London to act as witnesses during the very quiet and private investigation into the French spies they had uncovered during their rescue of Paul's friend, Dan. They, the housekeeper's sniff said, were right to come to the servants' door, if they must come at all, being outdoor servants.

"Are the Earl and Countess in, Mrs Mitchell?" Kitty asked, but she was to be disappointed.

"No, my lady. They were only here one night, and then they returned to Longford Court. They left a letter for you, my lady. We have had your bed made up these three days. Lady Chirbury instructed me to have a room ready for you and your son, Mr Mogg. She said you might be with my lady." The housekeeper's eyes were full of questions. She was too well trained to ask any of them, and Luke was certainly not going to volunteer any answers.

Lady Kitty was reading her letter and wrinkling her nose. Clearly, the message didn't impress her. "I'll need to write an answer to this." She opened her eyes wide as she looked at Luke, but he couldn't read the message.

"Lady Kitty has been travelling all day," he told the housekeeper. "She needs a wash and something to eat."

"So have Mr Mogg and his son," Lady Kitty added. "Darling Mrs Mitchell, could I trouble you for a bath in each of our rooms, and then supper set in the small sitting room? Mr Mogg, I have a couple of matters to discuss with you, so if you and Paul would join me for supper, that will save time. Mrs Mitchell, include a plate for my maid, if you please."

The housekeeper's nostrils flared, and Luke hoped she wasn't prone to gossiping with her cronies, for her speculations were running rampant behind curious eyes. "Yes, my lady," she said.

"Thank you," Lady Kitty said, nonchalant about her disreputable appearance.

Move right along. Nothing to see here.

Mrs Mitchell was not buying it, and neither were any of the other servants who were observing the conversation.

Luke could do nothing more than follow Lady Kitty's lead and hope that the servants' loyalty to the Chirburys would protect the lady's reputation.

He didn't find out what the letter said until supper, which was served by a footman.

Lady Kitty solved the problem of the audience by handing Luke the letter to read.

Kitty, if you get this, please write to us immediately, and then stay at Chirbury House until we get there. Rede has told the household staff not to talk about your presence if you arrive.

We will wait at Longford Court to hear from you. Matthew Baxter reports he captured one would-be assailant in our woods—the man was a hireling, and did not know the name of the man who hired him, but he confirms that the intent was murder.

I am very concerned the second man may have followed you and found you. It is silly of me to include my worries, since if you are reading this, you have clearly eluded the villain. Please be careful, Kitty. Whatever is going on, it is obviously dangerous.

I will not waste time berating you for taking off after Luke Mogg. I give him credit enough to assume he has done that already. We will fix whatever we need to fix, and you can tell us all about it when we are together again.

Your loving sister

Anne

"I've written a reply," Lady Kitty said. "Just a note to say that we arrived safely, and will do as Anne asked. Do you wish to add anything to that?"

Conscious of the listener, Luke just shook his head. "Nothing. I suggest you send it this evening. It will go on the morning mail coach, be in South Gloucestershire by nightfall, and delivered the next morning."

That fetched a wry chuckle from the lady. "Fast," she said, in an elusive comment to their own cross-country journey.

"They change teams fifteen times between here and Bristol," Paul offered, "so that's why they can go so fast." He'd spent most of the trip from Southend talking to the driver, who had proved to be an encyclopaedia of coaching knowledge.

Lady Kitty acknowledged the information with a nod, but returned to her main concern. "If Rede leaves straight away and travels without stopping, he could be here that evening. But more likely, it will be a day or so more." She covered her mouth with a hand and fought a yawn.

"We could all do with an early night," Luke said.

"I will write some notes to family and friends before I go to bed," Lady Kitty decided. "Just to see who is in London."

"Would the morning not be soon enough?" he asked her.

She smiled but did not reply. The stubborn female would do as she pleased, and there was no point in arguing.

"Please make sure that you get some sleep," he begged.

"I will," she assured him. "I am sure I will be asleep as soon as my head hits the pillow."

Kitty sent a protesting Millie off to bed, but managed to stay awake long enough to send off notes to all her cousins-in-law who might be in town. They were the daughter and daughters-in-law of Uncle Henry, Lord Redepenning. Her first intention—until she saw him with Baron Baldwin—had been to write to Uncle Henry first. Not knowing how close he was to Luke's enemy, she would wait until she could see him face to face.

Instead, she sent out letters to Susan Rutledge, Mia and Mary Redepenning, and Ella Renshaw. In case none of them were in London, she also wrote to her godmother, the Duchess of Haverford.

She said little in the notes. Just that she was staying at Chirbury House and that she wanted help with a problem.

Satisfied, she gave all of the notes to the butler and asked for them to be delivered tonight, then went up to bed, where Pierrot was already curled into a sleeping ball. As predicted, she was asleep as soon as her head hit the pillow.

Kitty was woken by a maid. The girl pulled back the curtains and the sun streamed in. Kitty sat up. "What time is it?"

The maid startled at her voice, and when she faced Kitty, she was wringing her hands in her apron and frowning. "Not quite seven, my lady. But Mrs Mitchell said to wake you, and to say you are needed."

She bit her upper lip and sniffed.

Kitty climbed out of bed, and hurried to her wardrobe. "Something is wrong. Tell me what it is."

"He said I wasn't allowed, my lady. He said if I told and you ran away, he would arrest me too." The maid clapped her hands over her mouth, her eyes round with horror.

Kitty paused with one hand on the green muslin morning gown she had been about to pull from the wardrobe. "Has Lord Baldwin come to call?"

The maid shook her head.

Kitty shrugged. Even if it was Lord Baldwin, she was hardly like to come to any harm under the care of her own family. There were some benefits to being closely related to an earl. "Fetch me a cup of tea, and then wake Millie and send her to help me dress," she ordered.

The maid bit both lips, and hurried from the room, bobbing a curtsey as she left.

Kitty shrugged into a robe in the time the maid would take to get to the stairs and beyond view of Kitty's bedchamber door. "Stay," she said sternly to Pierrot. She then crept down the main stairs far enough that she could hear what was happening in the entry hall below without being seen.

The voice she could hear arguing with Luke certainly did not sound like a baron. The accent was that of a working-class Londoner. Luke was saying, "You can have no reason to arrest Lady Catherine. Or my son for that matter. But you must see that arresting the sister of an earl without cause will stir a cauldron of trouble."

"I don't know about that," said the Londoner. A constable, Kitty had to suppose. "Arrest the females what was wiv the man known as Luke Mogg. That's what I was told. Arrest the boy, too. Don't know as the female upstairs is this Lady Catherine, do I? Just need to see the females what arrived wiv you last night and see if they fits the description."

Mrs Mitchell and the butler both cut in, arguing that the only women in the house other than the servants who lived here year round were Lady Catherine Stocke and her maid, who was known to them both, and was a daughter of the house.

"And what you think her ladyship would be doing coming in the kitchen door with the likes of these, I do not know," said Mrs Mitchell. From the sounds of his responses, the constable was not impressed.

I had better get down there. Kitty hurried back to her room. Millie met her at the door and helped her into front fastening stays, a petticoat, stockings, and the day gown. The maid who had woken her arrived with her cup of tea as she left the room for the second time. "Leave it," she said. "I do not have time."

Less than ten minutes after Kitty woke, she was dressed and walking downstairs, her hair in a simple roll at the nape of her neck and Pierrot in her arms. Millie followed anxiously behind her.

Mrs Mitchell and the butler were blocking the staircase, with half a dozen large men facing them, the one in the front red-faced and snarling. "If them females 'ave scarpered, I will 'ave you arrested for interfering wiv me in the hexecution of my dooty." Two more men were holding Luke and Paul by the door.

Pierrot objected to the man's tone with a loud bark, which had all eyes turned towards her.

"You!" Kitty used what she called her countess voice, copied from her sister Anne. "Shouting man. What is your name, and why are you threatening my brother's servants?"

"This," said Mrs Mitchell, triumphantly, "is Lady Catherine Stocke."

The snarl fell off the man's face and he gaped, but he recovered quickly and told one of his men, "Fetch the witness."

The man scuttled away, trying to keep an eye on Kitty's descent even as he hurried out of the door.

Kitty stopped on a level with Mrs Mitchell and frowned at the constable in charge. "Your name?" she demanded again.

The constable was rattled; she could see it in his eyes. Unfortunately, he appeared to be the kind of man who became more truculent when unsure of his ground, rather than less.

"All you need to know, my lady, is that I 'ave warrants for the h'arrest of the man known as Mr Luke Mogg, gamekeeper, of Longford, Gloucestershire, and his companions, a boy of h'about twelve years and two females, dressed in men's clothes, of about eighteen years."

Kitty raised her eyebrows and used her brother-in-law Rede's trick of speaking more quietly, so all of the burly men leaned forward to listen. "You will not save yourself from the earl's wrath by refusing to give your name, you know. He will be offended at your treatment of his sister and his servants, and he will discover the name of the man responsible."

The man's flush had deepened. Her attempt at intimidation was having the opposite effect.

"His name is Ronald Thomson," said the woman who had just entered the door. "Good morning, Lady Catherine."

Thomson spun to look at the newcomer, barking, "Mrs Wakefield? What in blazes are you doing 'ere?"

Prue Wakefield! Thank goodness. Prue and her husband David ran a firm of enquiry agents, and Prue was afraid of no one. Witness how she strolled into a hall filled with threatening looming figures, examining each of them with interest as they wilted before her. "One might ask the same question, Thomson. Who are these with you? I recognise Bill Marsh, but the rest of them are not with the Great Marlborough Street police office. Good morning, Bill. How is Sal's lumbago?"

Now that Kitty looked, she could see Thomson and the man addressed as Bill were neatly dressed, with clean linen, respectable clothing, and highly polished shoes, while the others were scruffier by far, their linen dirty, their clothing showing much wear, and their shoes down at heel.

Bill opened his mouth to answer Prue but subsided at a glare from Thomson, who drew himself up. "Special constables, properly sworn in. We was warned the suspect Mogg was a dangerous murderer. Look 'ere, Mrs Wakefield," he added. "I 'ave warrants for the h'arrest of the murderer Luke Mogg, the boy Paul Mogg, and two h'unidentified females dressed in men's clothing. These servants and this lady are keeping me from my sworn duty to search the 'ouse for the females."

Prue raised her brows and widened her eyes. "You have a warrant that allows you to search an earl's house?" Where Kitty would have delivered the line with scorn, Prue infused it with surprise, and for the first time, Thomson looked uncertain.

"No, in other words. In that case," Prue told him, "I suggest you station your hired muscle outside to catch these imaginary females when and if they emerge."

"Not h'imaginary," Thomson insisted. "I 'ave a witness—" He was interrupted by the messenger he had sent outside.

"No go, boss. He legged it," the messenger said.

# CHAPTER 9

After they left, Millie persuaded Lady Kitty to return to her room. "You'll want to wash, my lady, and to dress in something more appropriate for the day. I'll send for a cup of tea, for the other will be cold by now. I'll ask Mrs Mitchell to have breakfast served in the small parlour when Mrs Wakefield returns, for I imagine she'll not have had time to break her fast, coming as early as she did."

Thank goodness she did come, Millie thought. If she had not, Millie would herself be on her way to prison, for she had been ready to put herself forward to save Lady Kitty. Except that, if she had declared she had arrived with Mr Ogilvy and Master Paul, and with another woman who had already left, would that man Thomson have believed her?

He had believed Mrs Wakefield. She insisted on reading the arrest warrant, which had been only for Mr Lucius Ogilvy, also known as Lucas Mogg, gamekeeper.

When she pointed that out, he had argued. "My h'information is that the h'other persons are material witnesses, Mrs Wakefield. You must see h'I need to take them into custody in case they scarper."

Mrs Wakefield retorted, "I don't see that, Mr Thomson. Especially when the two women have apparently already scarpered. If they existed at all."

"I need to search—"

Mrs Wakefield widened her eyes and invested her tone with disbelief. "An earl's house? Without a warrant? For people who have only been seen by a witness who has himself disappeared?"

Millie had relaxed. Perhaps she would not be arrested, after all.

Thomson was not defeated. "I'll see about getting a warrant and I'll be back." He glared at Lady Kitty.

Mrs Wakefield smiled. "By all means. I shall advise the earl's solicitor to expect your note, telling him what time to meet you here."

Thomson's glare shifted to Mrs Wakefield and intensified. "I'll just be taking the man and the boy, then."

Lady Kitty moved, and Millie touched her arm, though how she was meant to stop her lady from doing something truly stupid she didn't know. Fortunately, her mistress paused for just long enough for Mrs Wakefield to speak again.

"The boy is not under arrest, Mr Thomson. You cannot put him in prison."

Thomson puffed himself up. "Protective custody."

Mrs Wakefield nodded at that. "I will just come along with you, then, to make certain that it is the sort of protective custody suitable for a twelve-year-old boy who has done nothing against the law. Lady Kitty, I shall return as soon as I can."

It would be an hour at the least. Probably more. Millie's task was to keep Lady Kitty from fretting the whole time.

Luke did nothing to resist the men who shoved and pushed him into the prison wagon and out again at the other end. Great Marlborough Street Magistrates Court. The cells there were probably a better place to wait than the hell that was Newgate Prison. *Something for which to be thankful.*

He was pleased, too, to see Thomson dismissing the special constables before they entered the building. He knew the sort; knives and fists for hire. He didn't trust the runners much, but he was reasonably certain they wouldn't take a bribe to beat him to death or stab him.

He had a lot to be thankful for, above all that Mrs Wakefield had persuaded Thomson that Paul was to be treated as a witness, and not as a suspect. It didn't save the boy from being taken into custody, but hopefully it would protect him from being locked up with the other accused.

Certainly, they were separated immediately; Thomson took Paul in one direction with a determined Mrs Wakefield. Luke was marched away in another between another two runners.

Thank goodness Mrs Wakefield was there. She had prevented Lady Kitty or Millie from confessing to being the scruffy females Thomson's witness had seen. She had shamed or cowed Thomson away from the violence that had been incipient before she arrived. She argued Lady Kitty out of insisting on accompanying the runner and his men to Bow Street.

And she had made it clear to Thomson that Luke and his supposed son had powerful allies, which should keep Paul safe, even if Luke had to pay for the crimes of which he was accused.

By his uncle, he had to suppose. Somehow, Baldwin had discovered their arrival, and made the accusations that led to the arrest. Perhaps he had seen Luke at the same time that Luke saw him, last night. Or perhaps he had someone watching the house.

It didn't much matter. Either way, here Luke was, his wrists shackled together, waiting for someone to unlock a door so he could be forced into a cell with a dozen other men. He would either survive what came or he wouldn't, but Lady Kitty and her allies could be trusted to look after Paul.

They freed his wrists before they locked him away.

He nodded to the other men in the cell, and found a free piece of wall to sit against. Now, he waited.

The morning dragged by, with nothing to do but think, except when he was approached by one of the other men.

The first incident followed a muttered conversation in the far corner. A large man with a shaven head, flattened nose, and cauliflower ears swaggered towards him and would have kicked his feet except that Luke pulled them back a split second before the man's boot struck, pushing off the wall with his back so that he could get his legs under him and leap to his feet.

"If you want my attention, mate," he said, "you have it." There was something familiar about the man, but Luke couldn't remember where he'd met him.

The big man sneered. "Don't he talk fancy, lads?" he said to his cronies. He bent closer, shoving his face close to Luke's. "What are you doing here, pretty boy?"

Luke suffered the assault of bad breath without flinching or drawing away. Any such reaction would be taken as weakness. He kept his tone pleasant. "I have been arrested on suspicion of killing someone," he replied.

The big man gave a crack of laughter. "And did you? Kill the person?"

Luke lifted one eyebrow. "I don't know," he replied. "They haven't told me the name of the person I'm accused of killing."

The big man straightened, his face showing reluctant respect. "So how many people *have* you killed?" he wanted to know.

Luke shrugged. He didn't know. Some, perhaps. Or none. Several villains died some five years ago during the rescue of Mrs Jules Redepenning and Lady Kitty, and he'd been one of the rescuers, but whether anyone had died at his hands, he didn't know. At the time, all that mattered was saving the ladies, and the other women and girls with them.

The big man must have read some of that in Luke's face, for he raised both his eyebrows and said to his cronies, with surprised respect, "He don't know. Pretty boy here don't know how many people he has killed."

"Might be a soldier," said one of the knot of people in the corner.

Big Man looked a question at Luke.

Luke shook his head.

"Humph," said Big Man. He turned on his heel and went back to his group. "He's not bad for a gent," he declared, and didn't pay Luke any more attention.

Luke sat again, this time with one knee bent and that foot flat on the floor. He almost closed his eyes, but was not fool enough to shut them all together. How much time passed, he couldn't be certain.

The second man made a sidling approach along the wall. Luke let his head loll to that side to keep an eye on him, and so was ready when the man began to swing his arm. He ducked within the swing, and pushed up from his foot. As the man's fist hit the brick wall behind where Luke had been sitting, Luke surged up fist first and punched his attacker in the belly, ducking past as the man bent double with the other fist already moving to clip the man's ear.

He strolled a few paces out of reach, but the man was gasping on the ground and had lost interest in picking a fight. Slugger left his corner again, walking up to stand over the man.

"Let that be a lesson to you," he said, and gave Luke a nod of respect.

The rest of the cell's occupants ignored both Luke and the man who had attacked him, though those nearest Luke moved further away. After some time, the assailant picked himself up and slouched off to the far end of the cell, not looking in Luke.

The third attack came out of the blue. Luke had begun to relax but he'd become used to the wide space around him, and the breach of that space alerted him at the same time as the intruder hurled himself at Luke, a sharp knife in each hand.

He caught the man's wrists, pushing them upwards, ignoring the sting as one of the blades sliced his face. The man struggled, shoving at Luke with his hip, kicking out with one booted foot and then the other, pushing against Luke's strength to try to bring the knives within striking distance.

"Guard! Murder!" yelled the big man who had challenged Luke first.

A few moments later, a shout from outside of the cell signalled that the call had been heard. Luke was too busy fighting for his life to see who had arrived, but when a shot rang out, his attacker fell back and he could take a cautious look, moving so he kept the attacker in view.

Several runners, including the warden who had locked Luke into the cell, were staring at a tall fair-haired gentleman who was pointing a smoking pistol at the man with the knives. Luke knew him. The Marquis of Aldridge, man about town and heir to one of the most powerful men in England. The marquis was a cousin of the Earl of Chirbury, and had stayed at Longford Court several times since the earl inherited.

"My lord!" The speaker was another gentleman, this one shorter, older, and plumper. Less fashionably dressed, too. "You cannot fire a gun in the Magistrates' Court!"

"A warning shot, only," Aldridge replied. "To stop the fight. However, I shall certainly fire it again if the man with the knives moves an inch." His tone was conversational, even a little bored. "It's a clever little thing. Fits in a pocket and fires three bullets without reloading. Good afternoon, Mr Ogilvy."

"My lord." Luke inclined into an almost bow. "A timely arrival."

Aldridge quirked one corner of his mouth into a grin. "Mrs Wakefield sent me, to retrieve young Master Paul, and to establish your welfare. Imagine my astonishment to find my intervention so necessary." He didn't take his eyes off the man with the knives as the warder opened the cell and two of the runners entered, to take the knives and secure the man.

The other gentleman puffed his chest out. "I am not releasing Mogg, or Ogilvy or whatever his name is. I have credible evidence that he murdered his infant brother."

Aldridge, even more bored, said, "We shall produce credible evidence that he is innocent of the charge, and that said brother is currently upstairs in your private sitting room, toasting cheese over the fire."

Kitty has been talking. Though Luke supposed his arrest meant his offer of going back into hiding and never challenging Baldwin for the title, which he had not yet made, had already been rejected.

The magistrate's eyes widened, then narrowed. "Until you produce your evidence, he remains in prison," he insisted.

"In a private room, as we agreed. And given this assailant, it seems necessary for his safety as well as his comfort."

"He is the third," Luke commented, "though I think the first was merely a misguided attempt at redressing class injustices." He addressed the magistrate. "You might like to ask that man," he pointed to the third assailant where the runners held him, "and that one," the second, who was pressed against the wall as if hoping it rendered him invisible, "who paid them to kill me."

Aldridge was making his pistol safe and putting it away, but he looked up at that and quirked an eyebrow at the magistrate.

"Yes, yes," the man said. "Very well. Your lordship will have his way. Take that man and that," he spoke to the runners while indicating the two assailants Luke had pointed out, "and question them. Report to me. And bring Ogilvy to my rooms."

Luke strolled towards the cell door, stopping before he reached it to hold out a hand to the big man. "Thank you," he said. "You very likely saved my life."

"Slugger Kelly!" Aldridge commented. "The Pride of the Fancy, as I live and die. What are you doing here? I heard you had set up a school for young boxers!"

That was where Luke had seen him! The man was a famous boxer, and Luke had once attended a match near Bristol.

Kelly was blushing at the marquess's interest. "That I did, your lordship. Good lads, too. Champions."

"Arrested for fighting," the magistrate told Aldridge. "Broke up a pub. They are here till they can pay the fine."

"That's not a problem, then," Aldridge replied. "I will pay the fine, as a thank you for many a won wager, and for saving the life of my friend Ogilvy with his shout. Tell me how much and who to pay it to, and let Slugger and his friends go, if you please."

The magistrate threw up his hands and looked up to the ceiling. "Is there any other criminal I can release for you, my lord?"

Aldridge looked amused by his heavy sarcasm. "That should do for the moment, sir. Come along, Ogilvy."

Kitty spent the rest of the morning worrying. She had poured out the whole story to Prue Wakefield over breakfast. Prue had been sent by the Duchess of Haverford, Kitty's godmother. Apparently, Anne had confided in the duchess about Kitty's letter, so Her Grace had jumped to the conclusion that the Wakefield's special skills might be needed. How right she was!

Prue said that a marquis trumped a baron, and the Duchess of Haverford's son, Aldridge, would take care of everything. She left to go and find that gentleman, who was also her husband's half-brother. Kitty hoped he would agree to exert himself for the sake of a gamekeeper.

It was hard to wait at home, but she knew Prue was right to say Kitty would be given no hearing at all at Great Marlborough Street, whereas the marquis had influence just because he was male and titled. It was unfair, but true. Prue said that, if she could not find the marquis, she would send her husband. David Wakefield was a commoner, but a highly-respected enquiry agent. And, of course, a man.

Halfway through the afternoon, the butler announced that the Marquis of Aldridge wondered if Lady Catherine was at home. The gentleman in question was standing at the butler's shoulder, one sardonic eyebrow raised.

Kitty leapt to her feet, but remembered her manners and greeted him politely. So did Pierrot, with a sniff to his boots and a sharp yap as he sat and offered his paw. Aldridge bent and gravely shook it.

"May I offer you refreshments, my lord?"

"If it pleases you," he said, amusement crinkling the corners of his eyes, "you may fetch your pelisse and bonnet, and have your maid pack what you might need for several nights' stay and bring it over to Haverford House. My mother has sent me to invite you for a short stay, for the sake of appearances. She also has another young guest whom I believe you shall be pleased to see."

Young. So not Luke, who had been at pains on several occasions to point out the decade and a bit that separated their ages. "Paul has been released?" she asked.

"Into my custody," he confirmed. "And before you ask, Ogilvy has been moved to a private room, where he shall have every comfort and a private guard to see to his safety."

Kitty felt as if she could breathe freely for the first time since she woke to Thomson's invasion. "I shall be five minutes," she said, and hurried up to her room, giving the footman in the hall a message for Millie to meet her there.

Soon, she and Aldridge were on their way in the marquis's exquisite high-perch phaeton, behind one of the sweetest-going teams she'd ever seen. Millie would follow with her bags.

With her anxiety lifted just a little, Kitty was able to enjoy her journey, especially when the buildings and crowds of London dropped behind them, leaving farmland and estates on either side of the road. Haverford House was on the Thames, several miles upriver from the capital.

The great house was in the shape of an H, with an ornate fence barring those without business from the huge front courtyard. Not Kitty and her conveyance, though. The gatekeeper heard the toot of Aldridge's groom's horn, and had the gates open before the team swept through without breaking pace.

Whenever Kitty came here to visit her godmother, she felt like a princess called to attend a queen.

They swung in a large arc and pulled to a stop before the flight of steps that led up to a pair of doors that Kitty, as a child, had believed to be created for and by giants. The butler was already opening one of them, and standing before it to await the entry of the marquis and his guest.

Another servant stood ready to conduct Kitty to the duchess, but Aldridge waved him off.

He picked up Pierrot, who made no objection. "I shall escort Lady Kitty myself," he said, and, with the dog in his arms, took her up four flights of stairs to the third level of the building, through the main wing of the house to the family wing, and then along a passage to the rooms that housed the nursery and schoolroom.

"We've made young Paul comfortable up here, with my sisters," he told Kitty. Sure enough, they entered a large comfortable sitting room, where Paul sat on the hearth rug with the duchess's youngest ward, Frances Grenford. Her Grace of Haverford and her other two wards, Jessica and Matilda, watched as Paul and Frances toasted bread and cheese over the fire.

"Again?" Aldridge asked him. "Good afternoon, Mama, ladies."

Paul returned Aldridge's grin. "You hauled me away from the bagwig's office before I could eat the last lot," he complained.

CHAPTER 10

It was beneath Titus to show emotion to such a lowly character as the constable he had bribed. His tone, however, could have frozen the Thames hard enough for another Frost Fair. "You promised. I am disappointed."

Disappointed barely touched the surface of his grief and anger. Lucius was still alive. Titus had paid this stupid wart on the rear end of humanity ten guineas, and had promised ten more, to arrange that Lucius would not survive the cells at Great Marlborough Street.

The man had arranged two assassins. If all had gone well, both Lucius and the boy would have died at the hands of criminals.

Titus had even practiced in front of the mirror, saying, *Oh dear. Now we will never know who the boy really is. What a pity. Never mind.*

But it hadn't gone well. First, the constable in charge had been persuaded not to lock up the boy. Second, Lucius had fought off both of the paid assailants.

As if that wasn't bad enough, the Marquis of Aldridge had turned up as Lucius turned tables on Titus's second assailant, and used it as an excuse to have Lucius moved to a private room. He'd put in his own man as guard, which put Lucius out of reach for the moment. He'd taken the boy, too. The brat was now staying at Haverford House, which was damned near impenetrable.

The constable was burbling apologies, but Titus waved them off. Of course, the man was sorry. He would not be seeing his second payment.

"That will be all," Titus told him. "You have failed me, and we shall not meet again."

He watched the man walk away, wondering if he should arrange an accident. But no. No need to overthink things. The man would not betray him, for two reasons. First, he could not explain what Titus wanted him to do without incriminating himself. Second, he had no idea who Titus was or where to find him. Thanks to a muffling scarf and a hat pulled low over Titus's eyes, he wouldn't be able to identify Titus even if they met again.

Titus would not return to this tavern, which was no loss. The beer was foul and the atmosphere worse. Its only appeal was that its denizens would kill their own mothers for the money he could offer.

There were dozens, perhaps hundreds, just as bad. Titus would just have to find another one. Or Dixon would do it for him. Dixon, his manservant, would not let him down. The man was nearly as clever as Titus, and looked enough like his master to pass for him when necessary. Titus had often used the resemblance to establish an alibi.

Titus had found Dixon in the stews in Newcastle, and was reasonably certain he must be the offspring of a brothel-visiting Baldwin—Titus's uncle or father, probably. Not that he'd discussed that with Dixon.

Dixon was his most useful tool, too valuable to waste in disposing of Lucius and the boy for once and for all. Besides which, Dixon refused to kill anyone. It was an inconvenient quirk on Dixon's part, since Titus had to deal with the criminal underbelly of London himself.

It would be worth it. Someone else would take the lives of Lucius and the boy, and swing for it when they were caught. He and Dixon would focus on his own class and their servants, blackening the reputations of the pair so no one regretted their loss.

He flipped a coin to the bar keeper and walked out the door with the firm step of a man it would not be wise to challenge. People clearly got the message, for they left him alone, which was almost disappointing.

It was late. He'd go home and start again tomorrow. Somewhere in this teaming city must be someone who could rid him of one annoyingly competent man and a helpless boy. One of his father's favourite sayings drifted through his mind and brought a wry curve to his lips. *It is hard to find good help.* If his father only knew how hard!

Luke's new prison was a pleasantly appointed bedchamber. Yes, the door was locked. But he shared the place with no one, he had a comfortable bed, and he even had chairs and a bookshelf, complete with books.

And the guard on the door was not just to make sure that he did not, somehow, break his way through the locks, but that no further assailants managed to get inside and finish him off.

Lord Aldridge's profession of friendship with Luke had so far impressed the magistrate that Luke was fed a very nice dinner, and an excellent breakfast the following morning. From the magistrate's own table, the servant informed him, when the guard opened the door for him to carry in the tray.

After all the travelling, Luke was enjoying the opportunity to sit with his feet up and read *Castle Rackrent*, a Maria Edgeworth novel he found on the bookshelf. When he'd finished that, the shelf offered two he had already read: the rather overwrought Shelley novel, *St Irvyne or The Rosicrucian* and, as a complete contrast, *Sense and Sensibility* by a Lady.

There was also a treatise on agricultural chemistry and a life of Nelson.

He was still on the third of the improvident heirs to the house of Rackrent when the guard knocked on the door and swung it open without waiting for an answer.

Luke came to his feet. "Uncle Baldwin," he acknowledged his visitor. From the corner of his eye, he saw the guard take up a post inside the door.

Baldwin stared at Luke, saying nothing.

Odd. Luke had somehow expected his uncle's murderous intentions towards his nephews to have written their story on his face. Not so. The man was older. He was balding, and grey sprinkled the hair that was left. Still, he was a fine figure of a man, and if Luke had met him without knowing the history, he would have guessed that honesty and kindness formed a large part of his character.

Which just went to show.

Baldwin broke the silence. "Lucius. I could not believe it when they told me… I thought you were dead."

Luke spread his arms. "Still alive. I plan to stay that way, at least until Paul is safe and in his right place again."

"Paul," Baldwin repeated. "Your son."

Luke lifted his chin in challenge. "My brother, and the true baron."

"Your son," Baldwin insisted. "That is what you told people in that village where you have been hiding."

"Your nephew, the true baron, whom I hid when it was obvious someone was trying to kill him." He cupped one elbow with the other hand and lifted the other to his chin, the forefinger stretched along the side of his nose. "I asked myself, who would have a motive to kill a little child who stood between him and the title?"

Baldwin's jaw dropped. His face cycled quickly from astonishment to hurt. "Lucius! You could not possibly have believed such a thing!" He sighed. "Of course, you didn't. You are trying to discomfort me. I did not want to believe the evidence, you know? But it pointed to you, Lucius. The magistrate agreed. Everyone agreed."

Luke shook his head. "I had the advantage of knowing I didn't do it. Indeed, since my brother is still alive, that should be obvious."

"There is no point in this discussion. It gives me no joy to say that you will not be allowed to pass your son off as your brother, and you will hang for the poor little lad's murder." He appeared to be near tears. "I loved you once."

He turned on his heel and marched out the door, followed by the guard. The guard touched his cap to Luke as he shut the door. The click of tumblers said he had turned the key again.

Luke sat back in his chair and picked up his book, but it was a long time before he opened it.

Prue Wakefield must have told Aldridge everything that had happened since Kitty overheard the plot to kill Luke and Paul. He, in turn, must have disclosed all to his mother. The duchess was full of plans to establish that Kitty had not been travelling with only her maid and two males to whom she was not related.

"We can leave the legal side of it to the Wakefields and Aldridge, my dear," she said. "You and I will make certain that your reputation is not harmed in any way. The first step is for you to come out in Society with us. We will make it clear to anyone who asks that you have been staying with me while Rede and Anne are out of Town."

"I have not brought any of my evening gowns with me, Aunt Eleanor," Kitty protested. The last thing she wanted to do while Luke was in prison was to go out on the town.

The duchess waved off the objection. "We can alter something of Jessica's. The two of you are near enough to the same size. Or, if you prefer, we can send to Chirbury House for more of your wardrobe."

Kitty tried to explain. "I do not feel right going out to enjoy myself while Luke—Mr Ogilvy is under this cloud."

"Enjoy yourself?" Aunt Eleanor raised both eyebrows in an expression that managed to convey both surprise and disappointment. "Dear Kitty, this is not about enjoying yourself, though you are welcome to do so if you wish. This is a campaign to ensure the whole world finds it impossible to connect you and your maid with the anonymous females who were travelling with Mr Ogilvy."

Kitty frowned. How would people know about Luke and his

incarceration, let alone that he had been travelling with two women?

The duchess appeared to read her mind. "The newspapers bribe people in the magistrates courts to tell them anything of interest that happens in and around the ton, and even if none of the constables talk to a reporter, who is to say that the person who gave them their information will not?"

"Oh." Kitty had not thought of that. Aunt Eleanor's mention of the informant reminded her of a question she had been pondering before Aldridge collected her.

"How do you suppose they knew we were at Chirbury House, Aunt Eleanor? Someone must have been watching it for Lord Baldwin, do you not think?"

Her Grace pursed her lips. "I find it hard to believe that Baron Baldwin is a murderer, Kitty, I must say. He is very well regarded at the Admiralty, and Lord Redepenning thinks highly of him."

Kitty knew the duchess and Rede's Uncle Henry were both shrewd judges of character, but in this case, they must have been fooled, for Kitty knew what she had heard.

The duchess hadn't finished. "However, whoever the villain is, I think your deduction is likely. I am relieved that the constables were not told to look for Lady Catherine Stocke. If the villain knows only that two women were with Mr Ogilvy and young Paul, but not who the women were, we need not fear him spreading rumours about you in the ton. Thank goodness you had the sense to take your maid with you and to travel incognito."

That caused Kitty to frown again. "The servants at Chirbury House know, but they have been told not to mention it to anyone. I think they will be quiet. I told them who I was at Selby Manor. The butler did not believe me, and turned me away, but some of the footmen also know. Mr Mexstead, the old stablemaster, recognised me, but he told his family not to tell anyone who I was. Said I should keep it a secret."

The duchess nodded. "Wise man. I think no harm has been done, Kitty. For one thing, who is going to talk to some footmen in Essex? The villain did not know where you were coming from, or he would not have needed to watch Chirbury House. For another, even if he did, by some random chance, discover that Mr Ogilvy and his party had been at Selby Manor, the butler's opinion is the one that will carry weight. Especially if we do a good enough job of convincing people that you were with Rede and Anne in London three days ago, and have been staying with me ever since."

Kitty supposed it was a good idea. She did not want to bring shame on Anne and Rede, or cause more trouble for Luke. "But not tonight, Aunt Eleanor," she begged. "I do not think I can smile and be pleasant tonight."

Her Grace looked appraisingly at Kitty and then nodded. "Stay at home tonight, and Matilda, Jessica, and I shall prepare the ground. We shall mention that you did not feel up to coming out with us tonight. Perhaps you have had a slight ague since arriving in London? Yes. That shall work very well, and will explain why you did not race off to Longford with your sister and my nephew. You shall be completely over this ague by tomorrow night, Kitty dear."

Kitty took the last sentence as a command, not a suggestion. "Yes, Aunt Eleanor."

CHAPTER 11

Luke's next visitor was David Wakefield. He arrived during an altercation between the guard Aldridge had set outside the door and a couple of other men.

Luke, who had been lying on the bed reading his book, had moved closer to the door to hear the dispute.

"Where do you think you are going with that?" the guard asked.

"Dinner for the prisoner," one of the other men barked.

There was a confusion of voices then, and Luke couldn't pick out all the words, but the sense of it was that Aldridge had arranged for the guard's relief to bring a meal from a cookshop when he arrived, so the guard was suspicious. The men with the meal were arguing that the magistrate was responsible for feeding prisoners and they were just doing their job.

Wakefield—Luke put his face to the hatch in the door and could see it was him—spoke firmly over the rest and imposed silence. "Mr Ogilvy will not require any foods provided here, but will eat what is sent to him by the Marquis of Aldridge," he said. "You must want your dinner, however, the pair of you. Sit down and eat."

There was a scuffle and a shout. At least one of the men had tried to run.

Luke sighed. Presumably, that counted as murder attempt number three for the day. (One could not include Slugger's independent attempt at intimidation.) His attempt at humour settled his disquiet.

After some more low-voiced conversation, the door was unlocked and opened.

"May I come in?" said Wakefield. He held a tray with a covered plate and an opened bottle.

"Please do," Luke said, "Is that my last supper?"

"Intended to be so, I suspect." Wakefield put the tray on top of a chest. "I've sent a message to my groom. He'll collect it and take it for examination. I have a chemist friend who may be able to figure out what is in it, and who will at least be able to feed it to a rat to see if my suspicions are true."

"My uncle is determined to see an end to me." Luke had thought he was over the sense of betrayal that had wounded him so deeply nine years ago. He was wrong. Seeing his uncle again today had brought it all back—the love, the disbelief, the agony of knowing the man was so false.

"Someone is, certainly," Wakefield agreed. "Aldridge told me about your assailants. He also told me to pass on to you to only eat and drink what is provided by his men. I thought he was being over cautious. I will need to congratulate him on his perspicacity. He will be unbearably smug."

Luke shrugged. "I will be cautious," he agreed. "Is Paul safe? Is Lady Kitty? And Millie Price?"

Wakefield was reassuring. "Your young charge, Lady Kitty and Miss Price are all staying with the Duchess of Haverford, and are well guarded." He pulled one of the two chairs out from the table and sat down. "I have some questions, Ogilvy, if I may. Lady Kitty explained the core of your story to my wife, who told me, but I'd like to go over it to see what threads I can tease out to find evidence for your acquittal."

Luke took the other chair as Wakefield added, "Or conviction. I should warn you that I serve the truth. I do not hide facts that inconvenience my clients."

"The truth will serve me well," Luke assured Wakefield. "I can't tell you what evidence has been given against me, but I believe you will be able to prove that the brother I was supposed to have killed is alive and well, and has been living as my son these last nine years."

"That is what Lady Kitty told my wife. It follows that, if a charge of murder is disproven or dismissed, whoever laid the information will claim kidnapping, which might be harder to defend."

Luke shook his head. "Not so. My father appointed me my brother's trustee and custodial guardian. I had every right, and it was my duty, to remove him from a situation of danger."

"An unusual arrangement," Wakefield commented.

"For a bastard to be appointed to that role?" Luke demanded. "My father knew I loved Paul. Or Julius, as he was called back then. I do love him."

"I know," Wakefield agreed. "I have seen you together. Ogilvy, Aldridge is sending a solicitor to talk to you tomorrow, and he can cover what you might be charged with, what your defences might be, and that sort of thing. Trust the man. My job is to investigate Baldwin and uncover a crime that has been buried for nine years. And with that in mind, I have some questions."

The cell door opened again, and Wakefield's groom entered with a couple of small boxes. Wakefield loaded the suspect food into one of them and gave him the bottle. The other box proved to contain Luke's dinner.

After he left, Luke said, "Ask your questions, Wakefield."

"I can do that while you eat, Ogilvy. Go ahead."

It was more of an interrogation. Each of the attempts all those years ago was finely dissected. Wakefield demanded even to understand Luke's feelings at the time.

"The wheel on the gig taking him and his nursemaid to church was possibly an accident. I thought the next was, too, or the carelessness of the maids. Perhaps it was. The little baron was a fiend for escaping from his nursery, so we had a gate across the door that adults could step over, and another, for safety, on the door to the servant' stairs. He could manage the main stairs, scooting down them feet first on his stomach, but the servants' stairs were too steep, and they had big gaps between the banisters."

Luke shuddered at the memory, though it was not as bad as what came later. "Both gates were down and the doors were open. Paul started down the stairs at full speed because the maids were already calling for him and he didn't want to be caught. If I hadn't been coming up at just the right moment, he'd have been over the side. If he was lucky, he'd have dropped a flight onto stone steps. But he was small enough to go down the gap between the flights—forty feet to the stone flags below."

"Where had the maids been when he got out? Who was the last person through those doors? How easy was it to unlatch the gates?" Wakefield had these questions and more, and Luke had to search his memory. He couldn't answer all of them. "Uncle Baldwin questioned the servants. He told me some of it—said no one was taking responsibility for the lapse, and that he had given them all a stern warning."

"And the next time?"

"Possibly the fraying of the ropes on his swing, but I noticed that before Paul could use it. We'd had a storm, and they may have rubbed against the tree." He shrugged. "If it was deliberate, anyone could have done it. Everyone in the house and on the estate could get to that tree. Visitors too."

"And no one was seen near the tree or touching the ropes, I take it."

Luke heaved a sigh. "No one remembered seeing anything, but I didn't ask until after the next incident, which was definitely not an accident." Luke could see the scene as clearly as if it had happened yesterday, and his heart lurched as it had then. "A fire in the nursery, but an open flame was never left there at night, and it started in a clutter of paper and wood shavings in the corner nearest to Paul's night nursery. The clutter should not have been there; wasn't there when I made my usual nightly visit. Nanny was a tartar about keeping the nursery clean and tidy. But Paul had had a slight temperature when I read him his goodnight story, and I came to check on him a second time. The fire was just taking hold. The clutter went up in seconds and the flames spread to the curtain above."

"What did Baldwin say when you told him that the fire had been set?" Wakefield asked.

"That I must have been mistaken. It was dark. I was in a hurry to get Paul and get out of there. He was right about that. I screamed for the maids and jumped the flames to fetch Paul. The servants confirmed where the fire was, but not the fuel that set it leaping high enough to reach the curtains."

Luke suspected that the curtains had been splashed with alcohol or something else to encourage the blaze that whooshed up them to scorch the ceiling, but they were ashes by the time the fire was out, so he had nothing to prove his suspicions except his own observations, and Uncle Baldwin refused to believe him. Or, at least, professed to do so. "The rumours started after that."

Wakefield teased more memories out of his brain, and then moved on to the rumours that began to circulate in the week after the fire.

"I noticed the looks first. And the nursemaids were suddenly very diligent in their work, never leaving me alone with Paul. Then a footman started to follow me around whenever I was in the house. My cousin told me people were saying I had tried to throw Paul down the stairs and set fire to the nursery. He didn't believe it, but he thought I should know about the gossip."

No, Luke told Wakefield, he had no idea how widespread the rumours were. He had not been able to find out where they originated, and had not suspected his uncle until Baldwin accused him directly, and tried to have him removed from the house pending an investigation.

"Even then, I trusted him. I'd known him all my life! I talked to him, described again what I'd seen. I agreed that someone was trying to kill Paul, but it certainly wasn't me."

Luke had thought he was getting through to the man. Baldwin acknowledged that the circumstances were suspicious. In addition, he agreed Luke had nothing to gain by killing the child, and much to lose.

"He suggested it was time to get the local authorities involved and I thought so too, and wanted to send a footman. But he said we should keep it quiet for the moment, so I rode over to ask the magistrate, the local squire, to call on us. On me and my uncle. On the way there, someone shot at me. Creased my shoulder and spooked my horse. Nothing worse, though. After that, I had to accept the truth. My uncle was trying to become baron, and Paul and I stood in his way."

Wakefield had more questions. Who else knew where he was going? Was the route he took his normal route? What time of day was this? On and on until they'd drained that incident of anything Wakefield could think to ask.

Another knock on the door was the groom returning with a report. "The rat died, Mr Wakefield." He backed out again. Wakefield nodded thoughtfully. "The fact that someone is desperate to kill you inclines me to believe you are innocent, Ogilvy."

Which was some comfort, Luke supposed.

"Back to your story. What happened next?" Wakefield asked.

Luke shuddered. "The next one might have succeeded, if Paul hadn't had a tantrum. He was a good little boy on the whole, but he did not like fish. Still doesn't. If the murderer had chosen a different meal, we might not be here now. Paul threw his entire dinner on the floor, and his puppy gulped down the fish before anyone could stop him. The dog went into severe cramps and died."

"More evidence in your favour," Wakefield said. "You would have poisoned something he would eat without fuss. I'm assuming you knew his preferences?" Another interrogation followed. Questions Luke had not considered at the time. He could have done with Wakefield back then!

"I take it your uncle took your concerns seriously after that?" Wakefield said.

Luke nodded. "My uncle sent his son for the magistrate. It was a disaster. The magistrate believed the rumours. My cousin and I both argued I had no reason to hurt Paul. I pointed out I had been shot on the way to fetch the magistrate. But he had made up his mind. My uncle was the respected second son of a baron. I was the base-born brat of the gamekeeper's daughter. In a dispute between us, I must be guilty. I was to be locked up pending investigations."

Wakefield's eyes widened. "The devil you say! He actually gave the circumstances of your birth as his reason for ignoring the evidence?"

"Not an uncommon point-of-view," Luke said. Wakefield was the base-born son of a duke. He must know how most people regarded those born on the wrong side of the blanket.

"Sadly true. So, you were locked up, and I suppose your brother was attacked again."

"Fortunately, the nanny believed me. She had taken to sleeping in the night nursery, and had persuaded a footman to sleep in the nursery itself. They chased off someone who was holding a pillow down over Paul's face."

Wakefield frowned. "I gather that didn't exonerate you."

"The devil of it was that someone had failed to lock the room they were keeping me in, and I escaped." Luke groaned at the memory. His only thought had been to protect Paul, and instead, he nearly got himself hanged.

Wakefield saw the implications immediately. "Doing exactly what your enemy expected."

"The nanny couldn't see the face of the intruder in the dark night nursery. The footman chased him to the window and got a better look, though the light was still poor. He could not swear that the man was not me."

Wakefield came to the same conclusion that Luke had. "I don't suppose they expected the nanny and the footman. The smothering attempt was meant to succeed."

"Yes. So I—

"Just a minute. We'll get to that. I have a few questions about your escape."

Of course, he did. Luke answered them.

Wakefield's last question on that topic was, "How did you come to hear about the nanny's precautions and what happened in the night nursery?"

"She told me, two nights later, when I broke in to steal Paul away. I managed to sneak past the footman, but he heard us talking. They believed me, Wakefield." Luke choked up, cast back into that dark hour when the whole world seemed arrayed against him and his death would mean the death of the person dearest to him in the world.

"I'm sorry." He took a deep gulping breath. "She believed me, and she persuaded the footman, who was her nephew. She agreed Paul and I needed to disappear. She sent her nephew to the kitchen for warm milk, drugged it with laudanum, and they both drank it and went back to bed. I never had a way to discover what happened to them, but if they are still alive, Wakefield, they can confirm that part of my story."

Wakefield nodded. "I will find out. I will talk to them if I can. So, then you staged your murder suicide."

Luke shrugged. "It seemed the only way to end it. It wasn't hard. I left our coats and my spare shoes on the cliff and jumped off, with Paul in my arms. I'd waited two nights because a storm had moved in the day I was arrested, and in any case, I needed both the high tide and moonlight. There's a particular spot on the coast near Ormswood Hall with a pool among the rocks deep enough to safely jump into at high tide. If I'd figured it wrong, the fiction would have become fact. But I'd been playing on that coast since I was knee high to a grasshopper. I knew we had a better than good chance of getting away."

Which led to more questions. Luke told him about the boat, full of things they might need, including money Luke had taken out of his bank weeks ago, fearing they might need to run. About sailing far down the coast, sleeping during the day and travelling on at night. About buying milk and bread for Paul from remote farmhouses and tiny fishing villages along the way.

He was exhausted when Wakefield ran out of questions and left. And when he finally managed to sleep, his dreams were full of the anguish and fear of those days, tied up in visions of Paul—the youth he was now—being repeatedly ripped from Luke's arms to a horrible death.

CHAPTER 12

Kitty took Pierrot to leave him upstairs in the nursery wing with Paul and the duchess's youngest ward, Frances.

"You look lovely, Lady Kitty," said Frances. "Doesn't she, Paul?"

"She always does," Paul replied, without much interest. He had produced a knotted rope from his pocket and he and Pierrot were tugging, one on each end, Pierrot growling with every evidence of delight.

It was a game that they'd invented during the few idle moments on their journey, and was obviously more interesting than Kitty's ballgown. Kitty rolled her eyes at Frances, and Frances giggled.

Downstairs, the marquis, who was escorting them tonight, was far more complimentary. Kitty told him that the praise was due to Millie, who had taken one of Jessica's gowns from last year and performed some magic with a needle to make it look as if it had been taken straight from the pages of *The Lady's Magazine*.

"All praise to the seamstress," Aldridge said, "but the damsel within graces the lovely dress, Lady Kitty."

Kitty bobbed him a curtsey. "Thank you, kind sir." She was not much interested in his easy compliments, but she did hope for a moment of his time to ask if he had any further news of Luke.

Not in front of the duchess and her wards, however. The girls were already far too convinced that Kitty and Luke were romantically involved, and wanted to be regaled with all the details. The duchess had made the same assumption, and disapproved. "You can do better for yourself, Kitty dear," she said.

Kitty would wait until she could talk to Aldridge alone. He might share his mother's and sisters' opinion, but at least he would keep his own to himself. There was no opportunity now, with everyone ready and the carriage at the door. Like it or not, she was off to a ball.

Her Grace was a stricter chaperone than Kitty's sister Anne. After five seasons, Anne allowed Kitty to leave her side as soon as they arrived at an entertainment, and Kitty spent most of the time at balls with the ladies she'd met in her early years as a debutante, all of them now married, or dancing with some of the men who had become friends over the years.

The duchess wanted her to stay close. "I know you are an adult, Kitty dear," she explained, "but I count myself responsible for you at the moment, so stay within my sight, please. To ease my mind?"

It was very hard to say 'no' to the duchess.

Fortunately, several ladies she knew came to talk to her. "Kitty Stocke," exclaimed the first arrival. "I did not know you were in Town. At least, I heard Lord and Lady Chirbury were here, but then I was told they were gone again."

"Kitty came to stay with me until her sister and brother-in-law return to Town later in the week," Her Grace said, smoothly.

"I haven't been out and about in Society," Kitty explained. "I was a bit under the weather." *Rain, wind, sunshine. It had been quite changeable weather.* Kitty rather liked the duchess's tactic of telling the truth in ways that led people to draw entirely false inferences.

The other ladies asked after her health, and she reassured them and enquired about their children, which successfully diverted the conversation. Before long, she was petitioned for a dance by a couple of gentlemen who had paid fashionable court to her in previous years, and who were still friends because they had never had serious intentions.

Her most persistent suitor, the reason she had left London early this year and not returned, was fortunately not at the ball. Lord Hardwicke-Chalmers was certain that her declared disinterest in his courtship was a ruse to make him more eager, for he could not imagine that any spinster of her age would turn down such an eligible gentleman. She could handle him, but the need to do so had ruined many an evening she would otherwise have enjoyed.

Part way through the evening, Lord Baldwin approached the duchess. Kitty saw them chatting as she returned on the arm of the gentleman who had partnered her for a vigorous quatre dance.

Almost, she lied, and claimed a need for the retiring room. But no. She would not run from the horrid man. She summoned her most pleasant social manner, and allowed her partner to escort her the rest of the way to Her Grace.

"Thank you, Lord Smithson, that was most enjoyable," she said.

The young lord bowed to her, then to the duchess before leaving to secure his partner for the next dance.

"Kitty, dear," the duchess said, "May I make known to you Lord Baldwin. The baron is an indefatigable servant to his duties at the Admiralty, Kitty. Lord Baldwin, Lady Catherine is the youngest sister of Lady Chirbury, wife to my nephew. I believe you know his uncle, Lord Redepenning."

The gentleman bowed. Up close, Kitty could see some resemblances to Luke. The shape of the eyes and the chin. The dark hair, now peppered with salt, with the same stubborn cowlick escaping whatever pomade he had used to control it.

"Your servant, Lady Catherine," he said. Was his the voice she had heard that day in the village? As near as she could remember it. Light. Cultivated.

She curtseyed. "Lord Baldwin. Have you known Uncle Henry long?"

"A number of years," he replied, vaguely. "I do not yet have more than a passing acquaintance with your brother-in-law, Chirbury. I plan to call on him, however, on his return to London. I gather some sudden emergency called him away? A problem with a servant, perhaps?"

Kitty widened her eyes. "Rede didn't tell me, Lord Baldwin? Whatever put that into your head? Did Uncle Henry say something."

"I heard that a gamekeeper in his employ had run off?" Baldwin said, fixing her with a frown.

Kitty opened her eyes even wider. "Rede said nothing to me," she stated, with perfect veracity. "But then, estate business is not a lady's domain." She creased her brow, as if in thought. "But if that was so, why did Anne go with him?" She put her hand affectionately on the duchess's arm. "I was so grateful Aunt Eleanor invited me to stay. I feared missing part of the season!" Many gentlemen found it impossible to believe a beauty could have any wits at all, which in Kitty's view, made them fair game for a display of imbecility.

Whether or not Baldwin was convinced, he must have accepted she was telling him nothing. "That would have been a tragedy indeed," he said, his disinterest imperfectly hidden.

"Yes, for I had new gowns," she confided, twirling a little so her skirts belled around her.

The man's eyes twitched, as if he wanted to turn them upwards, but he managed to make a few more civil remarks before taking himself off.

Aunt Eleanor lightly rapped Kitty's knuckles with her fan.

"You are a minx, Catherine Stocke," she said. "*Yes, for I had new gowns*, indeed!"

The following day, Kitty accompanied the duchess and her two older wards on afternoon visits and then to a meeting of one of the duchess's charities. Afterwards, Her Grace ordered the open carriage to stop at Gunter's for ices, sending a footman in to make the order. They ate the delicious confections in the carriage.

It was a sunny afternoon, and many other people had had the same idea. All four ladies were hailed by friends and acquaintances, many of whom came to chat for a time. Not all of them were welcome.

One of the younger ladies who persisted in regarding Kitty as a rival to be brought low asked Kitty, "Is it true that your brother's gamekeeper has been arrested for murder?"

Kitty opened her eyes as widely as she could. "Goodness, Miss Fairburn, who is spreading such a story?"

Miss Fairburn blushed. "I heard it somewhere." She looked up and past Kitty's shoulder. "I wondered if it was true."

Kitty frowned, and shook her head slightly. "It does not sound likely," she said. "I wonder which gamekeeper, and whom he might be supposed to have murdered? And why?"

Lady Juliana Meredith leaned closer. "I heard you were at the house when the man was arrested, and that the constable tried to arrest you, Lady Catherine."

Kitty answered that perfectly true statement with a burst of laughter. The Duchess of Haverford broke from her conversation with a couple of matrons to say, "I can assure you that no constables have attempted to arrest a lady staying in my house, Lady Juliana." She finished with a harrumphing sound that indicated her opinion of any constable foolish enough to try.

One could depend upon Miss Fairburn and her cronies to repeat juicy gossip, and to add speculation to make it more inflammatory. One could hope that the disapproval of the duchess might help to button their lips.

When Aunt Eleanor turned away again, Miss Fairburn changed the subject. "Such a pretty dress, Lady Catherine. Are you hoping to bring back the sleeve style from last Season?" She batted her eyelashes at the rest of the group as if hoping for applause.

Kitty chuckled again. "I am happy to leave the pursuit of fashion to you young ladies, Miss Fairburn. This is a gown from last Season. For some reason, I did not wear it, though I like it very much." She lifted one arm. "The sleeves are particularly pretty, do you not think?"

"You were very polite to her," Jessica said, after the group made their farewells and excuses, and moved away. "I wanted to scratch her eyes out, and she wasn't even addressing her nasty comments to me!"

Kitty smiled again. "My niece's nanny, Hannah, always said, *A soft answer turneth away wrath.* In my experience, a soft answer drives one's would-be persecutors wild with rage. Their barbs have failed to pierce my armour, and yet, I have said nothing to which they can take offence."

Jessica chuckled. "I shall remember that."

Jessica knew all about barbs from the likes of Miss Fairburn. She and her sisters, Matilda and Frances, had been raised amidst luxury and given every advantage, but in the eyes of Society's high sticklers, nothing could wipe out the stain of their birth. They were all three daughters of the Duke of Haverford by different mistresses.

"Lady Catherine! Lady Catherine!" The voice, a man's tenor blemished by a shrill nasal whine, could come from only one man. Kitty turned to look, suppressing the inevitable sigh.

Sure enough, Hardwicke-Chalmers came rushing through the crowd, oblivious to the child he nearly stepped on and the waiter whose tray of ices nearly flew up into his face. The waiter performed an aerobatic masterpiece of a manoeuvre and continued on his way as Hardwicke-Chalmers skidded to a stop beside the landau and looked up into Kitty's face with a delighted smile, sure of his welcome.

"You need to tell your brother to dismiss his butler, Lady Catherine. They told me at your house you were not in town," he said.

Her Grace answered the man while Kitty was still gasping at his impertinence. "I daresay, Mr Hardwicke-Chalmers, that they said she was not at home. And no more she is. Lady Catherine is my guest at Haverford House."

Hardwicke-Chalmers gaped at the duchess as if surprised to find her there, then blinked hard and gulped. "That would be it, Your Grace," he agreed.

He then turned to Kitty and asked what entertainments she was attending, as he wished to reserve as many dances as she would grant him, and if she was planning on taking in a musicale, he wished to claim the great honour of sitting beside her.

Kitty could scarcely believe the affrontery of the man, ignoring the existence of the duchess's two wards and even the duchess herself. "I must defer to Her Grace," she said, pointedly, "who has been kind enough to chaperone me, along with her wards, Miss Grenford and Miss Jessica Grenford. The choice of invitations is entirely over to Her Grace."

Hardwicke-Chalmers looked at the two Grenford girls, at the duchess, and then back at Kitty. "Awkward," he said. "I will have to think about this."

With that remark, he walked away. Even for Hardwicke-Chalmers, that was extraordinarily bad manners.

"Have you known Mr Hardly Charming for long?" Jessica asked. The nickname fitted perfectly.

Kitty giggled at the mangling of the oaf's name even as she answered. "He has been pursuing me all Season. He seems to think that I am too old to be selective. What is awkward? And what does he have to think about?"

"Us," Matilda provided. "If you are chaperoned by our guardian, he can hardly dance with you and refuse to dance with us. And he cannot possibly be seen dancing with such as us."

Kitty was quick to say, "Surely not. Would he say such a thing in front of you if that is what he meant?" *Yes*, she answered her own question. *He is that crass and dense.*

"A foolish and conceited young man, with little justification for either," the duchess said. "I believe him to have sufficient native wit if he cared to apply it, but instead, he depends on his mother to do all his thinking for him."

Kitty was surprised, for the Duchess of Haverford seldom spoke ill of anyone.

"Have a care, dear Kitty," Her Grace added. "Honoria Hardwicke-Chalmers' sense of ethics is bound up with her own self-importance. If she has set her sights on your dowry to drag her family out of the hands of the moneylenders, she will not hesitate to be underhanded in her methods."

"I will not give him the opportunity to stage a compromise," Kitty promised, adding, "and I would not, in any case, marry a man who tried to force my consent, even if it meant giving up Society. Living without invitations is much preferable to living with a tyrant and a liar."

She would have caught back the last sentences had she thought them through before she spoke them. The Duke of Haverford was both tyrant and liar, as well as erratic and a rakehell.

However, the duchess merely commented, "Very wise, my dear, but it would be advisable to avoid the need to make such a choice.

CHAPTER 13

They arrived home to a note from Rede, the Earl of Chirbury, Kitty's brother-in-law. The man himself was announced half an hour later.

"Did Anne come to London with you?" Kitty asked, after the initial flurry of greetings.

"She is following at a slower pace, Kitty," Rede told her. "She has the children with her. She didn't want to stay in Longford when you might need her, but she wouldn't leave without the children. She should be here late tomorrow." He addressed the duchess. "I'd be grateful if you could allow Kitty to stay until Anne reaches London, Aunt Eleanor."

"Kitty may stay as long as she likes," the duchess replied. She smiled at Kitty. "After our encounter with Hardwicke-Chalmers, I better understand why you were reluctant to join our social round, but I can assure you that I am more than capable of dealing with that young man and his mother."

"Horrid man," Jessica commented.

"Is he still making a nuisance of himself?" Rede asked. "Bounder. Perhaps I should have a word."

"Just tell him that my trustees have lost all my money, and that you and Anne have disowned me," Kitty suggested. "I guarantee he will have no further interest in me." Matilda and Jessica laughed, but Rede did not appear to find her comment funny.

The duchess stood. "Matilda, Jessica, we shall leave Chirbury to talk to Kitty about Mr Ogilvy and his younger brother," she announced. "Rede, I shall have Paul sent down to join you, and refreshments sent in. Come along, Matilda, Jessica."

Kitty wasn't quite sure what to expect from her brother-in-law. Would he be cross with her for chasing after Luke? "I could not let them just disappear, Rede," she blurted, as the door closed behind the duchess and her wards. "It was what Luke planned: to go somewhere else and start again, and hide for another decade or more."

Rede raised his eyebrows. "Instead of which, you persuaded him to come to London, where he has been arrested and will face trial for murder."

"His brother is alive and well, so he cannot be convicted," Kitty argued. "And Paul has the right to be recognised as baron, which was never going to happen if he and Luke kept hiding."

"Hmm," said Rede. "There seems to be a lot to the story that I had not heard. If I understand correctly, Paul is Luke's brother, and not his son, and Paul, but not Luke, is a baron. Please explain, Kitty."

Kitty briefly outlined Luke's history as she knew it, and what had happened since she overheard the plotting in Longford.

Rede nodded, thoughtfully, but said, "Might I suggest running or making a stand was their choice to make, not yours?"

"They made the choice," Kitty insisted. "I just pointed out that they had one."

"Hmm," said Rede again.

Kitty waited to see if he had anything more to say. When he just looked at her, his face showing no expression, she said, "I told Luke and Paul that you would help them; that they didn't need to hide any more. Luke was alone against powerful enemies when he first took his brother and fled, but I said that our family and our friends would believe Luke, and support them both to win what is rightfully theirs." She lifted her chin in challenge as she finished the statement. If Rede made a liar of her, she would appeal to Anne.

Rede's tone was mild as he replied. "It appears you have been marshalling support very competently without my help. Aunt Eleanor has clearly decided in Paul's favour. I have spoken with David Wakefield, and he is committed to helping Luke. And I understand that my cousin Aldridge is taking a hand. Well done, Kitty."

"You've spoken to Wakefield?" she repeated.

"Yes, and written to the magistrate letting him know that my wife has pertinent evidence in the case, and shall be available for an interview the day after tomorrow. Also, that I am happy to stand as a character witness for the accused."

Kitty flew out of her chair and bent over Rede's chair to hug him. "Rede! I knew you could be trusted to help them both."

He gave her a pat on her back, and released her. She was resuming her seat, a little flustered at her emotional response, when Paul entered the room, Pierrot at his heels.

"Ah, Paul," Rede said. "Or should I say, Lord Baldwin?"

Paul was bowing, but at that, he shot upright. "Oh, I say," he protested, and then, "I suppose I am. How strange."

Pierrot danced up to Kitty and demanded to be lifted onto her lap. Kitty settled him, happy to be an observer in this conversation. She would support Paul if he needed it, but Rede was a fond father, and she had confidence her intervention would not be called on.

"It's an unusual situation," Rede acknowledged. "You were confirmed as baron while you were still a baby, so your uncle's confirmation was based on the false premise that you were dead. It will make the House of Lords very uncomfortable, and I imagine that the current incumbent will argue you are an imposter."

Paul shrugged. "I am not an imposter, though. I don't remember it myself, but Dad has told me all about it. I am Baron Baldwin, whether my uncle likes it or not."

"Then it is up to us to find the evidence to convince the House of Lords," Rede agreed. "Paul, Kitty is coming home with me to Chirbury House when my countess arrives tomorrow. However, I would like you to consider staying here, at least until I can be sure we can keep you safe. Haverford House is better defended against intruders."

"Do you think he will try again to kill me?" Paul asked. His face lit with glee, as if having a target on his back was a cause for celebration.

"I do not doubt it," Rede replied. "He has two choices. Three, in fact, but I do not expect him to cede the field without contest. First, he can eliminate the challenge by eliminating the challengers. He is the heir in the event of your death, Paul, and he will assume, wrongly as it happens, that those who are currently supporting Luke will give up once you and Luke are both dead."

Kitty wished Rede would stop talking about the deaths of her friends. She would have said something, but Paul was not turning a hair. "And the second?" he asked.

"He is already pursuing that one, and I should have said that he can follow both choices at the same time. He will fight in the courts and, if necessary, in the House of Lords, to prove you are an imposter. If that works, you are no longer a threat."

He frowned a little. "Which means you and Luke also have two choices. I imagine Luke has already considered offering Baldwin a deal; signing something that says you are an imposter in return for Baldwin's promise to let you both leave the country and never come back. Has he discussed that with you?"

He hadn't mentioned it to Kitty, and she expected Paul to say "no", but he nodded instead. "Yes, and I choose to stand and fight, Lord Chirbury."

Rede nodded, as if that was the answer he expected. "Then be very careful, Lord Baldwin. It would be a shame to be proving your right to the barony over your corpse."

Kitty flinched, and this time, Paul looked slightly disconcerted.

"Good," Rede commented. "Don't treat this as a game, young man. It is not. My family and I will be very distressed if you and your brother were killed. My sister Kitty here, in particular. Take care, and we shall win through in the end."

Luke knew there were worse things than being locked in a clean room with regular meals, hot water for washing, and a small stack of books to read. As an active man who spent most of his days outside, he had to keep reminding himself of that fact.

The most difficult part was not knowing what was going on. He had to trust Wakefield's investigation to find the truth and Aldridge's influence to ensure that Paul was safeguarded. It chaffed him not to be able to act on his own behalf.

As the third day in custody dragged to a close, he was pacing the room. Twelve paces from the inside wall to the outside. Fifteen across the length of the room at a slight angle, to avoid the wall on one side and the chest of drawers on the other.

A knock on the door heralded a welcome interruption from his own thoughts, whether it was a meal delivered by David Wakefield's man, the enquiry agent himself, the magistrate asking some more questions, or even his uncle.

Though he hoped it was not his uncle. He had still not recovered from the last confrontation. Deep down, it seemed, he had always hoped that his uncle was the man he pretended to be, and there was another explanation for the events all those years ago.

He did not expect the gentleman who entered after the lock was disengaged, though he should have. Of course. His employer. The Earl of Chirbury. Brother-in-law of the lady who had masqueraded as his wife for one glorious—one ill-conceived—week.

"My lord," he said, in greeting.

Chirbury returned a nod. "Mogg. But it isn't, is it? Ogilvy, I believe?"

Luke bowed. "Lucius Ogilvy, my lord. At your service."

Chirbury raised an eyebrow. "But you are not, are you? At my service. You resigned in the letter you left on your table at the gamekeeper's cottage."

Luke couldn't tell the man's mood. Before the death of a cousin made him earl, Chirbury had spent years in the wilds of Canada, building a successful fur trapping business. He was an expert in concealing his emotions and thoughts behind a mild expression and half-closed eyes.

"I did, my lord." He kept his own face carefully blank. "The resignation stands." He probably no longer had the option of disappearing into anonymity again, but neither of the other possibilities included being Chirbury's gamekeeper.

Chirbury put one of them into words. "You'll be in Northumberland raising a baron," he suggested.

"That," Luke agreed. "Or dead. My lord, if the case goes against me, would you take Paul and protect him? I know it's a lot to ask, but—"

"Consider it done," Chirbury interrupted. "If things go badly, I will take him into my family. But we shall endeavour to ensure they don't, for my sister will be upset if they hang you by the neck until dead, Lucius Ogilvy. Speaking of which, what are your intentions towards my sister?"

Typical Chirbury. A soothing remark then a sneak attack. Two, in fact. Luke forced back the visceral reaction at the thought of his hanging, and tried to deflect the second jab. "Lady Catherine?"

Chirbury raised a single eyebrow. "You thought I might possibly mean my sister Meg or my sister Lady Bexley?"

Luke stopped jousting. "I cannot have intentions towards Lady Catherine."

The other eyebrow lifted. "*Cannot.* Not *will not*, or *do not.*" The earl's tone was contemplative. "Perhaps you mean *should not?* My question is *why not?* You travelled for a week introducing her as your wife. Some would say you owe her a proposal." He pulled out one of the chairs at the table, turned it around, and straddled it so he could rest his forearms on the back. "Take a seat, man."

Who knew that words could knife a man in the chest and, at the same time, lift him to the stars? Luke sat in the other chair without thinking about what he was doing. "Chirbury, with due respect, I am the bastard son of a baron and a gamekeeper's daughter, I'm a gamekeeper myself, I'm twelve years older than her, and to cap it all off, I've been arrested for murder. What do I have to offer her?"

Chirbury shrugged with his eyebrows. "What she wants, apparently. That is what Kitty says, and my countess agrees, so it must be true."

Luke gaped at Chirbury. "Lady Chirbury thinks Kitty and I should marry?" He had forgotten to call her Lady Catherine.

"Not what I said," Chirbury pointed out. "My lady thinks Kitty wants to be your wife, and that she—that Kitty doesn't care about your birth, your age, or the false accusations against you."

Kitty cared for him. Luke knew that. But Chirbury would never let her make such a mistake, and if Chirbury would, Luke wouldn't. "She is too young to know her own mind," he said, arguing with himself even as he said the words. She was twenty-three, almost twenty-four. Her family's trials had matured her early, and—except for her feelings about him—he would trust her judgement and her instincts ahead of those of most people he knew. The earl in front of him included.

Chirbury shrugged. "She was too young six years ago when she set her heart on you. Anne and I told her it was an infatuation. That she was reacting to the trauma of Selby's assault and then the kidnapping. That she fixed on you because you helped to rescue her, and because she knew so few other unmarried men."

"All true," Luke agreed, though reluctantly.

Chirbury shook his head. "Demonstrably not. She has been courted by a broad selection of English gentlemen, Luke. I've no wish to dwell on the number of suitors I've turned away. I asked her to consider anyone I thought she had even the slightest interest in, if they were honest and respectable. More than a score over the years, and she refused them all."

Luke, was it? They'd never been on first name terms, though that was more on Luke's side than Chirbury's. The earl had asked him years ago to call him by his nickname, Rede. Given that he lusted for the man's sister-in-law, Luke thought such familiarity a mistake. He had to remember that he was not a fit mate for Kitty.

But Chirbury apparently thought differently.

"Are you telling me you would permit Kitty to marry me?" he asked, though it came out as more of a challenge.

"It is Kitty's decision. And yours, of course. My countess and I would not oppose the match, and she would undoubtedly still marry you if we did. She will soon be three years past the age of needing our consent. You are twelve years older than her, and that age difference mattered when she was not quite eighteen. To us, at least, though even larger age gaps are common. Now? She is an adult, and to my mind, uncommonly mature for her age. You are base born, you tell me, but you are the acknowledged son of a baron and the guardian of another."

He shrugged. "Yes, some will believe she has married down, but not people whose opinion she cares for. Which leaves us with your current situation. That, of course, needs to be resolved. However, we are ahead of ourselves, my friend. I still need to hear what your intentions are towards my sister."

Luke groaned. Heaven was his for the grasping, except a hangman's noose dangled between him and it. "I cannot deny that I love her, Rede. Marrying her would be the greatest privilege I can imagine. Also, if I win my freedom and prove my innocence, I have my own estate, left to me by my father. That is, I hope I still have my estate. My uncle is a competent manager, so I assume so. It is not much compared to Longford, but I can afford to take a wife. If I can prove my innocence. My uncle is determined to see me hang."

"Whereas I am determined that you shall not," Rede replied.

Kitty and Millie took leave of Paul the following day, when Rede sent his town coach for her. Kitty was reluctant. She felt, somehow, that she was betraying Luke by not staying to protect the brother for whom he had sacrificed so much. It was silly. Aldridge had promised he would be safe, and everyone knew Aldridge was the real power behind the Haverford duchy these days, as his father slowly succumbed to old age and illness.

Paul seemed perfectly happy to let Kitty and Millie go, but his fond farewell to Pierrot contained a bit of a reproach. He and

Frances, the other occupant of the children's floor, had enjoyed having the dog with them while Kitty tagged along with the duchess and Frances's older sisters into Society.

Kitty was barely through the door of the Chirbury townhouse before her sister was hugging her, holding her at arms' length for a searching examination, and hugging her again.

"My dear," Anne said, "the troubles you get yourself into!"

Kitty had not expected the sheer relief of seeing the sister who had been half mother to her. She surprised herself by bursting into tears even as she laughed at Anne's remark.

Instantly, she was back in Anne's arms again, and Anne was patting her shoulders, as if she was once again ten years old and crying over a broken cup or a grazed knee.

"There, there," Anne soothed, which set Kitty laughing again.

"I do not know why that should be comforting, Anne, but it is. What does it even mean?"

Anne's eyes twinkled as she coaxed Kitty into the nearby parlour, her arm around her sister's shoulders. "In this case, it means that the entire Redepenning clan, and its connections, are rallying to support Luke and Paul, Kitty. At least those who are in England." She led her to a sofa and sat beside her.

Kitty found a handkerchief in her reticule and used it to mop her cheeks and wipe her eyes. "My goodness. I am embarrassed," she said.

"You have been brave and capable since you first overheard that villain, supporting Luke and Paul, and never letting them know how worried you were, lest you added to their burdens," Anne said. "Then you saw me, and for a very brief moment wanted me to bandage your scraped elbow again, and make everything better. Nothing wrong with that!"

Anne was uncannily right. "It is something more than a scraped elbow," Kitty said.

Anne kissed her cheek. "A scraped heart is worse," she agreed. "You have never wavered in your choice, have you, darling?"

"Much good it has done me," Kitty grumbled. "He doesn't think of me that way, Anne." Though the kisses would argue otherwise. Still, men kissed easily, or so she understood, and heaven knew, he'd hardly availed himself of every opportunity she had given him!

"He thinks himself too old and too unworthy," Anne observed, "or so he told Rede."

Kitty felt like stamping a foot. "Does he not think I should make that decision?"

Anne sighed. "Men and their pride. Rede wasn't going to tell you. He said it was for Luke to talk about his own feelings, as if they were not perfectly obvious to anyone who has seen him watching you."

Was Anne hinting that she might support the match? "Years ago, when I said I didn't need a Season because Luke was the only man I would ever love, you and Rede told me that I was too young to know my own mind. You said I needed to meet others—men of my own station, men closer to my own age. I've met them. I've been courted by them. If anything, I am even more convinced now than I was six years ago that Luke is the man I want." Kitty hoped she sounded determined, rather than petulant.

"I don't think we were wrong then, Kitty. You were young. You had not met many men. We would be wrong to say the same thing now. You know your own mind. If you and Luke decide to marry, Rede and I will support you."

Kitty sighed. "Sadly, Luke remains to be convinced that I know what is best for me."

Anne put her arm around Kitty's shoulder and squeezed. "First, we will see to these charges of murder. Once Luke is no longer under the threat of being convicted for something he did not do, and Paul is safe, perhaps Luke will see things differently."

She stood. "Now. I imagine Millie Price is hovering in the hall, restraining herself from breaking down the door to come to your rescue. Let us go and assure her that I have not beaten you. You were wise to take her with you, Kitty. She is a treasure."

"I did not mean to," Kitty confessed. "She refused to be left behind."

Anne laughed. "See? A treasure."

CHAPTER 14

Two days after Luke saw Rede, he was collected by David Wakefield, as well as the solicitor Wakefield had engaged on his behalf and two silent constables, and escorted down the stairs to the magistrate's court.

Luke was wearing the clothes of a gentleman, sent to him by Aldridge, though how the man knew his size, he had no idea. A valet had brought them, which was just as well, since Luke would have had no idea how to tie the cravat that was currently doing its best to strangle him. The rest was subdued but smart. Luke felt like a goose dressed up as a peacock—a drab imposter beneath the fine feathers.

"This is not a trial, Mr Ogilvy," the solicitor assured him. "Merely a preliminary hearing to decide whether there is evidence for the charges. If they cannot produce enough evidence, the case will be dismissed."

"And if the magistrate is satisfied with the evidence?" Luke asked. After all, how could he prove that the boy he loved was the baby he had supposedly killed?

"The case will go to trial, my investigations will continue, and we will win that case," Wakefield told him, confidently. "If it goes to trial, you will be represented by a barrister, but I am hopeful today will see the end of it. We also have the opportunity to present evidence."

The court was in a large room divided in two by an iron balustrade. On the side of the room that Luke entered, around a score of people talked quietly to one another or watched what was happening beyond the balustrade.

A quick glance around and he saw faces he knew. Paul, first of all, with Aldridge alert on one side and Kitty on the other. He was comforted and alarmed in equal measure. What if he was committed to trial? He didn't want Paul and Kitty to see that.

Millie was a pace or so behind Kitty, watching her closely as Kitty gazed at Luke. Uncle Baldwin and his son stood as far from Paul and Aldridge as they could get. Lord and Lady Chirbury were between the two groups.

At the far end of the room, the magistrates' dais on the left faced the dock on the right. The three magistrates were in conversation behind a large desk. The current accused was leaning on another balustrade in front of the dock, looking at the magistrates across the heads of the people in the two rows of chairs that faced the magistrates.

Between the chairs and the dais, two clerks wrote in ledgers at their own table. At a signal from one of the judges, one of the clerks called for order. "Committed for trial at the Old Bailey." said the magistrate in the middle, and the constable on the dock took the arm of the accused and hurried him down the steps towards Luke and out of the door.

Another case was called. Luke didn't bother to watch as someone read out the charge and the evidence against the accused. He'd been caught in a householder's parlour, with a sack full of that householder's silver and other small portable items. He said nothing and was bound over for trial.

Meanwhile, Luke kept his eyes on those he loved. Paul sent him a grin. Kitty smiled, but her eyes were worried.

His own name was called. Rather than take his arm, the constable gestured towards the dock. *The benefit of being regarded as a gentleman*. It might not save his neck, but at least it left him with the dignity of walking unassisted to his fate.

The dock raised him above everyone in the room except the magistrates. Kitty had taken one of the chairs below him, so all he could see of her was her bonnet. That must be her sister beside her. He hadn't noticed what bonnet the countess was wearing, but Kitty was holding the lady's hand.

Paul and Aldridge had moved to the balustrade that divided the room. Paul's grin had dropped away. He was studying Baldwin, his emotions concealed behind a grim expression that sat oddly on his youthful face. Millie was with them, and so was the Earl of Chirbury.

Luke's uncle and cousin had also taken a seat, at the other end of the row to Kitty and the countess. Both kept their eyes studiously on the clerk, who was reading the charge of murder and a further charge of kidnapping.

The chief magistrate spoke directly to Luke. "What do you have to say for yourself, Ogilvy?" he asked. Then, with a smirk at Aldridge, "Or should I call you Mogg?"

Not a good sign. Was the magistrate annoyed at the pressure brought to bear to give Luke preferential treatment? Or at being torn between two sets of demanding aristocrats?

"My name is Ogilvy," Luke acknowledged. "I deny both charges. My solicitor wishes to speak on the kidnapping charge, if your honours would be so kind as to permit it. We believe it can easily be put to rest."

That was the strategy they had worked through yesterday afternoon and again this morning. Produce the guardianship papers, which were a full and inarguable defence to the charge of kidnapping. And answer each question as simply as possible, then hand over to the solicitor for elucidation.

"Very well," the chief magistrate agreed, after a nod from each of his fellows. The solicitor stepped to the front of the room and handed one of the clerks some documents. The clerk passed them to the magistrates.

"Honourable sirs," said the solicitor. "Item A is a copy of the will of the former baron, Flavian Lord Baldwin, father of Julius Lord Baldwin, the child who succeeded him. Also, the father of my client, Mr Lucius Ogilvy, his acknowledged son by a mistress. Items B and C are letters from lawyers, in which Mr Ogilvy is acknowledged as the new baron's guardian. Item D is a note from Mr Marcus Baldwin, my client's uncle, with a similar acknowledgement."

He paused as the magistrates passed the documents between them, then said, "We submit, your honours, that a child's guardian cannot kidnap him. In answer to the other charge, we will show that Mr Ogilvy removed the child from his home for the child's safety. In response to this charge, we shall say only that Mr Ogilvy had the right to take that action, as his guardian."

The chief magistrate shot Luke a glare over the top of the glasses he had donned to read the documents. "Odd sort of an arrangement, I must say." He turned to Uncle Baldwin and his son. "Mr Baldwin? You brought the charges. Do you accept that Ogilvy had guardianship rights over the little baron?"

Mr Baldwin? It was his cousin who had him arrested? Luke stared, wide-eyed, at the back of the man's head. Eight years had changed him. He was broader in the shoulders than the twenty-one-year-old on the threshold of adulthood Luke had left behind. More serious, too, his eyes—from what Luke had seen of him as he crossed the courtroom—shadowed. But perhaps that was just the circumstances.

Luke had been the younger man's hero, once. It had been his cousin who warned him of the lies against him, of the magistrate's intention to arrest him. When had he stopped believing that Luke was innocent?

Uncle Baldwin whispered to his son, who replied to the magistrate. "I withdraw the charge of kidnapping."

"Then you may speak to the charge of murder," said the magistrate.

Luke listened in growing horror as his cousin stepped through all the attacks Luke had described to Wakefield, and even two more that Luke had not known about. He named servants who claimed to have witnessed Luke in the vicinity, or, in the case of the attempted strangling, to have seen him entering the nursery with a pillow. He even said he had witnessed the two attacks that Luke didn't believe had happened.

Those waiting for another hearing or just visiting the court stopped their quiet murmuring to listen to the damning litany, turning avid eyes from Baldwin to Luke, their belief in what they were hearing shown in the horror and scorn they directed his way.

Luke composed his face to impassivity, and endured.

At last, Baldwin detailed the scene that Luke had orchestrated on the clifftop. He then turned to glare at Luke. "He killed my little cousin. I thought he had killed himself, too, but when I discovered he still lived, it became clear to me he'd had a plan all along. My uncle provided a cottage and paid an allowance to a poor girl who had a child out of wedlock. Ogilvy's child, born just a few months before little Lord Baldwin. The girl fled the village with the child several weeks before Ogilvy."

He pointed to Paul and raised his voice. "And there *is* her child!"

He was rewarded by the gasps and then excited comments of the onlookers, so that the clerk had to shout repeatedly for order.

"Is that your testimony?" the chief magistrate asked, once the room was once again silent.

"It is," said Baldwin, "and every word of it true."

"What say you, Ogilvy?" asked the magistrate.

Luke had a thousand words teeming in his head: words to refute the lies, words to question the betrayal of the one family member he had believed to be on his side. He glanced at Paul, who smiled slightly as he looked back, his eyes warm and trusting. Kitty was glaring indignantly at Baldwin. Their belief in him steadied him, and he remembered the words of the solicitor.

"Address anything that people say that you know to be true, Mr Ogilvy. You can safely leave me to argue against the lies."

With that in mind, he knew what to say. "Your honours," said with a slight bow, "my cousin has mentioned eight attempts on the life of my ward. I knew of six of those, though I believed the first to be an accident at the time. It may have been, as might the second.

After the third, I warned my uncle of my concerns. After three more attempts, I took my ward and fled."

He looked down at his hands, marshalling his thoughts, and his cousin began shouting he was a liar. The chief magistrate shouted louder. "If you speak out of turn, Mr Baldwin, I will have you removed from my court. Continue, Mr Ogilvy."

Luke warranted an honorific from the magistrate! That was progress. "I have never and would never lift a finger against my brother. My father put him into my arms minutes after his birth, and made me swear then to protect him. With my life, if necessary." He returned Paul's smile with a warm one of his own. "My father's wife did the same thing just before she died."

"Mr Baldwin claims you killed your ward and fled with your son by this village girl," the magistrate commented.

"I did not," Luke replied. "He speaks, I believe, of Lucy Featherstone, the disgraced daughter of the local vicar. He does tell the truth when he says my father supplied her with a cottage and a small allowance after her father discovered her condition and turned her out. It is also true that my uncle and I agreed to continue the arrangement when we became trustees for the new baron."

He and Uncle Baldwin had agreed the child was probably another half-brother, though it was not like Father to dally with a gently-born girl, or to leave her unmarried if he did.

Mind you, by the time Miss Featherstone's condition came to light, Father had married another young lady, one with powerful relatives. Luke had come home from a trip to London to find his father had taken a wife; the father who had always said he would never marry, for Titus was heir enough.

The thought that crossed Luke's mind was both fantastic and obvious. He forced it back. He would need to talk to Wakefield about it.

The magistrate on the right attracted Luke's attention by asking, "And were you the father of this Lucy Featherstone's child?"

"No, your honour," Luke replied. "I could not have been, since I did not know Miss Featherstone in that way." Nor anyone else. As a bastard himself, Luke had sworn not to indulge in the activities that brought bastards into the world. "I do not know who fathered the child. Miss Featherstone would not say." Was it worth mentioning that Lucy had left to marry a farmer from north of the border with Scotland? The man was prepared to take her and the child, and Luke had given her ten pounds as a wedding gift.

"So that is your case?" asked the magistrate on the left. "You deny any wrongdoing and provide no answer to Mr Baldwin's accusations?"

"If I may," said the solicitor. "I would like to ask some questions on behalf of my client."

The chief magistrate gave permission with an inclination of his head.

"Mr Baldwin," said the solicitor, "you have provided a wealth of witness testimony. Or should I say hearsay testimony? Are any of the witnesses you mention present in the court to be questioned?"

Baldwin, with a look of affront, said, "No. Of course not. Most of them have moved on to other positions. Besides, they are all in Northumberland."

The solicitor raised his eyebrows and asked, "Any sworn depositions, perhaps?"

"I have given my word as a gentleman, sir," Baldwin declared. "That should be enough."

"If it please the court, I would be happy to provide character references for both my client and his accuser, addressing the point of trustworthiness," the solicitor told the magistrates.

Baldwin pushed his chair back with a screech as he stood to protest. "I say! I am not on trial here!"

But perhaps he should be. Luke looked at his uncle, who was staring at his son as if he didn't know him, even as the clerk called for order again.

"I next have several questions for the man currently known as Lord Baldwin," said the solicitor as soon as he could make himself heard. "Lord Baldwin, who is buried in the grave that bears the name of Julius Paul Baldwin, the former baron and Mr Ogilvy's ward?"

Uncle Baldwin stood to give his answers. "I do not know," he replied. "The body was that of a child of around three or four, but it had… some time had passed. It could not be identified."

"The body was found some distance up the coast?" the solicitor asked.

"That is correct."

The solicitor adjusted his glasses and studied the papers in his hands. "Fishermen at the time proposed searching in the other direction, down the coast, since that was the most likely direction for the currents to carry anyone who drowned in the sea off the cliff where your nephews had reportedly jumped."

"We found no bodies down the coast," Uncle Baldwin insisted.

The solicitor handed the paper he held to his clerk and addressed the magistrates. "Your honours, this is a copy of the coroner's report into the identity of the child buried as Lord Baldwin. You will see that the body was also claimed by the widow of a fisherman, whose child disappeared three weeks before Lord Baldwin. The coroner notes that he was inclined to release the body to the fisherman's wife, who positively identified a birth mark on the child's thigh. Other factors such as nutrition and the age of the child's teeth suggested that the body was older than the little baron. Then the mother withdrew her claim."

The clerk carried the report across the courtroom to the magistrates' clerk, and the solicitor turned again to Uncle Baldwin.

"Sir, did you believe the body to be that of your younger nephew?"

Uncle Baldwin glanced towards his son before replying. "I was unsure," he admitted. "The estate and the title needed certainty. I believed that my nephews were dead, and having a death certificate gave the Committee for Privileges comfort in proclaiming me the next baron. We thought—I thought—it best to… The child had an honourable burial, and no harm was done. I thought."

"Lord Baldwin, did you pay the widow to withdraw her claim to the body?" the solicitor asked.

Someone in the courtroom gasped, and Uncle Baldwin paled. "Not as such," he insisted. Another glance at his son. "We provided a sum of money to allow her to start a new life with her surviving children. A gratuity from one grieving family to another."

One of the magistrates raised both eyebrows, and another shook his head.

Luke expected the solicitor to make more of the matter, but he moved on to another question. "Sir, did any of the witnesses your son named come forward at the time of the attempts on your nephew's life?"

Uncle Baldwin's face could have been carved from granite and his voice was low and cold. "No, they did not. And after Lucius disappeared, dead, as we thought, we all agreed the matter was over, and nothing would be served by raking over the coals."

"Did you know of more than six attempts?" the solicitor asked.

"My nephew raised his concerns after the third attempt. As he said, the first two were passed off as accidents. I knew of three more. I heard of the further two only now, in this courtroom."

Baldwin protested. "Father! How can you say that? We have discussed these matters many times."

Uncle Baldwin looked at his son and then at the solicitor. "Is that all?" he asked.

The solicitor nodded to his clerk, who crossed the room with a sheet of board. "No, sir. I would like you to look at this drawing and tell me if you know the person in it." The clerk held the board up for Uncle Baldwin to examine.

From his vantage point, Luke could see it, and knew it immediately. He remembered the day it had been drawn. He suppressed any outward reaction, but hope burst inside him like a fountain.

Uncle Baldwin examined it carefully. "That is a drawing of my nephew, Lord Baldwin, as he was towards the end of his life." His voice choked, slightly. "I did not know one had been made. Can you tell me the name of the artist? I would like to buy it."

"As to that," said the solicitor, "We can ask Lady Chirbury, with the court's permission."

Kitty knew what the solicitor was about as soon as he handed the drawing to Anne. She had seen it before.

"Do you know the artist, Lady Chirbury?" the solicitor asked.

Anne nodded. "The artist is my friend, Miss Ruth Henwood."

"Were you present when the drawing was made?"

Anne nodded again. "I was."

The solicitor gave Luke a smug smile. "Lady Chirbury, can you please explain to the court where the drawing was made and when?"

"I can. It was in eighteen hundred and four at the Michaelmas Fair in the village of Longford on Nidd, in West Gloucestershire. My sisters and I offered to look after the little boy we knew as Paul Mogg, while Longford Court's recently appointed gamekeeper, the man known as Lucas Mogg, competed in the archery contest."

Anne produced another sheet from between the leaves of the folder she carried with her. "Ruth made several drawings, including the one you hold and this one." Kitty caught a brief glimpse of a young Paul and Anne's daughter Daisy, playing together on the edge of a blanket.

The solicitor gave the drawings to the clerk who took them to the judges.

"Your honours, I submit that the boy in those drawings has been identified by the child's uncle as Julius Paul Baldwin and by the Countess of Chirbury and Selby as the boy who grew up in Longford village under the name of Paul Mogg."

Once again, the clerk was called upon to exercise his lungs in restoring order.

The chief magistrate looked over his spectacles at Luke's cousin. "This would appear to disprove the charge of murder, Mr Baldwin, and we have already dismissed the charge of kidnapping. Do you have anything further to say before we decide the case?"

The cousin had turned pale. "The boy is Luke's son," he protested. "The Featherstone chit's child. Luke told me so himself! Besides, why else would my uncle pay for her cottage?"

"Enough, Titus," his father said. "No more lies. I cannot believe I let you deceive me for so long, when all this time…" He was shaking his head, his eyes full of tears, the grief ravaging his face adding years to his age.

"Your honours," he addressed the magistrates, "my brother supported Lucy Featherstone because he knew her seducer was my son. If my son is prepared to lie about this in court, I have to ask what else he is lying about. And the answer breaks my heart."

"Father!" Luke's cousin protested.

"Titus?" Luke exclaimed in a croak. Kitty craned her head around to see Luke's face, which mirrored the devastation on his uncle's. "It was Titus all along?" he asked his uncle.

"I am not remaining here to listen to such nonsense," Titus Baldwin announced, rising to his feet and barging across the court-room towards the gate in the balustrade. Wakefield, Aldridge and Rede moved to put themselves in the way. "Arrest that man," the chief magistrate commanded, and several constables rushed forward to comply.

Almost before many in the courtroom had realised that one man had been exonerated and another accused, it was over. Baldwin had been led away. The case against Luke had been dismissed. And Luke and all his supporters, plus his uncle, had removed themselves from the courtroom.

CHAPTER 15

Luke was reeling at the revelation that he and his uncle had both been duped by his cousin. Shaken as he was, though, it was nothing to the shock his uncle had received. Poor Uncle Baldwin seemed to have shrunk in on himself, he walked blindly, shaking his head. "I believed him," he kept saying. "How can I ever forgive myself. I believed him."

Wakefield ushered them into a room where they could be private. "You and your uncle need to talk," he said. "We will wait for you in the next room."

Rede shook his head. "I'm going to take Kitty and Anne home. Paul, too, if you wish, Luke. And there's a room in my home for the guardian of the true Baron Baldwin."

Uncle Baldwin shuddered.

Aldridge also spoke up. "Know you can call on me at any time, Ogilvy," he said. "Rede, I'll come with you and say hello to the children, if I may. Paul, you can travel in my curricle again."

Wakefield nodded. "Your solicitor and I will be next door, Ogilvy," he said. He nodded to Uncle Baldwin. "Lord Baldwin," he said.

That seemed to bring Uncle Baldwin out of his stupor. "Mr

Baldwin," he replied. "My nephew Julius—No, Paul. Paul is the true baron."

Wakefield regarded him with respect, and this time his nod was closer to a bow. "Mr Baldwin."

As the door closed behind them, Luke wished for Kitty's presence. Perhaps she would know the right thing to say to his uncle, who had betrayed Luke with his lack of trust and betrayed himself by trusting his son.

Uncle Baldwin lowered himself into a chair. "I am so sorry, Luke," he said, his voice hoarse with strain. "I cannot begin to tell you how sorry I am. Titus! It was all Titus."

"I believed him, too," Luke had to admit. "It was Titus who told me that you had decided to get rid of me by framing me for Paul's murder. It was Titus who opened my door so I could escape from jail. I thought he was helping me! He is the father of Lucy Featherstone's daughter? He must have been only, what, sixteen?"

"It was not long before his seventeenth birthday, and she only fifteen, poor little girl. By the time we knew, Titus had already compromised Alison Porritt at a house party. That's why my brother married her."

Luke shook his head in disbelief. "I knew he was a scoundrel with the girls, but I thought he confined himself to bargirls and the like, who knew what they were about."

Uncle Baldwin grimaced. "He did, after that. I promised to geld him if he ever again took a girl of quality without benefit of marriage, or any girl without her consent. Meant it, too. Especially once my brother secured the succession and Titus became the spare."

His words were another puzzle piece. Paul's birth had pushed Titus out of his place in succession to the barony. Paul's supposed death had put him back as heir.

"I thought he had grown up," Uncle Baldwin confessed. "I wanted to think so, of course. That summer, the summer he seduced one girl and attacked the other, you were away. I had refused to let him go with you, and I thought he was acting that way to try to punish me."

"I travelled to London on business for the Baron," Luke remembered, "and then on a tour of the Baron's various interests." He smiled at the memory. "The Baron said I needed a bit of polish, that I was his son, and would be a gentleman, by God, or he would know the reason why."

So much had happened since those long distant days that he'd not thought of them in years. "Titus begged to come with me," he remembered. "The Baron said the last thing I needed was a schoolboy tagging along."

"That's why he made you Paul's guardian rather than me," Uncle Baldwin explained. "He trusted you, Luke. He told me that, when it came to Titus, my judgement was…" He trailed off and covered his eyes with one hand. "I thought he had grown up," he repeated.

Luke hadn't questioned that, either. He thought it was of a piece with his father's insistence that the baby was his responsibility. The ancient history made sense of so much. Why the Baron had married so suddenly, and to such a young girl. Why Alison was never comfortable with Titus. Why Titus avoided the Baron. He had wondered at the time, but never sought to understand.

"If Paul is Titus's son, you are rightfully baron," Luke commented.

"Not legally," said Uncle Baldwin. "In any case, Alison was not with child when my brother married her. He waited after their wedding until he was sure she had not conceived." His face grew even bleaker. "He said he had to at least try to sire a son, since Titus was not fit to be baron. Julius—I suppose I shall have to get used to calling him Paul, now—is rightfully the Baron Baldwin. We will need to sort that out. We will need to make some decisions about Titus, too. There will be talk. Scandal. I am sorry, Luke. I do not deserve your forgiveness, but I am begging for it, anyway."

"You have it," Luke told him. "We will face these troubles together."

He put a hand on his uncle's shoulder, and Uncle Baldwin leaned into the touch. It was a comfort, but not the touch he needed. If only Kitty had stayed. Her clear-eyed thinking would be a help. Her presence would be a comfort.

He brightened as he realised that accepting Rede's invitation meant he would see her tonight. And the sooner he talked to Wakefield and the solicitor, the sooner he could go to her.

It was not quite as quick as he'd hoped.

Wakefield agreed to continue his investigation, this time with Titus Baldwin as his target, and the solicitor cautiously accepted the task of representing the man who was actually guilty of attempting the crime Luke had been arrested for.

The four of them then met with Titus, who had been locked in the room where Luke had spent the last three days.

He leapt to his feet when they entered, ignoring everyone but his father.

"Father! Thank God! You've come to get me out of here. This is all a huge mistake."

"Is it, my son?" Uncle Baldwin asked. "Then a thorough investigation will absolve you, though if that is the case, I cannot see why you lied about the poor Featherstone girl."

Titus sent a venomous look at Luke. "I might have known you would believe uncle's bastard over me. It was always so. Always Lucius, Lucius, Lucius. *I* was the heir." He struck himself on the chest as he paced angrily back and forth across the room.

"Did a message need to be taken? Ask Lucius. Is a tenant having trouble with the rent? Consult Lucius. On and on. Did my uncle take me on the rounds of the estate? Did you, Father? No. It was always Lucius."

Luke was struck dumb. Had Titus really been so resentful of the duties Luke gladly undertook? He never said a word!

"When you were a boy," Uncle Baldwin protested. "Later, when you were older, we invited you and you refused."

"Because Uncle had married. He had a son! It was never going to be mine." Titus's response was anguished. "It was meant to be mine," he whispered.

Uncle Baldwin shook his head. "You could not have believed that. My brother was free to marry and have children at any time. In fact, that's just what he did."

Titus almost spat his response. "Married a chit who spread her legs for me first, and claimed to be father to my bastard. What an irony. The cuckoo he planted in my mother supplanted by a cuckoo of my own."

Uncle Baldwin paled still further. "I suppose your mother told you that Flavian was your true father. It is a lie."

Aunt Baldwin was a sour and critical presence in Luke's childhood who glared at Luke whenever she was forced to tolerate being in the same room as him. She had been sent to live with relatives in Scotland when he was ten, but he never knew why. He remembered, though, that Titus spent two weeks every year with her, and had always come back angry and unhappy.

"My mother told me the truth," Titus insisted. "That Uncle Flavian wanted her but she had already promised to marry you, and so he raped her. She said you couldn't be my father because she refused you her bed. And that is why I have no brothers or sisters. You should have killed him. I would kill a man who did that to a woman of mine."

"This again?" Uncle Baldwin rolled his eyes upwards. "Your mother's lies?" He looked at Luke. "All lies. Flavian never had to rape a woman to get her into bed. And even if he had been attracted to Aileen, he would not have acted on it. Also, she did not deny me my rights until… Never mind when. It was after Titus was born, in any case."

"Liar," Titus accused. "Liar. You supported your brother and abandoned your wife. And then my real father stole my birth right and gave it to Alison's little brat. And Lucius! I used to think he was my friend, and then it was Julius this and Julius that. I expect Alison warmed his bed, too. Everyone conspired against me. Everyone except my mother."

Uncle Baldwin was slowly shaking his head. Luke, too, was having trouble believing his ears and was lost for words.

"Nothing to say?" Titus mocked. "Because you know I am right! Go away, then. You are all against me. I don't want your pretence of help when what you really want is to see me hanged. Betrayed, like my poor mother. Betrayed and dead." He pulled out a chair at the table, turned it so it was faced away from them, and sat down.

"Titus, listen to me," Uncle Baldwin urged. "Your mother was not right in the head. What she told you isn't true. You are my son, Titus, and I love you."

Titus ignored him. Uncle Baldwin made several more attempts, no more successfully. In the end, Luke put an arm around his shoulders and assisted him from the room. Wakefield and the solicitor, who had been silent observers through the whole disastrous scene, followed, and the guard locked the door.

Luke was focused on Uncle Baldwin, but knew that Wakefield was whispering something to the solicitor. Anything they wanted would have to wait. Uncle Baldwin couldn't take any more today.

Wakefield must have come to the same conclusion. "Get your uncle home, Ogilvy. We can discuss this further after a night's sleep."

"Thank you," Luke said. "Thank you to you both." He owed them both his freedom, though he currently felt as if it had been gained at too high a cost. His rational self argued it was better to be facing this heartbreak than to line up for a rope necklace. He wished it hadn't cost his uncle so dearly.

He could not send Uncle Baldwin back to his hotel on his own tonight. He should be in the company of family, not of servants. Luke might be a reminder of his son's misdeeds, but he was also the only family available.

"I'll come back with you," he offered. "If we go past Chirbury House, I can stop and let the earl know that I'm staying with you."

Uncle Baldwin's eyes showed gratitude and relief even as he shaped the words to refuse. "There's no need to do that, Lucius. I know you will want to check on your boy."

"I want to spend time with my favourite uncle, too," Luke said, which was an old joke between them, since Luke's mother had been an only child, and Luke's father had only one brother.

It was true; he did want to spend time with his uncle. He had missed the man like an amputated limb. Titus, too, though he wouldn't think about that now. He wanted to get to know Uncle Baldwin again, but he needed to see Kitty.

Perhaps he could catch a glimpse when he went in to make his excuses.

Kitty was hovering on the landing, near enough to hear the front door open. Paul was upstairs becoming reacquainted with Kitty's niece Daisy, who was only a year his senior, and allowing Anne and Rede's children, the twins and their little sister, to climb all over him.

Anne and Rede had disappeared somewhere. Into their bedchamber, she rather thought. They did not like being separated. Ruth had remained at Longford Court with Kitty's middle sister, Meg.

No member of the family was around to prevent Kitty being the first to greet Luke when he arrived, and other than Millie, who could be trusted to support her, none of the servants would comment. They could think whatever they liked.

When the knock came on the door, she started down the stairs, timing her descent so she was still several steps up when the butler let Luke in.

"Is the earl available, Wilson?" Luke asked.

"The earl is not in," said the butler, stiffly.

"Do not trouble yourself, Wilson," Kitty said. "I shall welcome Mr Ogilvy. Mr Ogilvy, shall I show you to your room, or would you prefer to see Paul? He is upstairs in the nursery."

"I'm sorry, Lady Kitty," he said, with a warning glance at the butler. "I just stopped by to say I am not going to stay."

Kitty, well aware of Wilson's inquisitive ears, beckoned Luke to follow her. "Before you go, you must tell me what happened between you and your uncle," she insisted, leading him into the little parlour used for visitors whose status the butler judged to be too low for the drawing room upstairs.

She shut them both inside. "Luke, is there something wrong?"

"My uncle is in the carriage outside. Kitty, I am going to his place tonight. His heart is broken and I don't want him to be alone. My cousin Titus played us off against one another. Uncle Baldwin is devastated."

"You believe him?" Kitty asked. If Baldwin was lying, Luke might not survive a night at his house.

"Do you not?" Luke asked. "You saw him in the courtroom."

"He seemed shocked," Kitty acknowledged. She still didn't think it was worth the risk, but there was another option. "You are right. He shouldn't be alone, but wouldn't it be better if he stayed here, where he is not reminded of his son, and where he can get to know Paul? Bring him in, Luke, and I shall have Mrs Mitchell make up a room."

"Should we not ask the earl?" Luke protested.

"Ask the earl what?" Rede said.

Kitty started. She and Luke had been so focused on one another, they had not heard him and Anne enter.

"My uncle is waiting in the hackney, my lord," Luke explained. "Kitty has suggested you might be willing to have him stay the night."

"Yes, of course," Rede said, easily.

"The poor man," Anne agreed. "He has had a terrible shock."

"He has. We went to see Titus and... I won't repeat what Titus said. Suffice it to say he blames my father, his own father, Paul's mother, me. Me most of all. Everyone but himself. He seems to believe he acted to protect himself, when all the rest of us were determined to steal what should have been his."

Luke heaved a sigh. "If I found it hard to hear, it was worse for my uncle. He is holding himself together, but he must be..." He shook his head, words failing him. "I won't leave him alone tonight. If he won't come in, I shall stay at his place."

"Tell him we, better than anyone, understand," Anne suggested. "My cousin tried to rape Kitty and kill me."

"And my nephew was his accomplice," Rede added.

Anne put a hand on Rede's arm. "Go with him, Rede, and make the invitation yourself."

The two sisters went with the men out into the entrance hall, and Kitty continued up the stairs as they exited the front door. Anne didn't follow. Kitty could hear her giving some instructions, presumably to Wilson.

When Anne caught up with Kitty in the drawing room, she said, "I have asked Wilson to speak to Mrs Mitchell about a room for Lord Baldwin, and to organise baths in their rooms for him and Luke. I've also ordered light refreshments to be served here. I doubt either man has thought of food today."

Kitty wasn't sure whether to trust Baldwin, but the man had won her sympathy in the courtroom, when he interrupted his son to do the right thing. His heart certainly appeared to be breaking, and if it wasn't true, he was a superb actor. Even with her reservations, her heart filled with compassion when he entered the room on Luke's arm, his whole body slumped in fatigue and defeat.

Luke saw him seated next to Anne, who plied him with tea and savoury tarts.

"I am grateful for your invitation," Baldwin told her. "I would like to meet the young baron." He covered his face with one hand for a moment. "So much to do to put this mess right."

"You shall meet Paul," Anne said, "but the rest can wait. Today, you have had a great shock. Let us care for you today."

He blinked away tears. "You are very kind to a stranger, Lady Chirbury."

"Luke loves you," Anne said, simply. "We owe him much, Mr Baldwin. Helping you in this sad time is the least we can do."

"We shall help how we can," Rede agreed.

"I will go up and fetch Paul," Luke said to Kitty in an undertone. "Will you come with me?"

She followed him upstairs, but once they were on the nursery floor, she delayed him with a touch, her hand on his. He turned to face her.

Kitty came right up to him, her eyes challenging him to turn her away. Luke held out his arms and then folded them around her when she stepped close enough to slide her arms around his waist and rest her head on his chest. "I was so frightened, Luke. But now you are safe."

He kissed the top of her hair, and then her lips when she raised them to him. "I should not," he murmured, though perhaps more to himself than to her, for he kissed her again. "I am still too old for you and base-born," he reminded her.

This again. "I am not a child, Luke. Nor do I care about your birth." Kitty pulled away from him and he let her go, his hands lingering on her waist as if reluctant. "Nor do Rede and my sister, incidentally, which leaves only one of us out of those who have any say who thinks those things are important. You might want to think about that."

"I have offended you. I did not mean to, Kitty."

"I forgive you this once, for you have had a difficult couple of weeks, but when you kiss me as if you mean it one minute, then tell me you are all wrong for me the next, it makes me cross, Luke. If you trust I am old enough to decide to grant you my kisses, then trust that I am aware of all the disadvantages of a match between us. And of the benefits. Now go and fetch Paul, and I shall not berate you any more tonight."

Luke bowed his head for a moment then nodded. "Yes. Very well."

He strode to the door that led from the stair landing to the nursery suite, then stopped, turned around, and took three quick paces back to Kitty to seize her for another kiss, this one fierce and possessive. "I surrender. I cannot live without you, Kitty Stocke, so if you feel the same, we shall have to make it work."

Her return kiss was a triumphant celebration, which he met with enthusiasm, so much so that they were both trembling when he ended it. "Paul," he panted. "My uncle."

"Yes. Yes, of course." Luke's uncle was waiting to meet his

younger nephew, and Rede or Anne would undoubtedly come looking for them if they delayed much longer. It would be both rude and impolitic to drag Luke down to her bedchamber on the next floor and discover the truth of the promise in his kiss.

He smiled at her. "I love you, Kitty Stocke."

"I love you, too, Luke Ogilvy."

CHAPTER 16

Luke watched Uncle Baldwin and Paul make a cautious reunion, Paul suspicious of the man and Uncle Baldwin wary of offending the boy. Over tea and refreshments, a conversation about horses spun a few cautious threads of connections and a tangential excursion into the wonders of steam engines strengthened them.

It helped Paul's acceptance that Uncle Baldwin made no bones about his contrition over believing his son instead of Luke. "Your brother has always been the better man. Looking back, I cannot understand how I was persuaded to believe him guilty," he said.

"I expect you didn't, at first," said Daisy, who had inserted herself into the afternoon tea and the conversation.

"That is true," Uncle Baldwin admitted. "Also, Titus had always looked up to his cousin. He was the last person I expected to lie about Luke."

"Dad says we are not responsible for other people's choices," Paul offered.

"My father says that, too," Daisy agreed, looking at Rede.

Uncle Baldwin objected. "He is my son. He was only twenty-one. I should have seen. Should have known."

"Hannah says should butters no parsnips," Daisy retorted. Hannah had been Daisy's nurse, and later servant to the entire family of sisters, before Anne married Rede. Now she was nurse again, this time to the children of one of Rede's cousins, but her sayings had remained with the Chirbury household, to be trotted out when needed by any of the children who had been under her care.

Uncle Baldwin chuckled politely, but it was clearly an effort.

Kitty, bless her, seemed to sense that he was near the end of his endurance. "Your room will be ready for you, Mr Baldwin, and I expect your valet has arrived with your things. Do not feel that you have to stay down here with us. It has been a stressful day for you and Mr Ogilvy, and I imagine you would both like to rest for a bit."

"Quite right," Anne agreed. "You and Paul will have plenty of time to become reacquainted."

Uncle Baldwin stood. "If you are sure it would not be rude, I would not mind going to my room for a while. Paul? We can talk again later?"

"I would like that, Uncle Baldwin," Paul replied.

Uncle Baldwin met Luke's eyes. "He is a fine lad, Lucius. Luke, I mean," he said.

"I think so, Uncle. Shall I walk you up?"

Paul leapt to his feet. "I will come too," he declared.

They saw Uncle Baldwin to his room, where his valet was waiting with warm water and a freshly made bed, the crisp sheets turned down.

"I will rest for a while, but I would like to talk some more, Paul," he said. "You, too, Luke. I would like to hear about your lives in the past nine years."

"Later, then," Luke agreed.

Luke had been assigned a room next to Uncle Baldwin's. "Can I come inside with you for a minute, Dad?" Paul asked. "I want to know what happened after Lord Aldridge took me away. Did you find out why Mr Baldwin did it? The younger Mr Baldwin, that is?"

Luke nodded. It was a fair question, and the boy deserved some answers. "Some of it, I didn't know myself until today. Some of it

I'm still not sure about. But I think it all began with Aunt Baldwin. She never liked me." Which was putting it mildly. "She didn't want to allow me anywhere near Titus, but my father and Uncle Baldwin insisted that we were cousins, and that we should be allowed to play together."

"You were older than him, you said," Paul commented.

"Five years, but he was a sweet little boy. I played blocks with him and swung him on his swing. Later, I taught him to ride. He used to love to go along with me fishing, or even just for a walk." *He followed even when he had been told to stay home.* Many a time, Luke had to give up a trip or an activity not suitable for a little boy, so he could return Titus to the house. Aunt Baldwin always blamed Luke, but Father and Uncle Baldwin knew better.

"Then, when I was ten, my aunt went away. Father said she had become unbalanced. Uncle Baldwin had sent her to live in Scotland, with relatives who would look after her. Titus used to visit her there."

"That sounds like a bad idea," Paul said.

"It was. Apparently, she convinced Titus that my father had had an affair with her, and that Titus was my father's son. Uncle Baldwin says it is impossible, by the way, in case you wondered. But Titus believed it made him the rightful heir."

Paul shrugged. "He was the rightful heir already. At least until our father married. That must have been a shock to him."

"Worse than you think," Luke acknowledged. "Father married Alison, your mother, after Titus assaulted her. I was away at the time. Father wrote me a letter to say that he'd taken a wife, but he didn't tell me the rest, then or later."

"Titus assaulted my mother?"

Luke guessed what Paul was wondering. "You are not Titus's get, Paul. Uncle Baldwin is certain of that. He told me today that Titus had been swiving the village girls, and you heard in court that he got Miss Featherstone with child. When your mother's father demanded that Titus marry Alison, your mother swore she would rather kill herself, so Father offered himself, instead. They sent Titus up to Scotland for a few weeks and then to friends of Uncle Baldwin's in Wales. Father said he would not expect Alison to live with him under the same roof."

They fixed up the dower house, and Uncle Baldwin moved into it. Titus had come home after six months, and Luke had been told only that he'd been travelling as part of his education. "By the time Titus came home, Uncle Baldwin had moved into the dower house and Alison was with child. You, Paul. My father's son and my dear brother."

"So, our cousin has been wanting to kill me ever since," Paul said. "Gruesome." The last word was said with relish rather than upset.

"Apparently so," Luke acknowledged.

"And Uncle Baldwin had no idea?" Paul asked. "I can tell he didn't, or he wouldn't be so distressed, but really? There was no sign of it?"

"Titus had me fooled," Luke pointed out. "I thought he was on my side. He warned me about what people were saying. He told me the magistrate was coming to arrest me. He helped me escape when I was locked up."

Paul whistled. "And it was all an act. All to make things worse for you. To clear the way so he could kill me."

"Apparently so," Luke said again.

Paul peered into Luke's face. "It has been a hard day for you, too, hasn't it, Dad? How about coming up to the nursery and playing with the twins? That'll give you something else to think about. Right pair of little devils, they are."

It was an unusual prescription for what ailed him, but Paul might just be right. Luke followed his boy up the stairs and was soon employed as the bear, blocking the way across the centre of the nursery, while squealing children made wild dashes from one side to another.

It certainly took Luke's mind off his grief for the loss of his faith in his cousin.

CHAPTER 17

Lady Kitty was upset, and doing her best not to take her feelings out on her maid. Millie understood. If Millie had not already known about her mistress's attachment to Mr Ogilvy, their journey across the width of England would have opened her eyes. It was equally obvious that Mr Ogilvy felt the same way, and now he had been revealed to be a gentleman, surely nothing stood in their way?

But Mr Ogilvy said nothing, and he and Lady Kitty barely saw one another, except at dinner. Everyone seemed to be conspiring to keep Lady Kitty and Mr Ogilvy apart.

For the first few days of Mr Baldwin's stay, he and Mr Ogilvy were busy dealing with the aftermath of the hearing—organising legal representation for the murderous cousin, commissioning an investigation into the villain's activities at the time of the supposed death of Mr Ogilvy and the child baron, setting in train the necessary processes to have the real Lord Baldwin reinstated as baron.

Lady Kitty was busy, too. The Duchess of Haverford had commanded her attendance at several social events. Lady Chirbury suddenly decided it was time to refresh their wardrobes, which entailed long visits to the modiste she patronised. The nursery set demanded Lady Kitty's company on trips to the park and to Astleys Amphitheatre. Millie was even busier, since she accompanied her mistress most places, and also looked after her clothes and her room.

Then one evening, Kitty returned to her room a seething kettle of frustration, which boiled over when Millie asked what she would be wearing the next day.

"Why should I care," Kitty demanded. "Pick anything, Millie. I probably won't go out at all. What is the point?"

"Has something happened?" asked Millie, bracing herself to be told to hold her tongue, though to be fair, Lady Kitty had never been one to blame a person for asking questions.

"Nothing has happened," Lady Kitty all but wailed. "Nothing is going to happen. Not if Luke goes to Northumberland without me!"

Millie had already heard from Mr Gibson, Mr Baldwin's snooty valet, that Mr Baldwin intended to return home at the end of the week. Mr Gibson had not said why, but Millie had overheard Mr Baldwin telling Lord Chirbury that he had resigned from his government position because of the scandal. "He is planning to travel with Mr Baldwin?" she asked.

Lady Kitty nodded. Her eyes were filling with tears, but Millie thought her more angry than sad. "They were discussing it at tea. Luke wants Paul to see his estate. Wakefield is sending some investigators, too, and Luke wants to be there to receive reports."

Millie nodded.

Lady Kitty's temper flared. "I know it is perfectly reasonable, Millie. You do not have to tell me. But what about me? Where am I in his planning?" In a whisper, more to herself than to Millie, she added, "He said he cared, but would he so completely forget me if that was true?"

Millie had four brothers, three of them older than her. She scoffed. "Just like a man," she said. "It is not that he has forgotten you, my lady. But men are not like us. We are used to juggling all sorts of projects at once. Mr Ogilvy loves you, but he is busy worrying about his uncle, dealing with all the business of coming back from the dead, making sure Lord Baldwin is established again, and the rest of the things that are clamouring for his attention. You are not making a fuss, so he thinks you are happy to wait."

Lady Kitty snorted. "Well, he is wrong. I am not."

Then you need to tell him so, Millie thought, though she did not say it out loud. It wasn't her place to give her mistress advice like that.

"I should tell him so, shouldn't I?" Lady Kitty mused. "After all, what is the worst that can happen?"

"He might ask you to wait," Millie cautioned.

"He might tell me he has changed his mind," Lady Kitty retorted. "Or he might agree to wed straight away and take me with him."

Millie blurted, "Can I come with you?"

Lady Kitty's eyes widened. "Would you wish to? Northumberland is so far away from your family! I thought…" She trailed off.

Millie wondered what her ladyship had thought. She didn't ask. Making her own opinion clear was more important. "I wish to, my lady. I like being your maid, and you will need someone of your own. I don't want to leave you." *I am your friend as well as your maid,* she wanted to say. But it wasn't her place.

Lady Kitty was smiling at her. "I am glad," she said. "And it won't be as bad as all that. I am sure we shall visit Anne and Rede. The roads are improving all the time. Why, I am told you can reach Northumberland in only two days, with good weather and good horses, so it cannot be more than three or four days home to Longford."

Millie returned the smile, relief settling in her heart. "Then it is settled," she said.

"Hardly," replied Lady Kitty, her smile fading. "First, Luke has to ask *me* to come with him."

Luke lay in the dark making a mental review of the list of things to do before he left London. Or at least trying to do so, with his thoughts distracted by how Lady Kitty looked when Uncle Baldwin asked about their journey north.

She hid the pain quickly, but not before he noticed. She didn't want him to go. He didn't want to leave her, either. *It is the right thing to do*, he assured himself. From what Uncle Baldwin said, all was not well on the estate.

Uncle Baldwin played it down. Servants whose families had worked for the Baldwins for generations suddenly seeking opportunities elsewhere. Several bad harvests. Mistakes in the accounts. "A fresh pair of eyes would be useful, Luke," he said. "I may have put too great a burden on Titus."

Or Titus might have been replacing servants loyal to the Baldwin family with his own men, and skimming money for his own purposes. He'd had the opportunity. Uncle Baldwin had been giving him more and more authority, in the hopes that he would rise to the occasion. Then, too, apparently, Uncle Baldwin had been very ill last winter, and slow to recover.

It was selfish enough of Luke to consider dragging Kitty to the other end of the country, far away from everyone she loved. How could he take her with him into a household he didn't trust and a situation that might take all his energies and attention to fix? What sort of a way would that be to start a marriage?

No. His plan was the best way for both of them. But Kitty was not going to like it.

Despite his whirling mind, he must have dropped off to sleep, for he woke to the realisation that someone was in his room. He was instantly alert, his every sense stretched to work out the dimensions of the threat. Then he detected the scent of rosewater and something subtle that was unique to one particular female.

Kitty was in his room. The muscles of his arms and torso relaxed. Another part of him stirred with interest.

He was about to speak when Kitty muttered, "He's asleep. Perhaps this can wait until morning." He heard the faintest of noises as she moved back towards the door. He could just see her, a darker shape in the darkness.

Then she stopped. "No. He'll just go off to another meeting, or closet himself with his uncle, or Anne will drag me out somewhere, and another day will pass without anything settled. Wretched man! He could make time to be alone with me if he so wished."

"I do wish," Luke said, sitting up in bed, "but no guardian with any sense is going to let me be alone with you, given how much I want you."

Did she stiffen? He couldn't tell in the dark, but her voice was strained when she commented, "We are alone now."

"You should leave," Luke told her, forcing himself to stay where he was instead of leaping off the bed and taking her into his arms.

"Not before we have had the discussion I came here for." She put up her chin. He couldn't see it, but he knew that tone of voice. He was not getting her out of this room without a fight, and he was far too pleased about the fact.

She shuffled cautiously across the room until she reached the chairs by the fireplace, where she sat down. Right, then. Luke pulled his sheet to remove the tail of it from between the mattress and the footboard, and tucked it into an improvised toga over his naked body. He had a banyan somewhere, but he wasn't going to find it without more light.

He fumbled along the top of the mantel until he found the jar of spills, then poked one into the pile of ash in the fireplace until it reached the embers and flared into life. He lit the candles in the pair of candle sticks that stood on the mantel. There she was. In—God help him to stay sane and strong—a soft silk robe that outlined every curve in delicious detail, her lovely eyes examining his unusual attire, her mouth sombre.

"Excuse me a moment," he said. He poked the spill back into the fireplace then hunted around until he found his banyan. A moment behind the screen in the corner to drop the sheet and don the banyan, and he was as decent as anything about this illicit meeting.

She had still said nothing.

"Would you like a brandy?" he asked. The Chirbury guest rooms were provided with glasses and decanters of various drinks for a late-night tipple. Luke had not so far availed himself of the courtesy, but if ever there was a time, this was it.

Just one, Luke. You can't afford anything that will loosen your control. Or, at least, loosen it further. It was more than enough that Kitty was in his bedroom, alone with him, in the middle of the night, dressed for bed.

"Just a small one," Kitty said, as if in answer to his own thoughts, but she meant for her, of course. He poured small portions into two glasses, and passed one to her on his way to the chair that faced hers.

"What can I do for you, Kitty," he asked.

She took a sip of her brandy without taking her eyes off him. There was that chin again, lifted in the air as a signal that her calm tone of voice hid a wealth of feeling: trepidation and irritation mixed, if he knew Kitty. And he did. "You said you loved me, and that you couldn't live without me. You said we would make it work. What did you mean?"

A fair question. The first part was easy. "I love you. I want you to be my wife, Kitty, to have and to hold for the rest of our lives." His voice had dropped to a low rumble as his love for Kitty and, yes, his desire threatened to overwhelm him. "I thought to wait to propose until I could make a home for you, but if you wish, I will ask this very minute." He set the brandy aside and fell to his knees at her feet to take her own glass from her unresisting fingers and possess himself of her hands.

She leaned towards him, moistening her lips so that a spear of lust shot straight to his groin, her eyes glowing in the candle-light.

"Will you promise to marry me, Kitty," he begged. "If I could, I would be a younger man for you, one with greater wealth and a noble heritage. But no one could love you more than I. No one will cherish you more than I. Will you be my future, Catherine Mary Stocke? My wife, my life partner, my reason for my work and my comfort in my leisure, the mother of my children, should God bless us?" He leaned to meet her, and if he was confident of her answer, it was not arrogance. She had given him good reason.

She did not disappoint. "My answer, of course, is yes." Then, being Kitty, she had more to add, leaning away from his kiss to say. "However, I have some questions." Her tone hinted she had better like the answers. He should have expected her to challenge him. He suppressed a smile. How he loved this woman!

He sat back on his heels. "Ask," he invited.

Luke had been about to kiss her, and then Kitty would not have had a thought in her head beyond the way she felt. Time enough for kisses when she knew what he planned!

"How do you see our future together?" she asked.

His response was prompt, though his eyes had turned wary. "Blissful."

He didn't add to that, so she remained silent and waited.

He knew what she was doing, of course. He had pointed out the trick himself, after seeing Rede use it on her. He didn't play games, but answered, a slight crease between his brows. "Kitty, it is as I said. I want us to be partners and lovers. Parents, God willing. I see us building a home and family together, caring for our tenants and our land."

"What of the immediate future, Luke?" This was the crucial question, and he knew it, too, the rat, for his eyes turned wary.

"Is this about what my uncle said at dinner?" he asked in that even, somewhat pinched, tone that indicated irritation. When he used it, Paul stopped asking questions. Kitty was not his child, and had no intention of allowing his irritation to stop her from finding out what she wanted to know.

She merely tipped her head slightly to one side and lifted her eyebrows in question.

Luke sighed. "Kitty, I need to go north with him. The estate has been suffering a run of bad luck, except from the sounds of it, I think the luck might be named Titus. I have to find out how bad things are, and what needs to be done to put them right. I'm sorry. I know it is not what you want."

Kitty smiled, cheerfully. "Of course, you must see to Paul's estate. It is your duty. And your uncle will need you, too."

His face cleared and he reached for her hands. "I am glad you understand." He leaned in to kiss her, and she kissed him back. It was as muddling as she expected, but at least it affected him, too.

She managed to retain sufficient control to pull away after several delightful minutes. She had come here with a mission, and it was still not accomplished. "How soon do we leave?" she asked.

Luke blinked, several times, the haze of passion fading as his brain made sense of her words. "You cannot come," he declared, firmly.

She was definitely going. Either with him, which would be her preference, or following him. Less desirable, but not as bad as letting him face all that work, and who knew what kind of hostility, without her.

Kitty was reasonably certain she kept those thoughts from her face, and her voice certainly sounded even and reasonable when she pointed out, "There will be no impropriety if we wed before we leave London." She picked up her brandy glass and had another sip while he gaped.

"That is why I asked when we were leaving. If you can wait a week, we could get a common license, but I understand one cannot marry for seven days after it is issued. If the matter is more urgent, then I suggest a special license. I am sure Rede will be able to get one."

"Marry?" Luke said. "This week?" He was torn, his face frowning as his eyes widened in speculation.

"Yes, for I shall tell you now, Lucius Ogilvy, I am not letting you leave me behind like an ornament you put on a shelf until you have time to dust me." She let a little of her irritation seep into her voice. "We shall be partners, you said. That means I stand at your side as you face whatever you find in Northumberland. I can help, Luke. I shall get the house in order while you manage the estate. I shall make sure Paul continues his schooling and eats well while you make sure he has an estate to grow into."

Luke took her hands again. "It could be dangerous, Kitty. Am I wrong to want you safe?"

Kitty took heart. That wasn't a no.

"Your cousin is locked up, Luke," she pointed out.

"If he has been stealing from the estate, he will have accomplices."

Kitty was tempted to snarl, but managed to keep her voice calm and reasonable. "You plan to rush straight into danger and take a twelve-year-old boy with you while leaving me behind? Think again, Luke. I am not a child in need of coddling."

He heaved a sigh. "Kitty, be reasonable—"

Kitty's temper flared. "You think you are being reasonable?" she demanded.

His jaw tensed and he opened his mouth with some retort on his tongue, then thought better of it. His shoulders deflated as he sighed. "No. I know I'm not reasonable. Not when it comes to you. It's not that I think you need coddling. I know how capable you are. It's just that..." He lifted her hands to his lips and kissed first one and then the other. "If anything happened to you, Kitty my love, it would destroy me." He let go and turned away, as if to hide his expression. His next words were in an undertone. "How can a man live without his heart?"

His obvious distress soothed her anger. "I understand," Kitty told him. "I do not agree, but I do understand, for I feel the same way about you. I know you have to go into danger, but I don't like it. And I can't—Luke, I simply cannot—let you go without me. If you do not want to marry yet, then we won't. If you leave without me, I cannot stop you. But I *will* follow. I promise you that."

In the next moment she was in his arms, and he was kissing her. "You will be the death of me, stubborn female," he muttered against her lips, before covering her mouth again, one hand on her lower back pressing her against him, the other gently cradling the back of her head as he ravaged her with his lips and his tongue. This time, he was the one to draw back. "We have to stop." His body belied his words. He was flushed and trembling, and the thin layers of their robes had not in the least disguised his arousal.

"Must we?" Kitty wondered, "If we are to marry within the week?" She had a theoretical knowledge of what came next. His kisses left her eager to put theory into practice.

She thought he would deny them both because she was young and innocent, and he would be taking advantage of her. What he said instead was unexpected.

"I am a bastard, Kitty. Got by my father on the pretty daughter of his gamekeeper. My only memory of my mother—or memories, because I think it happened many times—is of her crying after one of his visits."

Kitty didn't see the relevance. "You are not your father, Luke. And I am not your mother."

He shook his head. "That's not what I meant. I made a promise to my grandfather, Kitty. When he lay dying, he begged me not to be like my father—careless with women and ruled by my co— my lust."

Still not relevant, Kitty thought, but Luke hadn't finished.

"I promised that I would wait until marriage to experience physical intimacy with a woman, and would be faithful to my wedding vows once I'd made them. I swore it on the family bible."

She couldn't argue with that. *Wait. Did that mean he had never...?*

Luke was looking into some mental landscape—the past perhaps? "I've never found it hard to keep that promise, because I have seen so much misery arising from the behaviour my grandfather decried. My mother, and so many other women. Even the ones who were eager risked being left broken hearted. Or they gave themselves to a man who died before he could put a ring on their finger, and his good intentions didn't protect them or their baby from the consequences."

He was right, of course. Kitty had seen it herself. Indeed, if not for Anne's masquerade as a widow, she would have lived it, at least by association.

"Then along came you, Kitty. I have always struggled to resist you, and with each kiss it becomes harder and harder." He chuckled suddenly, and his voice dropped to a low growl that vibrated in the places that ached for him most. "In more ways than one." She caught the salacious reference, and her face heated. She licked her lips, which had gone suddenly dry.

Luke gulped and looked away. "Help me keep my promise, Kitty," he begged.

Botheration. An appeal to her honour. "Yes, of course." She turned her back on him to straighten the robe he had brushed aside during their kiss, drawing it closed high up her chest and belting it firmly. "Thank you for explaining."

Luke had tidied himself while she was rearranging her robe. He offered her another brandy, but she refused. "If I must be good, another would be a bad idea," she said. She returned to her chair, more determined than ever. "Luke, will you marry me and take me to Northumberland with you?" A special license was sounding more and more appealing.

Luke sat, too, smiling at her. "Are you going to argue with me for the rest of our lives together, heart of my heart?" His tone was one of enquiry rather than criticism.

"Only when you are wrong," she retorted, then amended the statement. "No, for sometimes I might be wrong, but believe myself to be right, as when I saw no reason why you should not bed me, tonight. When you explained, I changed my mind. I would hope, Luke, that we can disagree in a civilized manner, discuss things, and reach agreement."

"I beg you not to speak of bedding, my love," he groaned.

"A special license?" she suggested, hopefully.

"A common license. In the morning, I shall speak with Rede, and with Uncle Baldwin about waiting a few days longer. Now go to bed, Kitty. You have won."

Kitty widened her eyes. "I have won? That is not reaching agreement, Luke."

"I misspoke. We have both won. You are correct that it is not my right to decide to keep you from my life in order to protect you from a threat that might not even exist. But Kitty, if you are in immediate peril and we do not have time for a discussion, I want your promise that you will obey me in that moment. We can talk it over when we are safe."

That was fair, and quite a large concession. "I promise, Luke, unless you are the one in danger and I can do something to save you."

Luke heaved a sigh. "I imagine that we will have many more vigorous discussions in our future, my love."

Kitty blew him a kiss as she made her way to the door. "But imagine the fun we will have making up!" she told him, then slipped out the door, closing it behind her, delighted with her exit line.

CHAPTER 18

Titus paced the room in which he had been sequestered. Damn his father. Damn his uncle, who had married just to spite him. Damn the little brat who had supplanted him. Damn, damn, damn Lucius. How could a man escape death so many times? His mother had called Lucius a devil's cub, and he certainly had the luck of a devil!

Titus regretted losing control when the two traitors in chief visited him, but it was no wonder. He'd gone into the hearing expecting the brat to be disinherited and the bastard hanged, and it had all turned around on him. He could not blame himself for being so angry.

It was a pity, though. He didn't entirely remember what he had said, but he was certain he'd destroyed any chance of fooling Lucius again. His father, perhaps. His father was a gullible fool.

Titus could not rely on either of them to get him out of here. Just as well he didn't need them. Years of planning was about to pay off. He had money his father knew nothing about, tools who would not turn in his hand.

It would have to be escape. With his father against him, he was unlikely to be released on bail. Lucius would easily discover many of his little adjustments and hidden enterprises to supplement his allowance once he looked at the estate records and asked a few questions in Ormswood and the district.

And Lucius would do that. He had always been suffocatingly thorough. He might even find out about what happened to people who stood in Titus's way, though Titus had buried his tracks as deep as possible.

Yes, and he'd find a number of other matters that Titus needed to keep secret. If Titus waited to plead his case, he would hang. Titus had no intention of hanging. So, he would escape. Charming the guards and the magistrates should be easy enough. Titus had always been able to talk people into believing in him.

And his most recent visitor had brought news that would help. The witness who had broken his case against Lucius, the Countess of Chirbury and Selby, was sister to the woman Lucius was about to wed. He could use that to call into question her identification of the brat. He could claim to have been ambushed—which was true.

He could deny everything—after all, no magistrates or constables were in the room when he let his guard slip to the traitor and the bastard. He didn't need the magistrates to let him go. They just needed to trust him enough to relax their vigilance. His supporters would do the rest.

He would have to give up on being Baldwin of Ormswood, but he'd made wise investments with the wealth he had salted away. He could make a good life somewhere far away from England's shores.

But first, he was heading for Northumberland. He would not leave these sceptred isles without revenging himself on those who stole what should belong to Titus, particularly the bastard, the brat, and Titus's treacherous father.

CHAPTER 19

With two days to go until the wedding, Luke was worrying about the wedding night.

Now that he and Kitty were officially betrothed, Kitty's chaperones were more likely to leave her unattended, if only for a few moments, and he had made the most of every opportunity. He and she, that was, for she was his partner in their kisses and caresses, as eager as he.

Day by day, as the wedding approached, his desire ratcheted higher and higher, until he was certain he would fail Kitty when she was finally his wife. He would disgrace himself by climaxing at the mere sight of her, or lose control before she had found her pleasure.

More than anything, he dreaded hurting her. He'd heard various stories when men were drinking, and had no idea what to believe.

Which was why he had asked for a private meeting with the Earl of Chirbury, whom he'd better get used to addressing as Rede, now that he was marrying the sister of the man's wife.

It was late in the evening. Uncle Baldwin had gone to bed early, and the ladies were upstairs admiring the gown that had arrived this afternoon from the modiste: the one Kitty planned to wear for the wedding.

There was no time like the present, but for once in his life, Luke had no idea how to introduce the topic.

I am a virgin, and I would like you to teach me how to pleasure the lady you regard as your sister. That was it in a nutshell, and the stark terms showed him how impossible it was to talk about it. Not with Rede; not with anyone.

He opened his mouth to excuse himself, but Rede spoke first. "Spit it out, Luke. Cold feet?"

His response was instant and fervent. "Lord, no!" It was not the cold that was the problem, but the heat. "Quite the opposite."

"Something is wrong, though," Rede mused. "You're not an easy man to read, but I've known you long enough to know when you're fretting away at a problem. Are you going to tell me, or shall I keep guessing? You are free to tell me to butt out, but it was you who asked to speak privately."

Luke could not think where to start. Every opening line he'd imagined sent the discussion straight downhill.

Rede took a sip of his brandy, then said, "You have a mistress and five children, and you don't know how to tell Kitty. You prefer men. You are secretly an assassin for the British Crown and are being sent to India the day after the wedding."

Luke had to chuckle. "No, no, and no." Perhaps he didn't have to tell Rede the whole story. "Look, Rede, you've been married twice. I thought you might be able to advise me. I'm worried that…" It was no good. He ran out of words again.

This time, Rede said nothing. He waited, sipping his brandy, his expression bland.

"I have heard that some women find their first time hard," Luke blurted after the silence had stretched for what seemed like minutes. "I don't want Kitty… That is…" He must be as red as a beetroot. Until tonight, he hadn't blushed in years.

"You haven't been with a virgin before," Rede commented. "I am grateful for your restraint, for I don't think Kitty would have refused you had you pressed your advances."

Luke managed a nod. The last time he was this embarrassed, he was nine, and had been caught swimming naked in the lake at the estate in full sight of the dairy. The woman who supervised the dairy maids had chased him all the way home, whacking him with a switch, so he had no time to stop for his clothes.

Rede shrugged. "I was as nervous as you are now with my first wife. All I can advise is to make sure she has reached her completion before you enter her, and take it slow when you do. Stop when she needs you to and give her time to adjust. Given her age and how much she rides, she probably won't have a hard time of it."

That was reassuring. Luke wanted to ask a few more questions, but he'd listened to enough stories and read enough graphically descriptive literature to work it out from here. He hoped.

"You'll be fine," Rede said. "You have passion enough between you, from what I've seen when the pair of you thought yourselves unobserved."

The heat spread back up Luke's face. He had one more embarrassing question to ask, and he'd come this far. "That is part of the problem. What if I, ah, misfire?"

Rede shrugged. "That's not a problem, it's an opportunity—it makes it less likely that you'll forget yourself and rush her. Just keep giving her pleasure until you recover. I am doing my best not to consider that this discussion is about my sister, Luke, so unless you have some more questions, can we talk about something else? Politics, maybe? The weather?"

"Your next gamekeeper," Luke suggested. "I may have a couple of ideas."

K itty put on the gown to show Anne, who had been unable to attend the final fitting. It was made of blue silk. The modiste had suggested a gold to match the flecks in her eyes, but Kitty didn't like the idea. In truth, her eyes were a boring brown, a very similar colour to her hair. Not very exciting. The blue was the shade of a duck egg, and the piping that trimmed it was the blue of deep water, a precise match for the pelisse that had been made for her to wear with the gown.

It was an afternoon gown, so the neckline, with its cascading cream lace, was modest and the sleeves long. They were also trimmed with cream lace, though the lace on the hem was the same blue as the piping and the pelisse.

She turned in front of the mirror, modelling the gown for Anne while also examining it herself.

It wasn't the full effect, of course, because she did not have her hair done as she would for the wedding, and nor had she changed her jumps for the stays, chemise, and petticoats that had been made to go with the gown.

Millie brought those out for Anne to see. They were ivory, delicately embroidered in shades of blue and trimmed with a daintier version of the same cream lace as the gown.

After she had duly admired everything, Anne produced a flat leather case. "These arrived today from Longford Court," she said. "I have been saving them for your wedding—they were Mother's, and I think they will go beautifully with what you are going to wear."

The case contained a parure of exquisite pearls: necklace, earrings, brooch, bracelet and hair pins. Anne clasped the necklace around her neck. It had five gold lozenges decorated with leaves and six-petaled flowers made from sapphires, each lozenge supporting a drop pearl. Three strings of matched pearls connected the middle lozenge with the two on either side, two strings attached those lozenges to the final two, and one string each side led to the clasp, which was again of gold with sapphire flowers and leaves.

Millie set the earrings in her ears—an identical lozenge and drop pearl on either side. The bracelet was three rows of pearls connected by three lozenges, one of which concealed the clasp. It looked lovely on her bare wrist, but would fit better over her gloves.

Kitty sat for a closer look at the earrings, turning her head from side to side. She could just imagine the dainty pins in her hair, the pearls gleaming, the gold and sapphires catching the light as she moved. "They are lovely, Anne. Thank you for letting me borrow them."

Anne dropped a kiss on her hair. "I am giving them to you, darling."

Kitty spun round on her chair so she could see her sister face to face. "They are Selby jewels. Should they not go to John and his family?"

Anne shook her head. "This was part of Mother's personal collection. Papa gave it to her as a present when our brother was born, and she often wore it. It must have been stored with the Selby jewels, because I found the case among the jewellery we recovered after Selby died. I want you to have it, and to pass it on to one of your daughters. My heir will have the ones that have been handed down for generations."

Kitty admired herself in the mirror for a moment longer. Would Luke like what he saw? She watched her lips curve in a smile, smug and a little mysterious. She had been told often enough that she was pretty, but she knew she was nothing out of the ordinary.

Brown hair that insisted on curling. Brown eyes. *Item, two lips indifferent red; item, two eyes, with lids to them; item, one neck, one chin, and so forth.* Shakespeare's words described her well. Thinking of Luke and how he had surrendered to his desire for her made her feel beautiful in a way she had never experienced. Beautiful and powerful. The reflection in the mirror apparently agreed.

She was sure of Luke, at least as far as the wedding was concerned. Confident, too, she could be the partner he needed as Paul's guardian and steward of Paul's estates. Could she be his wife, though?

"Millie, will you undress me now, please, and put all this finery away? I'll put my night rail and robe on, and then you can go to bed as soon as you are done. Anne, will you stay for a cup of hot chocolate with me before bed? I have something I wish to ask you."

"Of course, Kitty," Anne headed towards Kitty's little sitting room. "I'll call a footman and order a tray sent up."

The maid who had delivered the tray was just leaving when Kitty joined Anne in the sitting room.

"Shall I pour?" she asked, taking the chair by the tray, which held a pot of chocolate, two cups, extra cream and sugar cubes, and a plate of little sweet treats.

Anne nodded. "Yes, please. Kitty, is there something wrong? This wedding is what you want, is it not? I'm sure Luke would agree to wait if—"

"I don't want to wait. Anne, I have been waiting six years." She passed Anne a cup of chocolate and the plate of treats as she searched for the words to explain her fears.

"Are you concerned about the wedding night?" Anne asked. "You know the basic facts, of course. I well remember *that* conversation."

Kitty remembered it, too. She had been seventeen, and curious about what happened between a man and a woman. She knew that men, even those who seemed to be gentlemen, must not be trusted; that she must never be alone with a man. She had faith that the sister who raised her, and who was the head of their little household, would not set a rule without a purpose. She just wanted to know why. So she asked, and Anne gave her a very brief lesson on male and female anatomy, and—most embarrassing of all—how they fitted together.

She gathered it had something to do with babies, and later learned more in bits and pieces, mainly through conversations between her married friends when they forgot that she was still a maiden. None of it, however, told her what she wanted to know now.

"Yes," she told Anne. "The basic facts are clear. We lie together. We connect our... you know. But how do I please him, Anne? And does it hurt?"

"You can trust Luke to guide you in what to do, Kitty," Anne said.

Not if he does not know himself. Kitty wasn't going to tell Anne that Luke had no experience. That was his secret. "I've heard stories," she said. Some of my friends make it out to be a chore, like darning socks. Something to be got over before going to sleep. Others look forward to it. Opinions vary on whether the ladies who enjoy it are wanton, or those who don't are deprived.

"It is not wanton for a wife to enjoy the marriage bed, Kitty," Anne said, firmly. "You will, I am certain. You like kissing, Luke, do you not?"

Kitty's face heated. She and Luke had not realised they had been observed. "I do," she confessed.

"And he likes it when you kiss him back." It was a statement rather than a question. A true statement.

"Yes, he does." That was reassuring. And helpful. "So I should not just lie flat on my back and think about the trim for my next bonnet, which is what one lady I know claims that she does."

Anne giggled. "I think I can confidently say that, if she has a single thought about bonnet trimming during a marital interlude, her husband is not doing his job properly. Kitty, the best advice I can give you is the advice Rede gave me our first time. Tell Luke if you like something or if you don't like it, and ask him to do the same. Rede and I have been doing so throughout our marriage, and it works."

That is actually really good advice. "I can do that. Thank you, Anne. Have I told you recently how much I love you?"

"And I you, little sister. I am going to miss you, when you are off in Northumberland, sorting out Luke's problems for him. If you need anything from me, anything at all, you need only write."

"I'll miss you, too, Anne," Kitty confessed, "but I'm only a few days travel away, and we will return to London from time to time, Luke says."

"We will write hundreds of letters, you and I, and keep the post busy going up and down the highway," Anne suggested. "And perhaps Rede and I shall invite ourselves to stay when the baby is a little older."

"I am sure that Luke and I will welcome you at any time, Anne."

How odd to be thinking of inviting Anne to her home, when for so long she had lived in Anne's. And it would be hers, would it not? At least until Paul grew up and married. Luke would be steward and guardian, and she would be chatelaine, and they would put to rights all that Luke suspected was wrong.

They would build a wonderful life together.

Luke followed James Mivart, the owner and manager of the hotel into the suite of rooms, his new wife on his arm, two other footmen entering behind them with their bags.

"How pretty," Kitty said, as she took in the flowers that adorned the sitting room.

"Very," Luke agreed, his eyes on her. *My wife*. His mind kept replaying the word. Perhaps if he said it often enough, it would begin to seem real.

Luke had taken a suite for three nights. When he asked Uncle Baldwin if he minded putting off their trip north for eight days because Luke wanted to marry Kitty and bring her north with them, Uncle Baldwin insisted he take at least a month. "Lady Kitty will not want to spend the first few days of her marriage travelling to Cumberland with me and Paul to play gooseberry," he objected.

Kitty, when consulted, retorted, "I am not such a ninny as that. As long as we do not share our room with them at night." She blushed, then, and hid her face with her hands, so that Luke had to gently pull them away to kiss her, and it was some time before he returned to the subject.

"I like the idea of some time alone with you before we make the journey," he admitted. Three nights, they agreed, and another three in London while they finished preparing to go North. They were fortunate that Mivart's Hotel, which rented by-the-month accommodation to wealthy visitors to London, had a suite left empty because the previous occupants had cut short their stay.

"The refreshments have been set out as you ordered, sir," Mivart said. "Please let us know if there is anything else you require."

Luke had everything his heart desired within arm's reach, and the only other thing he required was for Mivart to follow the two footmen out of the door. He looked at Kitty, referring the question to her, but she shook her head.

"Nothing at the moment, thank you," he told the man.

"Then it remains only for me to say, on behalf of the hotel, that we wish you a very happy stay at Mivart's, Mr and Mrs Ogilvy, and a long and prosperous life together." He bowed.

Luke and Kitty murmured their thanks and the hotel manager left. Luke locked the door, placing the hat he had removed on the shelf above the coat hooks to the right of the door, and shrugging out of his overcoat.

When he turned, Kitty stood where he had left her, still in her redingote and bonnet, her arms crossing her body, her hands clutching her elbows. She was ill at ease, poor darling.

"Would you like to give me your coat and bonnet?" Luke asked.

She looked down as if surprised to find she was still dressed for the outdoors. "Oh, yes. Of course." Her chuckle was more nervous than amused. "I am still wearing my gloves, even." She removed first one and then the other. She tugged at her bonnet ribbon, but somehow managed to pull it into a knot.

"Here," Luke said. "Let me help." She'd pulled it tight. He was tempted to find his pen knife and cut it, till he realised that focusing on the knot gave him a reason for semi-inadvertent touches that did not make her skittish.

He took his time, carefully picking at one edge of the ribbon until it loosened enough to give him a place to grasp. "There," he said at last, as he managed to work the tail of the ribbon back far enough that two more calculated pulls set it free. "Better?"

"Much better," Kitty assured him, and her next words made it clear she meant her nervousness rather than the ribbon. "I was being missish, Luke. I want this. I want you. I just hate being ignorant."

He knew that about her. She wanted to do everything perfectly, and became impatient with herself when she didn't learn as quickly as she expected. "We are both beginners, my love. I shall be patient with you if you will be patient with me, and we shall learn together."

The champagne he had ordered stood ready on a sideboard with two glasses and a tray of small savouries and cakes, cheese, dried fruit, nuts, and other snacks. "Would you care for a drink, darling?"

He poured their drinks and handed them to her to carry to the little sitting area, while he put the tray on the low table, next to a draughts board set up for a game. Settled beside her on the sofa, and looking for a way to bridge the awkwardness, he suggested, "How about a game of draughts?"

Kitty looked at him as if he had suddenly grown a second head. "You want to play draughts?"

"With forfeits," he added.

She tipped her head to one side, a hint of a smile playing about her lips. "Forfeits, my love? What sort of forfeits?"

"Let me see," he pondered, though mostly for show. The choice was an obvious one. "When one of us captures a counter, the other must drink a mouthful of wine and remove an item of clothing."

She raised her eyebrows, the smile broadening. "And does the capturer win a boon? A kiss perhaps?"

"A good idea," he agreed. "A kiss for a capture. Also, if our counter reaches the other side and becomes a king, we also win a kiss."

Kitty pursed her lips as she considered the suggestion, then nodded. "Very well, but we must decide the prize for the winner. A boon of the winner's choice?"

That could make the game very interesting. Luke nodded his agreement, and turned the board so that the direction of play was along the table. "Sitting side by side will make the kisses easier," he explained.

As it turned out, Kitty was wearing three petticoats, which meant a greater number of garments to remove. On the other hand, her increasing nakedness kept her from focusing on the game. She was distracted even more by Luke. Whether a kiss was won by her or by him, he made sure they were increasingly passionate, increasingly intimate.

Also, while Kitty removed her slippers and her stockings as her first four items, Luke's strategy was to leave his own shoes and stock-ings until last. By the time she was down to her last petticoat, with only her stays and her chemise to go, he was sitting naked but for one stocking and one shoe. He jumped two of her remaining pieces in one move, and that was the last of the game, for the next move was to the bed.

As it turned out, neither of them had anything to worry about. Luke had never doubted that he'd find his own satisfaction, only that he'd be unable to give pleasure to Kitty, and Kitty had feared she would disappoint Luke.

Love—and the willingness to talk—made up for lack of experi-ence, and if the first time was a little more rushed than Luke had intended, the two that followed made up for it. They finished the champagne in the early hours of the morning. They never did get back to the game of draughts, but they agreed that they had both won.

PART 2: AN ADVENTUROUS HONEYMOON

CHAPTER 20

As the son of a baron, Titus had been shown the same courtesies the Marquis of Aldridge had demanded for Luke: a bedchamber in the magistrate's house, guarded and locked; meals brought from a nearby cookshop; books to read; a laundry service.

He had his own servant with him, too, Uncle Baldwin had told Luke. A young man Titus had purchased as a boy from an orphanage in Newcastle. Perhaps that showed that the goodness in Titus was not completely extinguished. Or perhaps Titus just wanted a servant who was indebted to him, and who had no family loyalties.

Uncle Baldwin had apologised to Luke for paying to keep Titus in comfort. "I know his crimes against you and Paul are legion, but he is still my son, Luke."

"Of course, uncle. I understand," Luke had told him. Perhaps he might have felt more vengeful if he wasn't so happy. Since he and Kitty had agreed to wed, and especially since their three nights in the hotel, he'd been viewing the world through a haze of joy.

Even today, standing on the landing waiting to be admitted to his cousin's room, he had to remind himself not to smile. He was on a solemn errand, and he didn't need the constables and others who passed him to see him grinning like a loon.

He wiped the smile off his face when a warder approached him and said, "Please follow me, Mr Ogilvy."

Titus was not only being treated as well as Luke. He was incarcerated in exactly the same bedchamber. He stood as Luke entered. "Cousin! I understand congratulations are in order. An heiress, my father tells me!"

Luke's desire to smile evaporated completely. "Titus," he said.

"You can leave us alone," Titus told the warder. "My cousin is not a danger to me."

Luke could feel his eyebrows shooting up as the warder turned and left, but he did not object. After all, Titus was hardly going to murder him where he stood. With the pair of them alone in a locked room, he'd be a fool to try, and he wouldn't succeed if he did. In the years since they last met, Luke had led a hard physical life, but Titus was pale from indoor living and growing soft around the middle.

Titus strode forward and clasped Luke's hand. Luke braced himself for a fight, but Titus merely said, "I thought you were dead, Luke. When Father said he'd had you arrested, I was never more amazed. And Julius is alive, too! How wonderful. You must tell me how you accomplished it."

He released Luke's hand and waved to a chair. "More important, we must decide how to bring the crimes against you and Julius home to Father, where, I am so sorry to have to admit, they must belong."

"Paul," Luke said, as he took the chair, holding on to that one simple denial as a bulwark against the flood of lies. Titus used to do this as a boy, standing red-handed over the detritus of his latest foolish escapade, casting the blame on someone else with such conviction and charm his father and mother—and others too— would doubt the evidence of their own eyes.

Luke held hard to what he knew. "The young baron goes by the name of Paul, now." *And Uncle Baldwin is either innocent or the best liar the world has ever seen.*

"You must believe me, Luke," Titus insisted. "I had no idea that Father was trying to have your Paul killed and cast the blame on you. I just knew you could not have done what you were accused of."

He had tears in his eyes, and stopped to wipe them away. He had been able to cry on command as a child, too. "It never occurred to me—though it should have, the number of times I have been accused of crimes that he or uncle committed. Paul's mother, for example. It was father who was caught with her, though I was blamed."

His soft smile was full of memories and humour. "Not that I minded. The baron offered for her since his brother already had a wife. We had to rescue the family's reputation after all, and the girl became a baroness, so she didn't lose out. As for me, I was only seventeen, Luke. How did I know that the baron and father would keep doing it to me, until no reputable female was ever left alone with me, while they continued their rakehell ways in secret?"

Every line of Titus's face, of his body, conveyed outrage and regret. He was good. Very, very convincing. Luke might almost have been persuaded if his own memories and his long conversations with Titus's father had not given him a different perspective.

"You missed a great career on the stage by being born into the aristocracy, Titus," he told his cousin.

For a moment, Titus's performance failed. "You always believed them instead of me," he whined. Then the mask was firmly back in place. "I do not blame you, Luke. Father is very convincing. Even more so than Uncle, who had you as a visible sign of his real nature. Though you of all people should know he could not be trusted with women."

He sighed again. "I do not expect you to believe me. Just keep an open mind. Remember, I was the only one to speak up for you all those years ago. I remained your friend, Luke, even when you abandoned me for Julius. Paul, I mean."

Truly? They were back to that old claim? Titus had resented the time Luke spent with the baby, and even Luke's duties for the estate. "I invited you to join me, Titus. He was your cousin as much as I."

That sparked a flash of temper. "The brat is my usurp—" Titus broke off the last word, and shut his eyes while he took a deep breath. When he opened his eyes again, he had smoothed his face and resumed his gentle smile. "Is he your son, Luke? I have always wondered. I would not blame you. His mother was very desirable. I know you spent a lot of time with her."

Luke didn't dignify that claim with an answer. It had been a waste of time to come here. Titus was not going to admit his guilt, let alone explain his reasons. He stood.

"It's time for me to go. I trust you have all you need?"

"Apart from my freedom. So, you are going to abandon me again? This time with a rope at the end? My mother always said you would be the death of me." He managed to make it sound plaintive rather than accusing, and it was all the more effective for that. Luke had to remind himself that the fate awaiting his cousin was the one Titus had designed for Luke.

As to Titus's mother, if she still lived, she would undoubtedly curse him, but she had been doing so all his life, without effect. The harm done to him in the past had been by human agency, not supernatural. And he still survived.

"The courts will decide your fate, Titus. If you have evidence to support your innocence, you'll be given the opportunity to produce it."

Titus stood, shoving his chair roughly away, that and his clenched jaw the only sign of his temper. He crossed to the window and stared out at the street. "Go, then. I don't suppose I shall see you again."

"Probably not. My wife, Paul, and I are heading north in the morning." Luke thought of offering his hand in farewell, then clasped both hands behind his back. "This is goodbye, Titus."

Titus didn't reply, until the warder had come to Luke's knock and opened the door. Then, without turning, he said, "Goodbye, Lucius." His voice turned to a hiss. "And bad luck to you and the brat."

Kitty was visiting her friend Mia, who had come up from Portsmouth for the wedding. Mia was married to Rede's cousin Jules Redepenning and was staying with Jules's father, Rede's Uncle Henry, while they were in town.

"In Portsmouth," she told Kitty, "I have taken a townhouse. It was all very well living with one in-law after another when Jules was on the other side of the world and before the children came to England. Now that Jules is posted to the Channel blockade, and with three children and another due shortly," she patted her rounded abdomen, "we need our own home. Somewhere the children can have their own things around them, and where Jules can come when he is on leave.

"You must tell me all about it," Kitty said. "I wish I could visit, but Luke and his uncle are anxious to be home. We leave for Northumberland tomorrow."

"We will be at opposite ends of the country," Mia said, "but we can still visit one another. Susan travels even further when she takes her son to visit his estate." Susan was Uncle Henry's daughter, and had recently remarried. Her new husband's estate was halfway between Bath and Bristol, and her son Michael had inherited her first husband's estate near Edinburgh.

Paul was currently out in Uncle Henry's garden with Mia's stepson, Dan. It was a typical long townhouse garden, and the servants had set up archery butts for the two boys right at the far end, with a footman to keep an eye on them and to make sure that no one wandered down that way at the wrong moment.

"How are the girls?" Kitty asked. Dan had two sisters, Marsha and Ada. Mia had taken all three children into her heart, and they all adored their father's wife.

"The girls are well. Papa has taken them out for ices, with Hannah along to make sure they behave. I could not miss your wedding, Kitty, dear. How are you finding married life?"

Kitty blushed as she smiled. Married life had been a revelation.

If she had known what awaited her in Luke's bed, she might have pressed him to marry her, or at least bed her, a lot earlier.

"From the look on your face, I assume marriage pleases you," Mia observed.

Kitty's blush deepened. "I was only wed five days ago," she pointed out.

"You know perfectly well I was referring to the marriage bed," Mia retorted. Her smile broadened as her eyes focused into the middle distance. "Which has much to recommend it, if your husband knows what he is doing."

It had much to recommend it if one's husband was learning as he went along, but Kitty had no intention of sharing that with Mia, however good a friend she was.

"Luke has gone to visit his cousin," she said, to change the subject. "He is taking the betrayal very hard, even harder than when he thought it was his uncle."

"I suppose the horrid man thought that, with Paul and Luke out of the way, he would be heir and eventually baron. Then, when they disappeared, he believed he had won."

"It must have been an awful shock to discover they still lived," Kitty commented.

"How did he," Mia wondered.

"Uncle Baldwin. He admits he talked over the dinner table. He was one of the government officials on the Admiralty board that examined Jules, and he believed his son to be a safe pair of ears."

Last year, Mia's husband had been released from a French prison to act as guide for an English traitor and a group of French spies on a treasure hunting expedition that stumbled across the deranged naval captain who had kidnapped Jules's son Dan. After it was all over, Jules had to answer questions about how he had come to be in France in the first place, and why he had agreed to act as guide.

"Ah. And, of course, Jules spoke about Luke and his brave son, and the part they played in rescuing Dan and capturing Lady Carrington and the French spies. Did Mr Baldwin senior realise who the two of them were?"

"He says not," Kitty said. "He thought his lost nephews were both dead, and it never occurred to him to connect them with the heroes of Longford. Although, he did say that one of the reasons he mentioned it to his son was the coincidence of a gamekeeper called Luke who was an expert archer."

"I hear that Mr Titus Baldwin said in court he had never believed that Luke was dead," Mia commented.

Kitty nodded. "He was suspicious enough, when he heard his father's story, to travel to Longford on Nidd to see for himself."

"Where you overheard him talking to his accomplice," Mia acknowledged.

"Thank goodness. I have waking nightmares about what might have happened had I not thought to check whether sufficient violets were in bloom for the still room."

"Mr Titus Baldwin is in prison, you are married to Luke, and Paul has his proper identity again," Mia noted. "All is well that ends well."

Which was true. A bustle in the hall was Mia's two girls arriving home with their grandfather. Kitty and Mia went out to greet them.

When he heard his wife's voice, Luke focused on the door to the dressing room. Kitty was not yet in view, but he could hear her say, "Go to bed, Millie. We have a long journey ahead of us, and you will need your sleep."

Pierrot, who had accepted the addition of Luke to his mistress's bedroom with a nonchalance Luke had not expected, lifted his head from Luke's foot, then replaced it as Kitty came into the bedchamber.

Luke stood, careful not to dislodge the little dog, who nonetheless raised his head again to send Luke a reproachful look.

Kitty laughed. "He wants you to sit, my love," she said. "Do that, and I shall pour us a glass of brandy while you tell me about your visit to Titus." She busied herself with the decanter on the table by the window. "I know there is more than you wanted to say in front of Uncle Baldwin. What does 'He does not accept responsibility' mean?"

Luke shrugged. "He blamed his father and mine, and then me for good measure. I had forgotten that about him, or perhaps I assumed he must have grown out of it. Titus was always one to swear he'd never touched the cake even when he was caught with his hand in the tin and crumbs all around his mouth."

"You did what you could," his wife assured him.

"I am not sure what I hoped to accomplish," he admitted. "Perhaps I hoped he would apologise for trying to kill me. We used to be close, though we had grown somewhat apart as he grew older. My fault, perhaps. My father sent me away to Edinburgh to university, and by the time I arrived home, Titus was out of boyhood and into the wildest part of youth. He had friends he racketed around with; friends who would not have welcomed me. I was older, more sober, and of questionable birth. Also, my father had business interests all over Britain, and took to sending me as his deputy, so I was seldom at home."

Kitty carried over a glass of brandy for him, and half a glass for herself. "Your father married a girl Titus desired. Is that, perhaps, part of why Titus misbehaved?"

"That is what my uncle thinks. Alison had been my father's wife for four months when I first met her. I could tell that, whatever he said, Titus resented my father's marriage, and I thought perhaps he had been sharp with her, for she did not like to be left alone with him. He had an edge to his tongue, did Titus, and she was a timid little thing. No one told me Titus's assault on her was the reason she married my father." He accepted the glass and took the opportunity to drop a kiss on her hand.

She let her hand linger on his cheek for a moment, before moving to her own seat. "Then she had a son to supplant his father as heir. That must have added injury to insult."

Luke carried on with his explanation. "She was already with child when I got home. Titus told me he was delighted. He said he had always expected my father to marry and produce an heir for the estate, and we should all be very happy. My father said he'd take Titus away on his next trip. By the time they returned, the baby was six months old, and Alison had fallen ill with the disease that eventually killed her. After that, Titus was all charm, though Alison never warmed to him. I understand why, now."

"He knew there would be no more children to move him even further from the title."

He was startled at that but realised the probable truth of it, and the obvious corollary. "Do you think, even then, that he intended to kill Paul? He was only eighteen, Kitty."

She shrugged. "Who can know? Certainly, if he had been your constant shadow as a little boy, he must have resented your attention to the baby."

"Paul." His eyes softened, as they always did when he spoke of the child he had raised as his own. "His mother died before he was a year old, and his father ignored him. The baron never had much interest in babies. Then he died, too, and Paul was an orphan."

He admitted to Kitty something he'd never shared with anyone else. "And so was I. In truth, I had been since my own mother died. My father took me into his house, but I was never permitted to address him as father. He was to be Lord Baldwin or my lord. I was mostly left to the servants. When he noticed I existed, he regarded me as something between a pet and a poor relation. Kind, in a lofty casual sort of a way. When I grew old enough, he trained me as his steward. I was never treated as a son."

"I do not think I like your father," Kitty said.

There was not much Luke could say to that. "Have you finished your brandy, my love?" He asked. "As you said to your maid, we need an early night."

She downed the last mouthful and set the glass on the table. "Yes."

Luke stood and held out his hand. "Then come to bed, wife of mine. I need you."

The Great Marlborough Street Magistrate's Court, like the other London courts, had three magistrates. Titus invited each of them to dine with him, sending his manservant, Dixon, to purchase a very pleasant two-course meal from a local cook shop.

Two of the magistrates proved to be impervious to Titus's persuasions. One refused to see him at all, his response to the invitation saying he considered it inappropriate to fraternise with a prisoner. Another came to dinner and even stayed on to play chess, but would not listen to Titus's carefully prepared tale of victimisation and abuse.

"These are arguments for the court, Mr Baldwin. I cannot hear them until you come before the bench, when all sides will be able to present evidence."

The third was ripe for the plucking. Not only did he listen, he sympathised. He had an older half-brother, he said, who was the light of their father's eyes. He had often taken the blame for the other's wrongdoing.

"It is shocking, Mr Baldwin, that your father would prefer his brother's bastard to his own son."

"I think it is because he dislikes my mother, his wife," Titus confided, turning his face away from the light and touching a finger to his eye to wipe away a manly tear. "He sent her away when I was just a boy of five, and I have always been glad she escaped his cruelty, much though I missed her."

"Shocking," the magistrate repeated. "My own mother died when I was seven."

It was a bond, and Titus built on it that evening and during evenings that followed. He shared many of his boyhood escapades, ascribing them to Lucius. He agreed when the magistrate suggested that Lucius might be Titus's half-brother. "For that would explain why my father favours the ill-begotten scoundrel." He accepted the magistrate's apology for the way the hearing had turned out.

"My father can be very convincing," he assured the man. "You had no way of knowing he is a skilled liar and has always supported Lucius over me my whole life."

During the days, meanwhile, Titus and Dixon cultivated the guards. Titus was always polite and cooperative—a model prisoner. He ate well, thanks to an account his father had opened for him at the cook shop, and he shared his left overs with the guards. He sent his manservant out for fresh fruit, and shared that, too.

Dixon, who was not a prisoner and who was therefore able to leave the room whenever Titus pleased, spent time chatting with whoever was on duty, losing to them at cards, and sharing jokes and bawdy stories. Before long, they stopped questioning Dixon's comings and goings, and even trusted him enough to accept an ale from him of an evening, when he brought a jug back from the local tavern.

The magistrate's uncritical acceptance of Titus's story was reinforced by the guards' increasing sympathy for "poor Mr Baldwin", and his frequent visits encouraged the guards to forget about the revelations of the hearing and see Titus as a victim of his evil cousin and wicked father.

Their work paid off when Dixon had the opportunity to use the wax tablet he had been carrying for days, palming the key to Titus's room when the guard left it on the card table while he relieved himself. It was the work of a moment to take an impression.

After that, the rest of the plan was easy. A drugged mug of ale left the night guard asleep. Wearing Dixon's clothes, his cap pulled down over his head, Titus walked down the stairs and out of the front door. An hour later, after the changing of the guard, Dixon followed, joining Titus at the London docks. The ship on which Dixon had purchased passage sailed at dawn, bound for Newcastle Upon Tyne to pick up a cargo of coal.

Father and Lucius would pay for their treachery, and then Titus was bound for the United States of America, and a new life. After all, the former colonists owed the pair of them a refuge. True, they had paid for the information siphoned their way over the past few years, since Father was appointed to a position in the Admiralty. Paid even better than the French. But to Titus's mind, more was due.

Most of the money he'd received from the Americans had been paid to a bank in New York, for Titus had always been aware that one day, he might need to escape. If he was ever caught. If he was unable to shift his crimes onto someone else's shoulders.

"We shouldn't be going to Ormswood," Dixon grumbled. "If we

are caught, we shall be arrested again, and this time, both of us will be locked up in prison."

"We won't be caught," Titus assured the man. "I'm not leaving without the money and jewels I have hidden, and the rest of what I'm owed from the estate, and from Captain Relish and the Scot."

He also wanted to make sure that Lucius and the brat did not live to enjoy the estate that should have been his. His father, too. He would kill his father as a farewell gift to his mother. Dixon did not need to know any of that.

Dixon subsided at the promise of money. Greed was always a powerful lure for the manservant, which might make him useful enough to take to the Americas. On the other hand, Dixon knew enough of Titus's secrets that plan A remained attractive. No need to decide yet, but should Titus take a leaf from his cousin's book and fake his own death, Dixon would make an excellent facsimile of Titus as a corpse.

Uncle Baldwin didn't drop his bombshell until Luke and his party were half a day from Newcastle-Upon-Tyne, where they would stay overnight before the final day's journey north to Ormswood.

They had been riding in the morning, but rain had driven all but the outriders into the carriages, and they had not bothered to hire riding horses for the afternoon. They were quite a cavalcade. Uncle Baldwin travelled with his valet, driver, two footmen, and two outriders. Kitty had Millie Price. Rede had provided the other two carriages, complete with coachmen and footmen. And Luke had been persuaded by David Wakefield to add six guards to provide extra protection on the road and to be men he could trust at Ormswood Hall.

Thank goodness the delay in their journey had allowed time to write ahead for accommodation for the large party at the inns along the way.

Luke had been beguiling the afternoon by describing Ormswood Hall to Paul and Kitty.

At its core, it was a fortified manor, built around a Norman keep and approved by the reigning monarch in the 14th century to act as a refuge for the locals during raids from north of the border. It was between the Great North Road and the coast; four miles from the highway and a mile from the fishing village of Ormsmouth. The village of Ormswood abutted the estate, which was within walking distance of a vast ruined castle that had been part of the coastal defences in Norman times, though many of the stones had long since been taken away to build forts, other castles, and even Ormswood Hall itself.

Since its early days, the Hall had been extended five or six times, with wings built in styles contemporary to their era, meeting at different angles, each at a different level.

Luke didn't tell Paul, but he had already explained to Kitty, that it was also riddled with hidden rooms and passages: some built to be secret, such as priest holes and access ways to such refuges, some created when a new wing or an alteration to an existing room cut off servants passages and stairs.

"There used to be a book in the library with a map of them," Luke had told his wife. "Most of them, in any case. My friend Barn and I found at least two more in the Hall, and then there are the tunnels. A tunnel connects the Hall to its dower house, Primrose Cottage (which is a substantial house and not a cottage at all), and another runs to St George's Grange. Rumour has it that another tunnel runs all the way to the sea caves on the coast."

He'd have a promise from Paul not to go exploring alone before he told the boy any of that, and he'd certainly not tempt him with stories of the smugglers who supposedly used the caves.

"My father built the New Wing," Uncle Baldwin commented. "Or, at least, he began the building. My brother finished it, and reconfigured some of the others."

"He moved the master suit to the New Wing, did he not?" Luke asked. "I seem to remember visiting him in another part of the house. In fact…" he paused. "Uncle Baldwin, didn't I sleep in the Baron's bedchamber when I was sick, once?"

It was hard to be certain in the gloomy interior of the carriage, but Uncle Baldwin seemed to pale. His voice was steady, though. "You did. Your father wanted you under his eye."

Luke almost shrugged but resisted the impulse. His father had never been demonstrative, but perhaps he cared more than he showed. Still, Luke remembered another face by his bedside. Two faces. "His valet nursed me," he said. "Marsh. There was another man, too. I called him Patrick. I haven't thought of him for years."

Uncle Baldwin changed the subject. "I have sent instructions for my things to be moved from the master suite to the dower house. I do not suppose Paul will want to use the suite yet, though he has that right. But Luke and Kitty, you should use it. Better than leaving the rooms empty, and they are the best appointed in the house."

"You don't need to do that," Kitty protested. "Luke and I will be quite satisfied with another room, and—as you say—Paul doesn't want a whole suite of rooms all to himself."

"I suppose there is a schoolroom on the nursery floor, and bed chambers for boys of my age," Paul said.

"It would be better for you—and your tutor when Luke appoints one—to stay in the New Wing," Uncle Baldwin declared. "Kitty, that is kind of you, but I will still move to Primrose Cottage. It is for the best."

Luke leaned forward for a better view of Uncle Baldwin's countenance. Far from being pale, he had flushed, and he was not meeting Luke's eyes. "What are you not saying, Uncle? What is wrong."

Uncle Baldwin shifted uncomfortably. "I should have told you before. It's Aileen. She moved back to Ormswood some years ago."

For a moment, Luke didn't know who Aileen was, and then he remembered. "Aunt Baldwin? Your wife?"

Uncle Baldwin rushed into speech. "Her cousins died, and she was so much better. Titus and I thought we should bring her back under our roof. Paul's roof, as it turns out. She is still my wife, Luke, and I owe her care and protection. You understand, do you not?"

Luke agreed that he did. Indeed, he wondered what all the fuss was about. She had been unpleasant to him when he was a boy, but that was a long time ago, and perhaps it was part of her mental deterioration at the time.

Kitty was frowning, and her question to Uncle Baldwin was blunt. "Is your wife a danger to Luke or to Paul?"

Uncle Baldwin shook his head. "Oh no. I shouldn't think so." His anxious expression and his following words contradicted his denial. "She will be safely away in Primrose Cottage, after all. And I will have her closely watched."

Kitty met Luke's eyes and her expression showed the same realisation he had. Uncle Baldwin's true answer was yes. His wife was a danger. Luke resolved to set his own guards.

Paul must have reached the same conclusion. "I expect my aunt will be upset about Titus, and about not being a baroness anymore."

Uncle Baldwin's face set into harsh lines. "She must accept reality," he said. "You are the rightful baron, Paul. And her son planned to kill you. She owes you her respect, at the very least. Her love, if she has any in her. I have written to tell her what has happened. I have also written to the rector, who has been a great comfort to her in recent years. I trust she will have accepted things by the time we arrive."

Again, Luke and Kitty exchanged glances. She doubted the lady's compliant acceptance as much as Luke did. As much, in fact —his repeated protestations notwithstanding—as Uncle Baldwin did. Tomorrow would tell the story, but an angry and hostile aunt was not the welcome home Luke had hoped for.

CHAPTER 22

Ormswood Hall, Northumberland

Mrs Baldwin was with the welcoming party when their carriage arrived, dressed from head to toe in black, her face visible only in glimpses through the veil that enveloped her entire head, bonnet and all.

Millie guessed who she was, because Lady Kitty had shared her concerns about Mr Ogilvy's aunt by marriage when Millie helped her undress yesterday evening.

The lady was one of two black-clad females, but the one in the silk gown must be Mr Baldwin's wife. The other, in practical bombazine and a white cap, wore a bunch of keys at her waist that identified her as the housekeeper. Her allegiance was clear from the hostile stance and countenance with which she waited for her new master, and her position at Mrs Baldwin's shoulder.

Lady Kitty, as new chatelaine of Ormswood Hall, was going to have trouble with that one. Indeed, as Millie scanned the waiting servants, she saw barely subdued anger, fear, anxiety—a host of emotions, but little in the way of welcome for poor Paul. Lord Baldwin, she meant.

The Hall, though. That was something else. A great rambling house as big as several manors all put together, and looking like it, too, with ancient stone walls here, half-timbered walls there, and bricks somewhere else. And in many different styles. Towers round, square, and octagonal. Crenelations and pitched tiled roofs. Bay windows, evenly-spaced Georgian windows, French doors, and narrow slits with leaded diamond panes.

"You! Girl!" Millie didn't look around to see who was being addressed until the housekeeper bustled up and shook her finger in Millie's face. "Girl! I am talking to you. Stop gawking and help with the baggage. You will have to wake your ideas up if you are to work here at Ormswood Hall."

"Price," Lady Kitty called. "To me, if you please." In Lady Kitty's arms, Pierrot stirred as if to yap, but subsided again when his mistress patted him.

Millie hurried to her lady, ignoring the housekeeper, who squawked her indignation. Lady Kitty addressed the woman. "Mrs Embleton, I make known to you my dresser, Price. She is under my direction, and you will not give her orders."

She spoke with all the authority of her generations of titled ancestors, but Mrs Embleton bristled like an angry hen. "I am in charge of the Hall and its female servants, Mrs Ogilvy."

Lady Kitty gave not an inch. "Except for my dresser, you have that charge, Mrs Embleton. Under my direction."

"Take directions from the bastard's wife?" Mrs Embleton declared. "I will not."

"Very well," Lady Kitty responded, not batting an eyelid. "I accept your resignation. I will not expect you to serve out your notice. You may pack immediately and leave in the morning. See me before you go for your wages to the end of the quarter."

There was an indrawn gasp from those of the gathered servants who were watching the dispute between their housekeeper and the newcomer. The other servants, Millie realised, were trying to eavesdrop on a muttered and hostile exchange between Mrs Baldwin and Mr Ogilvy's uncle. Mr Ogilvy and Lord Baldwin were supervising the men they'd brought with them, who were unloading the luggage.

The housekeeper turned to Mrs Baldwin for support. "My lady. My lady. Mrs Ogilvy has let me go! She cannot do that. Can she?"

Mrs Baldwin abandoned her altercation with her husband and marched towards them, flinging back her veil. "How dare you dismiss my housekeeper!" Pierrot yapped and tried to wriggle his way loose, which distracted Lady Kitty for the moment it took to settle the dog.

Mrs Baldwin clearly thought neither dog nor lady to be a threat for she leaned in and hissed, "I employed her and no one else can dismiss her."

If she thought to intimidate Lady Kitty, she soon discovered her error. Millie's lady stood her ground, and replied to Mrs Baldwin's threatening shout with quiet aplomb. "You may employ whomever you choose at Primrose Cottage, Mrs Baldwin."

"Lady Baldwin," the woman hissed. "Your little imposter has not yet been confirmed by the House of Lords. Nor will he be, if I have anything to say about it."

Mr Baldwin interrupted. "The boy is Flavian's son, Aileen, and the true baron. The sooner you accept that, the better. And we are moving to the dower house."

Between one breath and the next, Mrs Baldwin changed from a dignified if angry matron to a screeching banshee who launched herself at her husband, claws out, screaming insults and accusations. "You devil! You betrayed Titus! My son; my son! Traitor! Coward! Imbecile!"

Lady Kitty passed Pierrot to Millie and hurried after the woman. Millie had her hands full trying to move closer while keeping the struggling dog from leaping down to protect his mistress from the threat. If Mrs Baldwin tried to hurt Lady Kitty, Millie would let Pierrot go and do his worst. Yes, and help him, too.

However, Mr Ogilvy was there in a flash, grasping Mrs Baldwin's wrists so Mr Baldwin could move out of her reach, blood running down one cheek from three scratches. He was a strong man, Mr Ogilvy, but he struggled to hold her as she turned her fury on him.

Lord Baldwin tried to help, but Lady Kitty put a hand on his arm to stop him, instead beckoning to two of the Redepenning footmen. "Assist Mr Ogilvy," she commanded them. "Be as gentle as you can. The lady is distressed."

Lady Kitty was more generous than Millie. If ever she saw a tantrum, that was one. The old harridan needed a good slap to bring her to her senses. It wasn't Millie's place to provide the slap. *But if the besom dares to attack my Lady Kitty, she'll find out what's what, and so she will.*

An older woman, neatly dressed in conservative grey with a lace-trimmed apron hurried from the house. "My lady, my lady, do not distress yourself. Let me take her, sir."

Mr Baldwin explained, "My wife's maid, Luke. She will take Aileen. You can let her go."

Sure enough, when Mr Ogilvy released her and stepped back, the maid helped Mrs Baldwin into the house, a supportive arm around her shoulders. Lady Kitty walked back to Mrs Embleton and the little group of servants who had gathered around her.

Well. If this is a promise of things to come, my lady is going to need me.

Millie squared her shoulders and fell into step behind her mistress, carrying the now quiet dog.

Uncle Baldwin's wife had not only *not* moved into the dower house, she had countermanded his orders to prepare the place for occupation. The steward was very apologetic. "But there it is, Lord Baldwin… Mr Baldwin, I mean. And Mr Ogilvy, sir. Lady Ba—, that is, Mrs Baldwin would not even let me have the place cleaned, and last time we had the maids in was three months ago, in the early Spring. It is in good repair, sirs, but the beds will need airing, and the kitchen will have to be stocked. We'll need to hire staff, too, sirs. I am very sorry, but…"

"Then what are we to do?" Uncle Baldwin wondered. Luke was worried about him. He seemed to have shrunk. He was pale and his hand shook.

"You and Aunt Baldwin will stay here tonight," Luke decided. "In the morning we shall decide what has to be done."

One thing was certain. After the display of temper and defiance outside, the woman could not stay under the same roof as Kitty and Paul. Furthermore, Luke was concerned about the servants and their loyalties. He had been ready to step in when the housekeeper was so rude, but Kitty handled it firmly and with dignity. Still, he had seen glares from others, including the butler.

Kitty had gone off with Mrs Embleton and the female staff. Luke had sent two of Wakefield's men after them. Not that he expected another physical attack, and Kitty could handle herself, in any case. But he would feel better when she was back within sight. However, his next task was to establish his authority with the male staff.

He'd take Paul with him. His brother was wandering the study, where they were currently sequestered with the steward.

"I think that shall be all for this evening," Luke said. "If you agree, Uncle Baldwin?"

Uncle Baldwin, who had barely spoken since the altercation with his wife, nodded. "As you wish, Luke."

Luke thanked the steward for coming to welcome them. "You must be anxious to get home for your dinner. We shall see you tomorrow. Shall we say ten o'clock? Please bring any of the estate's records you have in your keeping. Lord Baldwin and I shall begin a review of them tomorrow."

The steward frowned, but his face lightened when Paul commented, "That will be fun," in a tone that suggested it would be anything but.

"Boys will be boys," the steward commented to Luke. "I have three of them. Mr Ogilvy, sir, Mr Titus Baldwin keeps most of the records." Uncle Baldwin flinched.

Another problem to be solved. Luke set it aside for the moment.

"What ages are your boys?" Luke asked. The steward's sons

lived in a cottage not three hundred yards from the rambling main house. Perhaps they were potential friends for his boy.

Sure enough, two of them bracketed Paul's twelve years. The other was older, at nearly fifteen. The steward agreed to an introduction the following afternoon, responded well to a suggestion that the four boys might share a tutor, and bowed himself out.

"I hope you didn't think your break from lessons was going to last for ever," Luke commented, and Paul sighed.

"Forever might be boring, but estate records?"

"Yes," Luke told him. "Also riding all over the estate to see what the records are about. It's your land, Paul, and they are your people. You need to learn everything there is to know about the estate and every one on it."

"That doesn't sound too terrible," Paul allowed. "And I have to admit that Ormswood has not been boring so far."

That, Luke reflected, was an understatement. "Come along, Paul. It's time for us to talk to the butler and the footmen."

The scene on their arrival had shaken Kitty. She wanted to hide away in her bed chamber, wherever it was in this great rambling edifice. But she couldn't let Luke down. Or Paul, for that matter. Or Millie, stalwart at her side. Her leadership of the female side of the house had been challenged. She needed to establish herself now, for if she resigned the field, she would have a harder job tomorrow.

What would Anne do, or say? Kitty straightened her back and prepared for battle. The first step, she thought, was to give them the truth to balance against any rumours they may have heard.

"As you have heard," she began, "Lord Baldwin, son of Flavian Lord Baldwin, has returned and been recognised by Mr Marcus Baldwin as the rightful baron. Mr Marcus Baldwin has stepped down in Lord Baldwin's favour, and presented evidence to Parliament and the Prince Regent of the young lord's identity, which has been accepted. The formal letter to confirm his title should arrive in the next few weeks. Julius Paul Lord Baldwin is the true owner of Ormswood Hall, the entailed estates, and all other property bequeathed to him by his father."

"But what about Master Titus?" asked one of the maids.

"A good question, and I will answer it. But first, I wish to tell you why Mr Ogilvy fled with Lord Baldwin, and where they have been hiding." She looked around the group. Most of them were entranced, though Mrs Embolton and several others were sneering, as if to armour themselves in disdain against anything Kitty might say.

"You will have heard, I suspect, that Mr Ogilvy was accused of several attempts on the life of the infant baron. Those attempts were made, but not by Mr Ogilvy." She let a little of her impatience show in a stride back and forth that made her skirts swish as she walked, and swing as she turned. The irritation leaked into her voice, too. "No one appears to have asked themselves what possible motive the man might have had to kill a baby whose death would not benefit him and whom everyone appears to agree he genuinely loved."

There was a murmur at that. Grunts of agreement and snorts of disbelief, in almost equal quantities. *Change takes time.*

"Mr Ogilvy feared that, with his removal, the assassin would succeed in killing the little baron. He faked their deaths and went into hiding. He intended to remain concealed until the baron was grown, but the assassin found them and has made several more attempts to kill them both."

Muttering this time, as people wondered who the assassin might be. The maid who asked after Titus mentioned his name again, and Mrs Embolton told her to hold her tongue.

"My family met Mr Ogilvy and his brother when they arrived in our village, and Mr Ogilvy took the job of gamekeeper to the Earl of Chirbury. Lord Baldwin's uncle has seen a painting and drawings made at the time, and identifies the boy we knew as Paul with the little boy who was taken from this house. Julius Paul Baldwin, the true Lord Baldwin, saved by his half-brother." The point bore repetition.

Now to the present. "I am Lady Catherine Ogilvy. I am the daughter of the Earl of Selby. My sister, his heir, is Countess of Selby in her own right, and Countess of Chirbury as wife to the Earl of Chirbury. I have known Mr Ogilvy for eight years. He and Paul, Lord Baldwin, are valued friends to the Chirbury and Selby families, and I married Mr Ogilvy a little over ten days ago."

She gave a short laugh. "So far, my honeymoon is not what I was expecting." It was a bid for sympathy and succeeded, at least with the younger maids.

"Mr Ogilvy was appointed guardian to his younger brother by Flavian Lord Baldwin, their father, and is also one of the three trustees of Lord Baldwin's estate. Mr Baldwin, who was declared baron when Lord Baldwin was thought to be dead, is another trustee. He has stepped down from managing the estates, and Mr Ogilvy will be acting as custodian of all of Lord Baldwin's holdings until he reaches his majority."

Now to the crunch. "As Mr Ogilvy's wife, I will be chatelaine of Ormswood Hall until that day."

She was silent for a long moment, surveying the servants while they stared back at her or avoided her eyes, according to their natures.

"I will expect and reward loyalty and diligence. Those who cannot offer me both can give me their resignation." She fixed Mrs Embolton with her gaze, and then each of the woman's supporters in turn. "I will not tolerate disrespect or disobedience."

"Mrs Baldwin, known to you as Lady Baldwin, will be moving to Primrose Cottage. Her refusal to acknowledge her husband's authority or the change in her status is perfectly understandable and deserves our sympathy. Particularly given that her son, my husband's cousin Titus, is currently in prison awaiting trial on multiple charges of attempted murder."

She waited for the buzz of exclamations to fade away. "Yes," she said. "Mr Titus Baldwin was responsible for the attempts nine years ago. He also manipulated evidence to make it seem as if the villain was Mr Ogilvy. He has tried again to kill Mr Ogilvy and Lord Baldwin on several more occasions in recent months, since he discovered that Mr Ogilvy and Lord Baldwin were still alive."

"It is all lies," Mrs Embolton declared. "Everyone knows that Lucius Ogilvy killed his baby brother. It's clear to see he faked his own death, for here he is, just as arrogant as ever, the jumped-up bastard, stealing the place of his betters and cozening his own uncle till the man turns on his own flesh and blood."

"I have changed my mind, Mrs Embolton," Kitty announced. "Hand me your keys. You shall pack and leave immediately. I shall provide a footman to carry your possessions to the dower house. Whether your mistress chooses to keep you when she moves there herself, I care not, but I will not have you and your impertinent tongue under the roof for which I am responsible."

Mrs Embolton's jaw dropped. "But… It is not ready. It hasn't been cleaned, and who knows what condition the linen is in. Lady Baldwin told me to let it all rot."

"The steward was instructed to prepare Primrose Cottage for Mr and Mrs Baldwin's occupation," Kitty pointed out.

Mrs Embolton flushed, her eyes darting to her supporters. "I take my orders from my lady," she insisted, jutting her chin. "Lady Baldwin said she was not leaving the house to that ill-begotten c— to Mr Ogilvy."

The more Kitty heard about Aileen Baldwin, the more she agreed with Uncle Baldwin that the woman could remain in Paul's house.

She addressed the three maids closest to Mrs Embolton, who had looked at her with hostility and sneered when their ringleader defied her, looking at each one in turn as she said, "You, you, and you. Your names? Your roles in the house?"

She had to face down their defiance to discover the names, and that they were all parlour maids. Good. She had hoped she was not about to lose any of the kitchen staff, for there were already too few servants for a house of this size. She knew enough to be her own housekeeper, but heaven help the household if they were dependent on her cooking!

"Very well. You may all collect your things and go with Mrs Embolton to the dower house. Take what you need to clean at least one room for the four of you to sleep in. Take linen and blankets suitable for your beds. Fortunately, at this time of year, it will not be dark until ten o'clock, so you have at least six hours. I imagine you may have problems with some of the mattresses. If so, do what you can for the night and we shall address it in the morning."

She considered for a moment, while the maids in question gaped at her, then turned to the two Wakefield men. "Can one of you find me two of our footmen to escort these women while they are in Ormswood Hall and accompany them to the dower house to carry what they cannot carry themselves."

The boldest of the maids said, "You cannot dismiss us. We have done nothing wrong."

Kitty raised one eyebrow, an affectation she had practiced in a mirror after admiring it on Rede's cousin Lord Aldridge. She did not reply to that maid, but to the rest of the female servants, all watching with wide eyes and expressions that ranged from horror to satisfaction.

"As I said earlier. I will not tolerate disrespect and disobedience. If I ask a question, I expect it to be answered politely and immediately. If I give an order, I expect it to be obeyed without delay and competently. If you serve me well, you will find me a fair and appreciative mistress. If you do not, expect immediate dismissal."

Mrs Embolton and her cronies were still standing there. Kitty held out her hand. "The keys," she demanded. For a moment, she thought Mrs Embolton would defy her, but Millie moved up on one side of her, and the guard who had remained on the other. The woman reluctantly unhitched the keys from her waist and handed them over.

"You will regret this," Mrs Embolton threatened.

Kitty waved a hand in the direction of the door. "Off you go and pack your things. Or do I have to have you thrown bodily from the house?"

The guard she had sent away arrived back with two of his fellows as well as the footmen she had asked for. Mrs Embolton glared at them and then at Kitty, then turned to stomp from the room. The others scurried after her, followed by the two extra guards and the footmen.

Kitty turned back to the waiting servants. "Now. I would like to meet each of you. First, which of you is my cook?"

CHAPTER 23

Kitty had reason to be grateful for the long midsummer evening. Nothing had been prepared for the arrival of her party. Rooms had not been cleaned or aired. Beds had not been made. The cook threw her hands up in horror at the number of arrivals and the state of her pantry. The stable master, Luke said, had shown the same reaction to the number of horses that would need to be fed and accommodated.

Luke solved the stable master's problem by setting some of the men to hauling hay and oats, and straw for bedding from the storage barn.

Kitty's problem was feeding the people. She and the cook surveyed the pantry, the kitchen garden, and the chicken yard and decided on a menu for both upstairs and down that would make the best of the resources they had. The pantry was half empty. The kitchen garden, which should be brimming with food at this time of the year, was mostly fallow beds with a few neglected plants struggling against the weeds. And the chicken yard was ten times the size needed for the few elderly fowl that occupied it.

Tomorrow, Kitty would see whether the home farm had a beast ready for slaughter. If need be, the nearest market town would provide much of what they needed to replenish the stores. Someone in the neighbourhood was surely selling laying hens and ducks. The kitchen garden could always be dug over and planted—and certainly the stables had a dung heap the size of a small mountain which should have long ago been distributed to benefit the soil.

The cook was nearly in tears with relief that the new lady had a solution, and that she had not been held to blame. "For indeed, my lady, I have protested many times."

Kitty then toured the house with a couple of the senior maids, deciding on bedchambers, and the whole house was soon humming with maids and footmen running up and downstairs with mops, brushes, dusters, buckets of water, and other supplies.

The place was a disgrace. If Kitty had not already fired Mrs Embolton, she would have done so after her inspection. Rooms that were in use had grimy corners and furnishings much in need of maintenance. Rooms that had not been in use had been shut up and ignored. And there were lots of them.

The servants' quarters in the attics—men in one roof space and women in another—were the most neglected of all. Kitty stopped feeling sorry for the maids she had exiled to the unknown dilapidation of Primrose Cottage. If this was how they lived in the great house, they would find themselves right at home in the lesser.

Mrs Baldwin had locked herself into the baroness's chambers. A guard patrolled the passage outside, to ensure she stayed where she had put herself. The lady's maid emerged as the day drew on, to demand a cup of tea and some soup, then disappeared into the chambers again.

Uncle Baldwin had retreated to the baron's chamber, after apologising profusely and repeatedly to Kitty, Luke, and Paul. For his wife, for the state of the house, for the attitude of some of the servants, for his own failure to warn them to expect trouble. "I had no idea," he insisted.

Kitty privately thought he must have been closing his eyes, his ears, and his mind in order to be ignorant. There was no point in saying so. The man had aged a decade since he discovered his son's perfidy, and today's dramatics had been another hard blow.

"Go and rest, Uncle Baldwin. We'll see our people settled, and all else can wait until morning," Luke told him. He went off to familiarise himself with the study, and particularly the desk Titus used. Kitty needed to check on the maids who were cleaning the rooms that she and the rest of the arrivals would need tonight.

The first cleaning job had been the two bedchambers she had selected, one for Paul and one for her and Luke. Much though she would have liked to choose rooms far far away from those in which Mrs Baldwin seethed with resentment, Luke insisted on staying in the New Wing, and for good reason. The New Wing had been built without any hidden ways through its walls.

An hour's solid work had the chosen rooms stripped of their dust and cobwebs, and the beds made with sheets from Kitty's trousseau, since a cursory examination of the linen room had disclosed mould, moths, mildew, and other mayhem.

From there, she sent the maids in pairs to prepare the rooms for her servants and the Wakefield guards, moving from room to room to supervise them. They made good progress, and even had time to move on to the passages in the New Wing, so Kitty would be able to walk from her bedchamber to the public rooms without spiders dropping onto her from the ceiling or dust and worse clogging her skirts.

Pierrot had attended Kitty on all her rounds, and the thaw in the servants' attitudes was at least partly down to the friendly dog, who had charmed most the maids and several of the footmen. He was tired, and had taken to finding a corner to sleep wherever they went, though he was quick to leap to his feet to escort her when she was ready to move to another room.

Millie came to fetch Kitty half an hour before the time that the cook had agreed to serve dinner. *Is it worth changing?* It would only be her, Luke, and Paul. She was tempted to remain as she was, just removing her apron and washing her hands, but could almost hear her older sister's voice. Anne would say, "The servants will be watching you for anything to criticise. Donning an evening gown when dining en famille may seem silly, but it is part of winning them over."

"I am going to change for dinner," she told the maids she had been directing. "When you have finished up here, go down to the servants' hall for your own meal."

Luke was in their bedchamber before her, looking tired. He held out his arms, and she walked into them. "This is not the homecoming for you I envisaged," he said, as she rested her head on his chest.

He dropped a kiss on her hair, and she lifted her face for one on her lips.

"We will work it out, Luke. How did you get on with the search?"

He grimaced. "I found the ledgers. They were hidden in the priest hole off the library. Titus had it set up as an office. I have not read them in detail, but I've seen enough to believe he has been stealing from the estate. It is a mess, my love."

He bent down to ruffle the ears of the little dog, who had been waiting patiently for them to finish their embrace.

"We shall fix what is wrong," Kitty assured him. A knock on the door presaged Millie, with a jug of water for washing. She had a footman with her who carried a much larger jug.

"This is William, my lady and Mr Ogilvy. He has washing water for you, sir, and Lord Baldwin."

"I'll take my clothes through to Paul's room," Luke said. "Come along, William. I'll introduce you to the master. I shall see you at dinner, Kitty."

The next day's drama was evicting Aunt Baldwin, who was determined not to go, and who tried to marshal Uncle Baldwin and the butler to her support.

Uncle Baldwin, looking frailer than ever, appealed to Luke to deal with it. Hedley the butler was even more dour than he'd been yesterday, and ignored his former mistress's commands and then pleas.

Luke wouldn't order Hedley or any of the footmen to lay hands on the lady, but he was also reluctant to do so himself. Clearly Uncle Baldwin was going to be no help at all. Still, Luke wasn't prepared to have his aunt in the house with his wife and his brother.

He was about to send for Wakefield's men when Kitty arrived on the scene. "I have been over to Primrose Cottage," she announced. "It is as well we arrived in the summer, for the roof will need to be seen to, and I have written a list of other jobs." She waved a sheet of paper, with her neat handwriting covering both sides.

"However, Uncle Baldwin, you and your wife will be able to move in today. Mrs Embolton and her maids have finished cleaning the main bedchamber, the two downstairs reception rooms, and sufficient servants' rooms. I have sent over provisions and linen from the main house. And I have hired a temporary cook and enough servants to manage the kitchen."

"You insolent imposter! You wicked harlot!" Aunt Baldwin shrieked. "I'll not go! You will have to carry me out of this house, and I will scream every step of the way."

"Your clothes and all your possessions will leave this house immediately," Kitty replied, calmly. "Furthermore, so will your maid, if she wants to keep receiving her wages and, for that matter, food and shelter. No one will lay a hand on you, Mrs Baldwin, unless you attack them first. But nor will anyone feed you in this house, nor will we allow you a bed to sleep in or clothing to wear."

Luke would not have thought of that. It was brilliant. Firm and non-violent. As long as the servants did as Kitty commanded, Aunt Baldwin would not have a choice but to go.

Aunt Baldwin stared at Kitty, her mouth open. "You would not dare."

It was more a question than a declaration. Kitty met it with raised eyebrows and a solemn, "I suggest you do not try me."

Aunt Baldwin turned on her husband. "Marcus! Tell that female to get out. I am Lady Baldwin. I am in charge here."

Uncle Baldwin grimaced and took a step backwards, but he stood up to the woman. "No, Aileen. You are not Lady Baldwin.

You are not in charge here. My nephew Luke is manager of the estate on behalf of his ward, and Lady Catherine as his wife is chatelaine of the house."

Aunt Baldwin clapped a hand over each ear. "It is not true. It is not true."

"I have told Gibson to pack my things," Uncle Baldwin said to Kitty. "I will tell Aileen's maid to pack hers."

"Why are you supporting them?" Aunt Baldwin demanded. "Even if you have decided to surrender your barony to the bastard's imposter brat, why should I leave Ormswood Hall? What have I done?"

Uncle Baldwin's face suffused with colour and his eyes flashed. "You can ask that? After you poisoned Luke? Do you think you can stay in the same house with Lord Baldwin when I know what you are capable of?"

She tried to kill me? Luke met Kitty's questioning eyes, and shook his head. He had no idea what Uncle Baldwin meant.

In the next moment, Aunt Baldwin satisfied his curiosity. "He should have died, the unnatural monster. Any other boy would have eaten all the treat I prepared for him." She cackled, and an icy chill ran down Luke's spine.

"Turkish delight, my own recipe," she cackled again. "With a very special ingredient. What boy could resist it?" She whirled to point a finger at Luke. "But you only took two pieces and saved the rest for my son, you bastard! My darling little boy!" Her visage dissolved into grief and horror. "Even one piece might have killed him."

Luke suddenly realised what she was talking about. "When I was ten?" he asked Uncle Baldwin. "When I was so sick? She poisoned me?"

Aunt Baldwin threw her hands up in the air, spun on her heel, and stepped into the baroness's bedchamber, slamming the door shut behind her.

Luke barely noticed. "Uncle Baldwin?"

His uncle would not meet his eyes. "It was why Flavian sent her away. The first night you were sick? She offered to nurse you.

Flavian came to see you just as she was trying to force more of the sweet down your throat."

Kitty gasped, and slid her arm around her husband's waist. "Why did you not tell us?" she demanded.

"Ancient history," Uncle Baldwin assured him. "At least, I hoped… She is better now, truly. She wouldn't really hurt Paul, Kitty. She was upset. We all say things we don't mean when we are upset." Tears were rolling down his cheeks. The blood had drained from his face again, and he was holding his shoulder as if it hurt.

Kitty let go of Luke and put her arm around Uncle Baldwin's shoulder, instead. "He is ill, Luke. Uncle Baldwin, you need to sit down."

"Send for the physician," Luke ordered Hedley. "Tell him that my aunt is hysterical and my uncle appears to be having some kind of attack." He and Kitty assisted Uncle Baldwin down to his room, where Gibson helped to put him into his bed. The old man lay stranded on his pillow, taking shallow breaths, his face tight with pain.

Rocked by the revelations of one concealment after another, Luke couldn't untangle his emotions. He fell back on being busy, ordering Hedley to set some of the footmen onto the task of beginning the move.

"Mr Ogilvy!" Hedley exclaimed. "Surely you will not expel the bar— your aunt and uncle while they are ill."

Kitty came up from behind him and slipped a hand into his arm. "I will instruct Gibson and Mrs Baldwin's maid to pack them an overnight bag each," she said. "We will wait for the doctor's opinion before making a decision about when they leave this house. Most of their belongings, however, can be moved immediately."

Hedley managed, without arguing, frowning or sniffing, to give the impression of all three from a nearly impassive face.

Luke frowned at the man, but spoke to Kitty. "My dear wife, given these most recent revelations and my aunt's behaviour, I cannot allow her to remain under the same roof as the young baron. I fear for his safety. As for my uncle, I would prefer him to remain, but it must be up to him." His words were intended for the servants who had been attracted by the fuss and were hovering in the background. Some of them nodded while others just looked bewildered.

"I am of your mind in this, husband," Kitty told him. "However, in the meantime, we can make certain that Lord Baldwin knows what is toward, and that a guard is with him at all times."

That was good thinking. "I will see to it," Luke promised. "Hedley, you have your orders. The rest of you, back to whatever you are meant to be doing."

The doctor reminded Kitty of a badger. He was short and burly, but the thickness was muscle rather than fat. He had slicked-back hair and a long pointy nose that twitched as his beady eyes darted around as if searching for something juicy to report. However, he appeared to know what he was doing.

The groom who had ridden to fetch him had clearly told him about the changes at the Hall. He showed no surprise when he was shown into the study. Paul and Kitty were helping Luke and the steward to sort some of the folders and boxes Luke had retrieved from the priest hole, while the Wakefield guard assigned to keep Paul in sight at all times watched from one corner of the room.

The doctor challenged Luke as soon as he stepped into the room. "You're Lucius Ogilvy, right enough. I thought the groom must be out of his mind. We all thought you dead. Why aren't you in prison for murdering the little baron?"

"Because I am not dead," Paul answered him. "Luke took me away to protect me from our cousin Titus."

The doctor narrowed his eyes and examined Paul. "You are a Baldwin, right enough. What's this about the baron? Marcus Baldwin, I suppose I should say."

Luke took a step out from behind the desk. "Lady Catherine, allow me to make known to you Doctor Pelham. Doctor Pelham, my wife, Lady Catherine Ogilvy."

The doctor nodded a greeting and gave a slight bow. "I will show you up to Mr Baldwin's bedroom," Kitty offered. "He has had a spell of some kind. A faintness, some pain in the chest and arm, breathing difficulties."

The doctor huffed. "The groom said something about his wife. A tantrum of some kind?"

"An emotional breakdown," Kitty said, diplomatically. "Mr Baldwin intends that they move to the dower house. She was not in favour of the idea."

The doctor's nose twitched again. "A tantrum," he repeated. "I will see Mr Marcus Baldwin first." He added, as an afterthought, "My lady."

"This way," Kitty said, ignoring the hiccup in his courtesy.

She led him out of the door and up the stairs, also ignoring the Wakefield guard who fell into step behind them. If she wanted Paul to accept his constant shadow without complaint, she had better not balk at having her own, but she would have a word with Luke about assigning the man without consulting her first.

All was quiet as they passed the baroness's suite. The guard who sat at the door nodded as they passed. In the baron's suite, Gibson was sitting by the bed, watching Uncle Baldwin, who looked to be asleep. Pierrot had chosen to curl up at his feet. "How is he," she asked Gibson.

Uncle Baldwin opened his eyes and spoke before Gibson could. "Kitty, my dear. And Doctor Pelham. My wife needs you, Pelham. I fear she is having another of her episodes."

"I will examine you first, Baldwin," Pelham insisted. "I told you last time this happened, no sudden shocks or exertions."

He has certainly had a few shocks, Kitty reflected.

"If you will excuse us, Lady Catherine," the doctor said, gesturing towards the door.

She inclined her head and left the doctor with Uncle Baldwin, gesturing to the Wakefield guard to stay and observe. "I shall be out in the hall," she told him, so he would know she was staying with the other guard. He nodded his understanding.

Pelham must have thought she was talking to him. "Yes, yes. I will call you in again when I am finished."

Pierrot jumped down from the bed and followed her out into the hall, keeping close to her heel as she walked restlessly up and down. The guard at the other door pretended not to watch her. Perhaps she should not object to Luke assigning her a guard; after all, he was the one man in the room she had just left who could be relied on to truthfully convey whatever was discussed within.

And here was Luke. "I've left Paul and the steward sorting the accounts," he said. "Titus appears to have been given a free rein, and has taken full advantage of it. I'm so sorry for the mess I've brought you into, Kitty."

"Don't keep apologising for marrying me, Luke," Kitty snapped, her anxiety transmuting into irritation. She took a deep breath and let it out. Her anger was at the situation, and not at Luke, after all. "I would rather be here, helping you solve the problems with Paul's estate than mouldering into old maid-hood at the other end of England. And we will solve them, my love."

Luke took her hand and lifted it to his lips for a kiss, but his mind was not on romance. "How did Uncle Baldwin let him get away with it?" he mused. "I cannot see how he did not know. Was he part of it, or did he just ignore what he didn't want to see?"

Kitty cupped his face with her other hand, and didn't say what she was thinking. *It doesn't matter which. He is not to be trusted, whether he helped his son and his wife or just turned a blind eye to what they were doing.*

The door to the bedchamber opened, and the doctor emerged. "Lady Catherine— Ah, Mr Ogilvy! Good. Your uncle has confirmed your story." His brow creased as he shook his head. "Sad."

That was one word for it. Kitty brushed away the others she thought of—*wicked, terrible, cruel, awful*—and asked, "How is Mr Baldwin, doctor? Are you able to tell us what is wrong with him?"

"It is his heart, Lady Catherine," Doctor Pelham said. "Angina Pectoris. Pressure in the chest. I told him, no anger. No strong emotions. But his son; his wife—" He shook his head again.

"Will he recover?" Luke's worry for his uncle coloured his voice.

Kitty slid her hand into his arm and gave it a squeeze. Whatever her private thoughts about Uncle Baldwin, Luke cared.

Doctor Pelham shrugged. "If he rests. If he avoids any upsets. No arguments. No sudden shocks. I want him to stay in bed today. I will visit again tomorrow." He sighed. "Mr Ogilvy, he will not die of this attack, but he may do so next time, or the time after."

Luke stiffened. "You mean he is dying?"

"We are all dying, Mr Ogilvy," Doctor Pelham intoned. "Mr Baldwin will die, very likely of a heart attack, within the next decade. Perhaps the next year or two. You must be prepared. Now. I presume my second patient is in her suite?"

"Mrs Baldwin," Kitty said. "Yes. She has locked herself in, but if you knock, I hope she will see you."

"Best if we move out of sight," Luke suggested, and led Kitty down the passage. As they passed the door to the baron's suite, the Wakefield guard beckoned them inside. "Sir? My lady? Mr Baldwin wants to speak with you."

CHAPTER 24

Kitty hoped the doctor would not take long. She had a lot to do. She wanted to take another brief trip to Primrose Cottage to check on progress, and then she intended to spend the day at Ormswood Hall, supervising the maids and trying to make sense of the housekeeper's account books.

However, Luke's uncle was insisting they go into the village of Ormsbridge. "You must be seen, Luke. You, too, Kitty, and young Paul. Give them a chance to meet you and make up their own minds before other people tell them what to think. The villagers will have heard by now about you dismissing Mrs Embolton, Kitty."

"I had no choice," Kitty pointed out. "I cannot have a housekeeper who takes her instructions from an enemy of my husband and my brother."

Uncle Baldwin sighed. "You had no choice, but that is not how some will see it. And now there is the doctor, in there with Aileen, listening to her poison."

"You think he will believe her?" Luke asked, taking a step towards the internal door that led from the baron's suite to the baroness's.

"I do not," Uncle Baldwin insisted. "He has treated Aileen

before when she flies into these fancies, and he knows what she is like. He will persuade her to take her laudanum and she will sleep it off. But the doctor will tell his wife what we have said and what Aileen says, and she will gossip to the whole village."

Kitty understood the point he was trying to make. She had lived in a village when she and her sisters were in hiding, and she had heard politics discussed at the dinner table since Anne married Rede —the politics of Britain and the more domestic but equally cutthroat politics of Society.

They had met the hostility at Ormswood Hall with firmness, kindness, and the truth. Already some of the servants had begun to thaw. Kitty assumed some of the tenants and the villagers would also be against them from the start. The longer she and Luke waited to meet the locals and the neighbours, the more of them would be convinced of the truth of the rumours floating out from the Hall and the dower house.

"We will need to visit the tenants, too," she said. "And visit the local gentry. Luke, I will need a list of the tenants. The list should note who is most likely to listen to us. The steward might be able to help, and I shall speak to cook and the maids. Uncle Baldwin, who are the leaders of local Society? Who are the villagers with the most influence over the others?"

She took a good look at the man. He was lying back, nearly as pale as his pillows, one hand clutching his shoulder. "But that can wait, Uncle Baldwin. Today, we shall go to the village and you shall rest."

A knock on the door heralded the doctor. "Ah. Mr and Lady Catherine Ogilvy. You are here, too. Lord— Mr Baldwin, your wife's humours are seriously out of balance. I have given her laudanum and she is asleep. I suggest you sleep, too. Leave the problems to these young ones. I will call again tomorrow."

"Yes," Luke agreed. "Sleep, Uncle. We shall go into the village as you suggest. You have nothing to worry about."

They walked Pelham down to the front door, where he frowned at Kitty and said to Luke, with little subtlety, "Perhaps you would be kind enough to walk me to my horse, Mr Ogilvy."

Of course, Luke told Kitty what that was about as soon as he returned inside. "Pelham thinks we should move my aunt today, while she is still asleep. He also thinks we should hire a couple of nurses to live with her, and that my uncle should stay here. He says the strain of living with Aunt Baldwin could be deadly."

Kitty nodded. "Then that is what we will do, if your uncle agrees. How will we find nurses at such short notice?"

"Pelham has promised me a list of names, and some letters for me to collect this afternoon when we visit the village. I'll send someone down to Newcastle with them, and we will find out who is available and willing. It may take a couple of days to get them here but in the meantime, Aunt Baldwin's maids will manage. We might have to loan them a couple of the Wakefield men, but I would, in any case, want someone who answers to us keeping an eye on things."

On an impulse, Kitty asked if he'd like to walk over to Primrose Cottage with her, to see if it was fit for occupants. He agreed, and even invited Paul and the steward to join them, but insisted on going armed and taking two of the guard with them.

It proved to be useful and not at all dangerous. On the walk over, they told the steward that Uncle Baldwin had urged them to woo the locals. The man enthusiastically agreed, and proved to be a fount of knowledge about the people who might be hostile, those who would make their own judgements based on the evidence, and those who would side with the majority, whichever group that happened to be.

At the house, a sullen Mrs Embolton had nonetheless proved effective, at least in the rooms Kitty had directed her to clean. The finest bedchamber had been prepared for Mrs Baldwin, one of the reception rooms was pristine, if shabby and sparsely furnished. Apparently, though Kitty didn't see them, the housekeeper's room was now habitable and so was the room shared by the maids.

This was more than could be said for the kitchen and its larders, pantries, and scullery. A thorough clean would only be a start. The cavernous fireplace had no closed stove, no bread oven, little to differentiate it from its medieval counterpart. The huge kitchen table sat unevenly and wobbled, since some of the sturdy legs were a different length to others. Broken shelves and bent hooks hung empty on the walls. Pierrot's fervent interest in corners hinted at rodents.

"I'll find out from the rector who would be glad of a week's cleaning work," Kitty planned.

"The estate carpenter can see to the repairs," Luke decided.

"I will arrange for the chimneys to be cleaned," the steward offered.

Kitty nodded her agreement. "Your mistress will be in residence this afternoon," she told Mrs Embolton. "I will have meals sent over from the main house until we have the kitchen ready and working again, and a kitchen staff. You will need to make ready a room for Mrs Baldwin's maid."

"And one for Mr Baldwin," Mrs Embolton grumbled. "And one for his valet."

"Indeed," Luke told the woman. "However, his heart is troubling him, and the doctor has said he is not to be moved at the moment."

Mrs Embolton muttered about a wife's place being with her husband, but it was half-hearted at best.

Even Mrs Baldwin's supporters don't believe her husband should be burdened with her when he is sick. It was an unkind thought. Kitty decided they had seen enough, and suggested to her menfolk that they head back to the Hall.

CHAPTER 25

The three of them walked into the village: a ten-minute stroll. Luke was glad that Kitty had left Pierrot with Millie. Luke might call him a rat to tease Kitty, but the dog was well trained and had an easy temperament. Even so, Luke didn't trust his reactions if the villagers showed any hostility shown to his beloved mistress.

Luke chose the fastest way, through the southern end of the wood that gave the Hall its name. On another day, he would take Kitty and Paul to see the gamekeeper's cottage where his grandfather had lived out his life, and where Luke had learned the skills that had earned him and Paul refuge these past nine years.

"The name Orm means dragon in the Viking tongue," Luke told them. "Legend has it that a dragon used to lair in a spring in the most ancient part of the wood. In fact, some say that the brave man who fought the dragon and built the first Hall did not kill it, but only wounded it so badly that it crept back down into the earth to heal, and one day it will burst forth from the wood and take its revenge."

"Not this week, I hope," Kitty retorted. "We have dragons enough to slay."

"St George's Abbey was built to honour the dragon killer, or so they say. It was torn down in the dissolution, but St George's Grange is built on the site of the granary that used to belong to the abbey."

At first sight, the village seemed little changed. The same huddle of cottages. The same public house, though someone had touched up the white swan on its shield with some fresh paint. The same smithy. The same village green. The same little church with its oversized stone keep tower, hovering over all from its rise. The ubiquitous stone in shades of brown and autumn gold.

The old rector had insisted that the church—and perhaps the inn and the cottages, too—had been built from stone salvaged from the castle and the abbey, as had Ormswood Hall. Luke's father had argued that perhaps the stone had been quarried from these same hills, and who could tell after so many centuries what had been first used by the Vikings and the Normans and what had been hewn from the hills for a new building?

Nine years had wrought changes in the people. Apparently, the inn was in new hands, though from the same family. The rector Luke remembered had retired and been replaced by a younger man. Those who had been youths with him were now men in their prime, many of them doing the work and taking the places in the community passed on by their fathers.

The doctor and his wife lived in a substantial cottage on the other side of the village. Some previous owner had been fecund and prosperous enough to add a substantial lean-to at the side, with a loft over, to accommodate at least part of his enormous brood. Village wisdom said he and his wife had produced more than a score of children, all of whom lived.

Luke, telling Kitty and Paul the story, added, "But the number grew even in my lifetime. I am sure there were only an even dozen when I first heard the tale as a lad."

The doctor had repurposed the three rooms in the lean to—two downstairs and the loft above. One downstairs room was a reception room for patients. One was the doctor's office. The loft upstairs had large dormer windows, and could be used for surgery or as a bedchamber for patients who required round-the-clock medical care. Luke had stayed there overnight after breaking his arm when he was eight.

A note on the clinic door said it was closed, and anyone requiring the doctor should ask at the house. A path led from the clinic along the front of the cottage, so Luke beckoned to Kitty and Paul, who had waited outside the gate with Paul's guard and the groom who was to carry the doctor's letters to Newcastle.

A maid Luke knew opened the door to the cottage. "Maggie Brown, as I live!" Luke said. "My dear, this fine lady is Miss Brown, who was a nursery maid at the Hall." He spoke to Paul who had joined them. "Miss Brown was one of your attendants, Paul. Maggie, my wife, Lady Catherine, and you will not recognise Lord Baldwin. He has grown a bit since last you saw him."

The woman curtseyed and smiled, with tears in her eyes. To Paul, she said, "My lord, I would know those eyes of your'n anywhere. Here you are! Alive and safe! I could not believe it when I heard…"

"You were one of my nurses?" Paul asked. "I am so pleased to meet you, Miss Brown."

"Mags, you used to call me, my lord." She gave a deep sigh. "And now you are home, and so tall!"

She suddenly realised she was leaving them standing on the door step, and stepped back. "My lady, sirs. I beg your pardon. The doctor said you would be stopping by, Mr Ogilvy, and that I was to show you straight in to the drawing room. This way, my lady."

Mrs Pelham greeted them with avid eyes and obsequious words. "Lady Catherine! And Lord Baldwin, too. How honoured I am that you called to see me. Ah! Here is Maggie with the tea. Please, Lady Catherine, do be seated. Now, you must have tea! Do you take milk, my lady? Is it true that you are related to the Earl of Chirbury *and* the Earl of Selby?"

Kitty asked for a slice of lemon instead of milk, and agreed that she was a daughter of a former Earl of Selby and a sister-in-law of the Earl of Chirbury. Luke was tempted to list the other family titles. Rede's uncle and his cousin Alex had both been granted titles for their services to the country, and Rede's cousin Susan had married first a Scottish laird and then a viscount.

"Would you care for tea, Mr Ogilvy?" Mrs Pelham asked.

"I expect Mr Ogilvy would prefer an ale," said the doctor, "but we have business to transact first. One moment, Mr Ogilvy. I shall fetch the letters." He went through a side door into another room.

Mrs Pelham turned her attention to Paul. "And Master Julius. Lord Baldwin, I should say. What would you like to drink, dear? Milk, perhaps?"

"Cook has made lemonade, Ma'am," said Maggie.

"Lemonade would be very pleasant, if you do not mind, Mrs Pelham," Paul said.

"See to it, Maggie," the doctor's wife commanded.

"What a pleasant room," Kitty said.

Mrs Pelham fluttered her lashes and beamed.

Kitty continued to charm the lady while she sipped her tea. Doctor Pelham returned with a satchel. Luke excused himself, and he and Pelham walked out to the groom to send him on his way, then stood in the garden drinking the ale the maid brought out to them until Kitty and Paul emerged from the cottage. They were ushered on their way by a delighted Mrs Pelham who saw them to the gate and took the opportunity to wave to a couple of her neighbours.

"That went well," Kitty told Luke as they headed towards the vicarage, which was on the other side of the church.

"Yes," Paul said, "and not just because you have titled relatives. When she started talking about Titus Baldwin and his poor mother, I thought… I am not sure what I thought, but I thought it couldn't be good."

He looked away from Kitty to grin at Luke. "Kitty was marvellous, Dad. She agreed that it was tragic, and said how upset Mrs Baldwin was. Mrs Pelham immediately told us that the doctor was worried about the balance of Mrs Baldwin's mind."

"I hope you do not mind, Luke," Kitty said, "but I told her you had suspected your uncle, and how you were relieved it was not him and at the same time grieved it was your cousin, whom you had believed to be your friend."

She frowned. "Luke, she was ready to believe us, for she does not like Titus, though she did not say what he had done to offend her."

Their steps had taken them to the vicarage. "Let's see how we are greeted here," Luke suggested.

The next meeting was even more promising than the first. The rector and his wife welcomed them warmly, and assured the three of them of unequivocal support from the vicarage.

Apparently, in the short time Kitty, Paul, and Luke had been at the Hall, word had spread that Luke was devoting himself to the estate and Kitty to the house. The steward and the servants, Kitty assumed.

The vicarage pair refused to speak ill of any individual, but managed to convey that the change of stewardship at Ormswood Hall could only have positive results for the servants, the tenants and the village. Their attitude spoke volumes about the mismanagement of Hall and estate in the past few years.

The visit went far better than they had expected, Luke and Kitty agreed, as they set out visit the village shops.

"The doctor was on your side, Luke," Kitty said, "and his wife came around. The rector and his wife are firmly in the Ogilvy camp."

"This is a strangely peaceful war," Paul joked, "but the weapons are dangerous enough. A glass of lemonade and a cup of tea? I will not have to drink something more at the inn, will I, Dad?"

They were passing the coach yard of the inn, and a man stepped out of the shadow of the gate, facing them with a glare, his shout a bark of glee. "Hah! It is as I thought!"

His triumphant exclamation had drawn others from the coach yard, and several villagers who had been watching from a distance drew closer. It was to them he addressed his next remarks. "The murderer's boy calls him 'Dad'," he announced. "What further proof do you need? This supposed baron is an imposter, taking advantage of our poor lord while he is sick with grief."

Paul drew himself up, surveyed the man from top to toe with a curl of his lip, and replied in the crisp upper-class accents he had learned from the Redepennings and his tutors. He addressed his words to the on-lookers. "Good people, my brother Luke is the only father I have known for most of my life, since he took me away from the foul traitor who would have murdered me, your infant baron, and blamed it all on my brother. Calling him 'Dad' was part of my disguise, and has become a habit, but there is a deeper truth in it, for he has been more of a father to me than our own."

"The brat claims to be the baron, but we all know who killed the little baron," the sneering man shouted. "The boy called this fiend 'Dad', I tell you. Like breeds like. A bastard son to the bastard son."

Kitty put her hand on Luke's arm. He was relaxed beside her.

"Arthur Dawkins," he said. "Drunk are you, then? At two in the afternoon?" He leaned forward a little and sniffed. "Some things never change." That fetched a laugh from some in the gathering crowd.

Dawkins' face contorted with rage. "He had his own cousin thrown into prison!" he screeched at the crowd.

In Kitty's opinion, no good ever came from arguing with drunken bullies. "Step aside, Dawkins," she ordered, crisply.

He moved one foot, obeying the tone of command before his brain caught up, then stopped. "Bitch," he hissed, and spat at her feet.

Kitty tightened her grip on Luke's suddenly rigid arm. He somehow managed that trick that some men had of widening their shoulders and their chests so that they took up more space. He gently removed Kitty's hand and took a pace towards Dawkins.

Face and tone were grim as he said, "I'll not allow insults to my wife, you drunkard."

Dawkins was too inebriated to take warning. "I spit on your whore," he crowed, and attempted to do so. He didn't see Luke's fist coming, a swift upper cut that knocked him staggering backwards. Luke followed up with a shove that sent the man flying into a horse trough. He must have hit his head on the stone surround, for he collapsed, unconscious.

Luke turned to Kitty. "I apologise, Lady Catherine." His voice was still pitched to reach across the crowd. "Both for that blowhard's behaviour and for committing violence in your presence."

Kitty inclined her head. If they were giving a performance, she could play her part. "How could I ever blame you, my love, for defending me from an attack?" She raised an eyebrow as she examined the scene. "Is he alive? Should someone fetch the doctor?"

"It is like your kindness to be concerned," Luke said, approvingly. "You, boy. Run and let the doctor know that he has a patient here outside the inn. He turned to look at the crowd. "Barnaby Pattison, is that you?"

The man who nudged his way through the crowd was as broad as Dawkins, but tall and fit. "Aye. So, you've come back, Mr Ogilvy?"

"Luke, to you, Barn. Glad to be home." He turned to Kitty. "My love, may I make known to you my friend Barnaby Pattison. Barn grew up on the home farm at the Hall. We call him Barn because—well, just look at him! Barn, for some reason, for which I bless the Heavens, Lady Catherine has seen fit to grant her hand to this unworthy recipient."

Kitty held out her hand. Mr Pattison ignored it. "Pattison will do, Mr Ogilvy. Mr Pattison, if you want. I have my own farm now. I'm not beholden to Ormswood Hall, and you are no friend of mine. Friends don't disappear for nine years without a word."

He glowered at Luke. "Mind you, Mr Ogilvy, you had us all fooled with that little scene on the cliffs. Even I thought maybe an accident. Not murder, never that, but not escape, either. You should have told me."

Luke shook his head. "I didn't want you involved, Barn. Pattison. Someone was out to get me and my brother, and I didn't know how far they would go."

"Friends don't lie to friends," Mr Pattison insisted. The doctor bustled up before Luke could respond, and Kitty's attention turned to the miscreant in the horse trough, who was stirring and groaning.

"Drunk again, Arthur?" the doctor said, as he felt around the man's head, then directed two of the bystanders to lift him out of the trough for a fuller examination. Dawson came round enough to struggle, and Pelham ordered his helpers to hold him down, and continued checking the man's injury despite a stream of foul language. "He'll have a headache, Ogilvy, and not just from the gin he has undoubtedly been guzzling. His pupils are reactive and his manners are as bad as ever." He addressed the people who were still holding Dawson in place. "Take him home, boys. Let him sleep it off."

That accomplished, Kitty, Luke and Paul set out with their guard to explore the village shops. Luke was quiet, his jaw stiff. The attitude of his friend clearly bothered him. "I thought if there was one person whose welcome I could count on, it would be Barn," he told Kitty, keeping his voice low.

"He will come around," Kitty soothed, hoping it would prove to be true.

After the altercation with Dawson, Kitty was alert for more trouble, but the storekeepers and their customers made no overt attacks or unpleasant remarks. With some of them, the guard might have discouraged misbehaviour—she certainly caught some glares and a few sneers. Others were friendly and welcoming. Most fell somewhere in between, watching and cautious.

They had reached the bakery when the next incident occurred. A portly man in the garb of a gentleman was already being served when they entered, so Kitty moved to one side to wait while Paul stepped forward to take a better look at the variety of food on offer.

The man at the counter glanced at him, then turned just as Luke came in the door. His hair was receding from his forehead and inexpertly dyed black, some of the colour adhering to the bald patch. He had the florid nose and poor complexion of a heavy drinker, and the immaculately tied cravat and green and primrose striped waistcoat of a Town tulip.

"You!" The portly man nearly spat the word at Luke, his face flushing with anger. "You dare to show your face in Ormswood again?"

Luke's face went blank, all expression wiped away. He inclined his head. "Sir Thaddeus."

So, this was Sir Thaddeus Frayne, the magistrate who had arrested Luke. Clearly, he intended to do so again. "Hoy! Shopkeeper! Call the constables! This man escaped legal custody!"

The guard who had followed them into the shop took a step forward, and Luke gestured for him to stand down.

The shopkeeper hunched his shoulders, as if trying to hide his head like a turtle. The magistrate did not look to see if his order had been obeyed, since he was occupied glaring at Luke.

"Nine years ago, as I understand it," Kitty pointed out. "Mr Ogilvy has since been tried in a court of law and found innocent of all wrongdoing."

Sir Thaddeus turned on Kitty. "I was not addressing you, missy. Keep out of the business of your betters."

Paul gave an indignant gasp and the low growl came from Luke, but the magistrate's words tickled Kitty's sense of humour. She was strongly tempted to ask where she might find her betters, but these troubled waters needed oil rather than wind.

Luke must have made the same assessment, because he spoke calmly. "My wife is correct, Sir Thaddeus. If you speak to my uncle, who preferred the original charges, you will find he was present in the court room, and will swear to my innocence."

"Or Dr Pelham," Kitty suggested, "to save Sir Thaddeus the ride to the Hall. He can vouch for what Uncle Baldwin told him."

Sir Thaddeus was looking bewildered, though his colour was still high. He turned on the shopkeeper. "I gave you an instruction," he growled.

The shopkeeper's eyes darted from Sir Thaddeus to Luke to Kitty and then to Paul. "Word is they arrived up at the Hall yesterday, Squire. Lord Baldwin told all the servants that he isn't Lord Baldwin at all; that this young laddie is. Said that Master Titus is in prison on charges of attempted murder. Multiple charges, including the old stuff Mr Ogilvy was thought to have done. Reckon if I help you arrest him, I'm in trouble with the young baron, and if I don't I'm in trouble with you." He ducked his head in a brief bow to Paul. "Begging your pardon, milord, but I'm staying out of it."

Paul was sympathetic. "I understand your dilemma," he said. "It will take time for people to realise that I can be trusted, as can my brother and his wife, Lady Catherine."

The shopkeeper addressed his next remark to Kitty. "They say as how you're an earl's daughter, milady." The gossipers had been busy.

"I am," she said, with half an eye on the squire. She was also closely connected to a score of other titles, by marriage or blood. With fewer than 500 families in the peerage, all intermarrying, most daughters of noble houses could say the same. Furthermore, she had a godmother who was duchess, another who was a countess, and her godfather was a royal prince. Again, nothing uncommon for an earl's daughter, especially an earl who had been a playmate of the Duke of Clarence when he was a boy.

The squire was looking uncomfortable. Kitty wondered if she could drop the names of a few of her august relatives, and whether Sir Thaddeus would back off if she did.

Before she could do so, he recovered his pompous arrogance, leading with a snort of disdain and sneering, "As if an earl would allow his daughter to marry the bastard get of a gamekeeper's harlot daughter."

Kitty saw the rigid line of Luke's jaw and spoke quickly, before her controlled and patient husband lost his temper. "My love, I know you told me to give the people here a chance, but this man's insolence and lack of regard for the law are beyond enough. And that is to say nothing of his manners. It is not to be tolerated that he is permitted to remain a King's Man. I will write immediately to my godfather and ask him to speak to his brother."

Paul picked up her verbal ball. "Isn't your godfather the Duke of Clarence?" That was name dropping with a vengeance.

The curtain behind the counter twitched. Whoever was listening had reacted to that, as did the lady who bustled into the shop from the street.

"Oh, Sir Thaddeus!" The arrival was a lady perhaps fifteen years younger than the squire—Kitty put her age at about forty years—and buxom rather than portly, though her figure was disguised in a froth of frills and flounces that would have been excessive on a young girl. "Oh, Sir Thaddeus. Did you hear? Dear Lucius's wife is a goddaughter of the Duke of Clarence! A royal prince!"

"We have no proof that she is who she says," Sir Thaddeus grouched.

His wife giggled. "Silly! I know all about Lady Catherine Stocke. She is the sister of Lady Chirbury and Selby, who is married to the Trapper Earl. He is one of the Golden Redepennings, you know, that they write about all the time in the gossip columns. I read about your wedding, my lady, and you look just like the illustration. Well. Not just like, of course. Your nose is not nearly as pointed as they draw it. Did you really take your little dog to your wedding? Do you have him with you? Oh, but how rude of me. We have not been introduced. Lucius, dear, please present me to your wife. We are so excited to have you back, dear."

She giggled. "Poor Titus. I cannot say that I am surprised! Aileen Baldwin must be beside herself! And just think, Sir Thaddeus! Now that Aileen is no longer a baroness, I am the highest-ranking lady in the village, am I not? For a lady takes her husband's rank, and mine is a baronet. You do not mind, Lady Catherine, do you?"

She paused, perhaps for a breath, her head cocked on one side like a hopeful sparrow. Luke took advantage of the moment. "My love, may I make known to you Lady Frayne, and her husband, Sir Thaddeus. Sir Thaddeus and Lady Frayne, Lady Catherine, my wife."

Lady Frayne bobbed a curtsey and Sir Thaddeus, who had deflated during his wife's monologue, gave a bow that was closer to a nod. "We are so delighted," Lady Frayne assured Kitty. She nudged her husband in the ribs with an elbow. "Are we not, Sir Thaddeus?"

Sir Thaddeus mumbled something that might have been, "Delighted," his expression suggesting the opposite.

"To answer your questions, Lady Frayne," Kitty said, "Pierrot did attend our wedding, and he came to Ormswood Hall with us. He did not accompany me to the village today, but you will surely meet him soon. As to your ranking in the village, mine is only a courtesy title, and I imagine that Lord Baldwin has at least a dozen years before him before he will consider taking a bride."

Lady Frayne beamed and nudged her husband again. "Perhaps as much as a score. More, if he takes after his father, who was a wicked man with the ladies, and reluctant to settle down. We were all surprised, Lady Catherine, when he wed Alison Garrison, though I daresay he had no choice, for everyone knows that her father, Lord Illforth, was threatening to gut Titus Baldwin after he ravished the poor girl, and Titus was the only son of Baldwin's heir. He is a very naughty boy, is Titus."

She turned on her husband, who had made a sound of protest. "Now, now, Sir Thaddeus. You know I am right. And with Titus in prison and Lady Catherine in charge in Ormswood Hall, we have no need to bite our tongues and pretend that all has been well."

How interesting. When Lady Frayne said that, she'd sent a sharp look at Kitty that hinted she was judging Kitty's reaction. Lady Frayne was not the garrulous fool she was at pains to appear.

"Perhaps you would care to come to tea at the Hall tomorrow, Lady Frayne," Kitty said, "and meet my little dog." *And tell me some more about the naughtiness of cousin Titus and why the neighbours felt the need to keep quiet about it. You may be more forthcoming away from the listening ears of your husband, the shopkeeper, and whoever is lurking behind that curtain.*

CHAPTER 26

On the whole, Luke reflected as they walked away from the village, the visit had been a mixed bag. A couple of overt attacks, though Lady Frayne had effectively deflected her husband. A few supporters, fervently pleased to see them but not open about why. Quite a bit of imperfectly hidden hostility. Most people carefully neutral.

Perhaps Kitty could read his mind, for she tightened her hand on his arm. "We have made a start," she said.

The guard opened the gate that led from the lane into the path through the woods, then took off through the gate at a run. Luke was tempted to follow, but he would not leave Kitty and Paul unprotected.

Some crashing in the undergrowth hinted at a scuffle, and a moment later, the guard called out. "I have him, Mr Ogilvy. Do you want to question him?"

"Luke!" Barn's voice reached the lane. "I just need to talk!"

Luke sent a glance towards Kitty. She understood, for she said, "Paul and I will wait here."

Barn was face down on the ground, the guard's knee in his back and his wrists shackled by one of the guard's hands. He wasn't struggling, just watching the gate, and Luke when he came through it.

"Let him up," Luke told the guard, who narrowed his eyes but let go of Barn's wrists and stepped back.

"He's good," Barn said as he stood, rubbing one wrist with the other hand.

"They're good," Luke replied. "Six of them. Men I can trust."

Barn eyed the guard up and down. "Can you be bought, I wonder?"

The guard's impassive face relaxed enough for one corner of his mouth to quirk in a smile. "Can you?"

"That's why I'm here," Barn told Luke. "Your twisted cur of a cousin thinks he owns me body and soul. I need him to believe that's true. No one can know I've talked to you."

He scowled at the guard, who unbent enough to say, "I stay bought and so do my mates. If Mr Ogilvy tells us we didn't see you, then you weren't here."

"Is he armed?" Luke asked.

The guard shook his head.

"Then let me speak with him alone. Wait by the gate."

The guard considered that for a moment, and then backed away to the gate, keeping Barn in view the whole time.

"So that was an act, back in the village?" Luke asked his one-time friend.

"Partly." Barn shrugged. "It's true I was I was up a height you didn't tell me what you were doing. You must have known I would help you. I thought you were dead. All these years, while Baldwin lets his thrice-bedamned son do whatever he wanted! We needed you, Luke. And you abandoned us."

It had been years since Luke heard 'up a height' to mean angry. He'd missed the Northumbrian dialect.

"Did I have a choice?" He asked. "I didn't think so at the time."

Barn heaved a sigh. "I suppose not. But if I'd known you were alive… Well. No matter. I didn't lie in wait to rake over cold coals. Luke, watch your back. Titus has dozens of people in his pocket, and more than half the parish kept silent through threats or bribery.

People who speak out have nasty accidents. Houses burned. Fields ruined. Children or wives attacked and hurt. We can't even combine to fight him, because no one knows who is loyal to him, and who will betray anyone against him for a few coins."

"He has been stealing from the estates," Luke said. "I haven't checked the enterprises yet. I don't doubt he's had his greedy fingers in those, too."

It wasn't a question, but Barn treated it as one. "Yes, he has. He and that witch his mother. They have their fingers in all the business around here, Luke."

Luke could feel his eyes widening. "Smuggling?"

Barn shushed him, his eyes darting about the undergrowth as if to catch a listener. "I didn't say that. Just be careful, Luke. I'm not against you. Believe that. But I can't be *for* you, either. I have a wife and two daughters. I cannot put them at risk."

"He is in prison, Barn. In London. He's going to stand trial for attempted murder and any other crimes we can discover here.

Barn shook his head. "Titus's men will obey his mother. She frightens them more than he does, and that's a fact."

"She has been exiled to the Dower House, under guard."

"She was in the village not thirty minutes before you were. I saw her myself, talking to the squire."

"Sir Thaddeus? You're sure?"

"Certain."

"Did she have a couple of guards with her?" He flapped a hand in the direction of the man standing by the gate—they had different colouring, the Wakefield men, but were much of a height and of the same muscular build.

"She had no one with her except Sir Thaddeus, Luke. I was out the back of the baker's helping Charlie load yesterday's scraps onto my cart. We give them to families who are struggling. We heard them coming down the lane and got out of the way, right quick, so they wouldn't know we heard them. No one wants to get on the wrong side of either of them. Charlie ducked back inside and I hid behind the cart. She and Sir Thaddeus went into the bakery through the back door."

Barn was mistaken, or he was lying, or Aileen Baldwin had a secret way out of the Dower House, for Luke was certain Wakefield's men would never have let her go without their escort.

"You need to know what they were talking about, Luke."

"What did you hear?"

"Titus Baldwin is out of prison and on his way home."

Titus had been in worse bedchambers than the attic in the dower house, but for purposes other than sleep. The space was divided into three rooms, two for storage and one for servants. At least as far as most people knew. Titus had been hidden in a room behind the smaller of the two storage rooms: one with a low sloping ceiling, a concealed door and no access except for a slender path through the abandoned and dusty detritus of generations.

The little secret room was big enough for a full-sized mattress, which he and his mother had hauled through from the other room, and the tiny window opened to let in a trickle of a breeze to counter the heat. Mother and her housekeeper had kept the other servants busy in the kitchen, and Mother's maid had made him a bed with clean sheets. Yes. It was not the worst bedchamber he'd ever been in.

Only he, his mother, and her two closest servants knew he was here, and they had all sworn to tell no one else. "Not even your closest allies," he had warned.

He'd sent Dixon with a letter to Captain Relish or the man known only as the Scot. Dixon had acted as his courier before, and knew which taverns and brothels might be able to get a message to one or both, seeking a meeting. Dixon could be trusted to collect whatever the scoundrels had for Titus, whether it was his share of the proceeds from recent cargoes, or a bullet in the back.

Titus was quite prepared for either. If Relish honoured their agreement, the letter offered him half of what Titus was owed for two favours. The first was passage for Titus and Dixon on Relish's ship, the Ghost. The second, Dixon would disapprove of, so Titus didn't tell him.

The smuggler captain would probably come through. Titus knew secrets Relish and the Scot wanted to protect. But it didn't much matter. If they killed Dixon, Titus would lose both Dixon and the money from the smugglers. However, the two almost cancelled one another out. Dixon, if he lived, had been promised his share of the money.

Titus had more important matters to address. Mother agreed they needed to destroy Lucius's brat before they left. Mother wanted to kill the brat and Lucius's wife, and leave Lucius to suffer, which would have been sweet, but Titus saw a flaw.

The brat had to die, clearly. Titus's father, too. Titus was not about to leave either of them in possession of the title and the rest of the inheritance that should be his. Titus's only objection to killing Lady Catherine was her powerful family, but Mother pointed out that they must have cast her off now she had married to disoblige them, which was a reasonable assumption.

But leaving Lucius alive was dangerous. He was unaccountably fond of the brat and the servants reported that he and his wife were besotted. He would undoubtedly follow Titus to seek revenge, and Titus was not prepared to take the chance that he might catch up. Besides, though Mother did not know, she would be remaining behind. Titus might not wish to take her with him, but he was not so unfilial that he would leave her to hang. No. He would need to kill all four them, plus any witnesses, plus anyone who might even suspect his hand in the deaths.

Better still if no one even knew they were dead. It would take careful planning, and he'd need to calm his emotions. Revenge was a dish best served cold.

But how exciting!

When Luke and his family arrived back at Ormswood Hall, a messenger from David Wakefield was waiting, with news that Titus had escaped custody, and disappeared without a trace. "This confirms what Barn overheard," he said to Kitty, Paul, and Michael Palmer, the head of the team of guards.

"He'll hide," Kitty mused. "The question is, where?"

Luke frowned. "Wherever it is, he'll get in touch with his mother. Watch the dower house, find Titus." *But if Mrs Baldwin was in the village this afternoon, there must be another way out of Primrose Cottage, and therefore into it.*

"I had better go over there and see if the men on duty have seen anything. Paul, you stay here. With Titus on the loose, I want you and Kitty protected at all times."

He half expected one or both of them to argue, but they exchanged a look and nodded.

"We will not cause you further worry by refusing your sensible commands," Kitty said, "but you be careful, too, Luke."

"He has no reason to go after me," Luke argued.

"He has more reason to go after you than after me," Kitty retorted. "He knows you well enough to be able to guess what would happen if he hurt either one of us," her gesture linked her and Paul. "As long as you breathe, he could not rest easy."

His clever wife made a good point. "I will be careful, Kitty," he promised.

A cascade of sharp yaps announced Pierrot, his nose poking out between two balustrades as he tried to peer down at Kitty from the landing on the next floor. Kitty's maid Millie could be heard scolding him for escaping from the room he and Kitty shared, and the next moment, Millie looked over the balustrade.

"I will go up and change," Kitty said, with a smile. "Paul, would you come and check on Uncle Baldwin with me once I have taken off my coat and bonnet?"

Above them, Pierrot was complaining vociferously, with Millie's voice in counterpoint, telling him to shush and that he could not get down. Luke guessed that the maid had picked up the little dog to stop him from rushing down the stairs.

"Go and reassure your little rat that you are well," he said. "I will report back soon."

Kitty offered her cheek for his kiss.

"You mentioned a map of the secret rooms and tunnels, Dad," Paul said. "Would it be in the library, do you think? I'd like to see if it includes the dower house."

"Good thinking," Luke approved. "It used to be in the library. Green leather cover, quite worn. About twenty-five inches high and twenty wide. Try the shelves to the left of the window. If it hasn't been moved in the past nine years, that's where it will be. In fact, I will come with you."

Kitty took a step towards them, then changed her mind at another chorus of yaps. "I will see the two of you later," she said. "Luke, be careful. Paul, promise me you will not explore without permission from Luke and whatever company he decrees, nor without making sure that someone reliable, someone who isn't with you, knows where you are going."

Luke darted a glance at Paul as the boy gave the required promise. The chagrin in his expression told the story. Paul would keep his word, but hadn't wanted to give it.

The book wasn't where Luke expected it to be. He left Paul searching the rest of the library and he and Palmer, the head guard, walked over to the dower house, both of them constantly surveying their surroundings for anything hostile.

That was how they saw Gibson, Uncle Baldwin's valet, hurrying away from the house behind the shrubbery that bordered the path, hunching to stay hidden. Luke went a few more paces until he was no longer in the valet's line of site, then ducked and doubled back. The head guard, without a word between them, did the same.

Gibson continued to scuttle through the shrubbery until a turn of the path brought it across in front of him. He stepped onto the path, resumed his usual straight stance, and slowed his forward momentum to a solemn strut. He was clearly headed towards the house.

"I'd like to ask him where he went this afternoon," said Palmer.

"Do so," Luke invited. "If he lies, we know he cannot be trusted."

Palmer glanced at him, raising an eyebrow. "Progress of a sort to be certain of one enemy," he responded. "I don't trust any of them. Including your uncle and Pattison."

Luke had to agree with the man. "True."

At the house, the housekeeper wanted to refuse them entrance, but a glare from Luke and the very solid presence of the guard had her swallowing her complaints and stepping out of the way. One of the guards on duty had stepped into the hall to check who had arrived.

"Any visitors? Anything else of interest?" his leader asked.

"Come through to the kitchen," the man said. "I'll brief my partner, and we can take a stroll around the perimeter while I report."

One of the guards had seen Gibson make his surreptitious arrival and departure. The man had spent thirty minutes in the housekeeper's room with the door shut. "Not an assignation, for the mistress's maid joined them for more than half that time," the guard reported.

The other piece of news concerned the previous evening. "Mrs Baldwin summoned all of the servants downstairs, and she and the housekeeper spent nearly an hour interrogating them about a missing bracelet. She didn't point the finger at either of us. I half thought she would, and she may yet."

"Or something was happening elsewhere in the house she did not want anyone to see," the Palmer suggested.

"That's what I thought," the guard agreed. "Especially since the maid was missing. I left my partner to watch in the kitchen and I went to find her. She was up in the attics. Searching the servants' room, she said. But I've seen her and the housekeeper go up there three times since, and I don't know what for. They both have rooms in the basement."

"What's up there?" Luke asked.

"The servants' bedchamber and two storage rooms, sir," the

guard replied. "The storage rooms are full of all sorts of clutter. I checked, but without knowing what they are hiding, I can't find it."

"I'll take a look myself," Luke decided, which led a few minutes later to a confrontation with his aunt by marriage, her maid, and her housekeeper. All three loudly objected to his incursion up the stairs, and tried to stop him by putting themselves bodily in his way. When he lifted Aunt Baldwin from his path, she fell into hysterics, and the other two women bent to her assistance, which left him free to check the attics. Like the guard, he found nothing that meant anything to him, and demanding answers from the three harridans would get him precisely nowhere.

He'd have to come back with the estate carpenter and do a more thorough search. In the cellar, too. Any secret way out of the house probably started there.

CHAPTER 27

Millie's opinion of the servants of Ormswood Hall was low after the first day and sank further in the days that followed. They obeyed Lady Kitty reluctantly and slowly, but the rapid expulsion of Mrs O must have left an impression, because they did obey.

Slowly, and with as little competence as possible.

Millie had never seen such a number of spills and breakages. And out of Lady Kitty's sight—and Millie's—they grumbled constantly about the new regime. Lady Kitty had decided on a full clean of the house, top to bottom, one room per day. The fuss they made was ridiculous. Even the people hired from the village to supplement the staff proclaimed, out of Lady Kitty's hearing, that cleaning rooms that were seldom used was a waste of time.

In Millie's opinion, it was ridiculous to have more rooms than any family could possibly want to use, but since they existed and belonged to the young master, they needed to be clean. Dust and mould and insects had no place in a person's house, whether the room was used or not.

She assumed, as did Lady Kitty, that the tension in the house would decrease as the servants got used to the new regime. Instead, it grew. Millie felt she was under a gathering storm; one about to break over her head at any moment.

The house was occupied by several camps, most of them hostile. The cook refused to take sides, and her staff followed her direction. The parlour and chamber maids felt aggrieved at what they saw as extra work since, as far as Millie could tell, neither Mrs Baldwin nor her housekeeper acolyte had actually attempted to keep house.

The butler and the senior footmen thought it beneath them to be serving the base-born son of the gamekeeper's daughter, so kept referring anything Mr Ogilvy told them to do to Mr Baldwin, though Gibson would not let them into Mr Baldwin's room, so Millie could not say whether the gentleman actually reinforced every one of Mr Ogilvy's orders, or whether Gibson did it to avoid his master being disturbed.

The junior footmen had turned against Millie when she refused romantic overtures from several of them. They were united in accusing her of being proud beyond her station, since a maid took her mistress's status with the household and a wife took her husband's station in society. "You work for the son of a whore, Price," said their ringleader. "That makes you the lowest servant in the house, by my reckoning."

"Insult the man who pays your wages?" Millie commented. "That makes you the stupidest servant in the house, by my reckoning."

He took a swipe at her, but she ducked and stepped out through the servant's door into the entrance hall, where Lady Kitty's voice could be heard, discussing with Master Paul where they would search next. Lady Kitty and Master Paul were searching the house for a book that showed the plans for the Hall and all of its secret passages.

Mr Ogilvy knew some of them, which he showed to his wife and the young lord, as well as Millie and the guard. Mr Baldwin told them how to find some Mr Ogilvy didn't know about. "But there are others, Luke," he told Mr Ogilvy. "I've seen them on the maps. The book of maps? It's in the library."

It wasn't there, and Lady Kitty wanted to find it. It was a big book bound in green leather. Millie kept her eyes open as her duties led her around the rambling mansion, but she did not see it anywhere. She stepped with care, since she did not want to be caught alone by the footman she had insulted or any of his cronies. As a result, she heard more than a few conversations that would have hushed immediately if the speakers had known she was listening.

Meanwhile, Mr Ogilvy and Mr Palmer, the head of the guard, were riding the neighbourhood, and receiving a similar mixed reaction from the tenants, the villagers, and the neighbouring gentlefolk. Mr Ogilvy generally gave Lady Kitty a report on what had happened during the day as he and Lady Kitty dressed for dinner. They knew they could speak freely in front of Millie, though they kept their voices down. Mr Baldwin said there were no secret passages in the walls of the New Wing, but Mr Ogilvy was taking no chances.

One evening, as Millie went over the day clothes her lady had just removed to see if anything needed repair, she pondered whether she should tell them both what she had overheard that afternoon, or whether she should wait until she had her lady alone.

"I've been told twice more today that Titus is here," Mr Ogilvy was saying. "Somewhere in the neighbourhood. No one knows, or at least they won't say, where he is, but they're all scared of him, Kitty. And with reason."

"He's just one man," Lady Kitty protested. "If they hate him so, why don't they stand up to him?"

Mr Ogilvy shook his head. "From what I've heard, he has enough of them charmed that they do whatever he wants. And he has a gang of bullies to back him up. If someone stands against him, bad things happen. Their barn burns down. Their prize sow dies. Armed people in masks assault their wife or their daughter. In one case, their mother. Nothing that can be connected to Titus. They don't know, or they won't tell me, who he has in his pay."

"Smugglers," Millie said, and both Lady Kitty and her husband turned in surprise, as if they had forgotten she was there. She curtseyed and blushed. Servants were not meant to insert themselves into the conversations of the gentlefolk, but Lady Kitty had always been interested in her opinion. Millie was unsure of Mr Ogilvy, though.

"I beg your pardon. I should not have interrupted."

Mr Ogilvy flapped his hand as if to wave her apology away. "Never mind that. What makes you say smugglers?"

Millie shrugged. "The footmen speak of them when they think no one is listening. Some of them help with transferring the cargoes from the rowboats to the donkeys. Or the other way around when the whisky is going out."

"I asked Barn," Mr Ogilvy said. "He said… No. What he said was that he wouldn't say smugglers. My father closed down the last smuggler gang operating from Ormsmouth a dozen or more years ago. Lax as my uncle's management has been, I can see how they have started up again. Thank you, Millie. It helps to have confirmation. I don't suppose you know who their leader is? Perhaps we can persuade him not to let his men work for Titus."

"Titus is their leader," Millie exclaimed. Then corrected herself. "At least, he is one of three partners. I just heard them talking about it this afternoon. He put up the money to buy the first ship. In return, he takes a share of each cargo. The footmen who help on the runs are very proud of him."

Mr Ogilvy narrowed his eyes, though he was looking into the middle distance, at something in his own thoughts, and not at Millie. "And the other two?"

"One man, they just referred to as the Captain," Millie replied, "and they call the other Jock or the Scot."

Mr Ogilvy fell silent. Millie and Lady Kitty watched to see if he was going to say anything else, and then Lady Kitty asked, "Does it help?"

"I should say it does." Mr Ogilvy grinned at Millie. "Smugglers, by George!" He gave his wife an enthusiastic kiss. "Smugglers have brought gin and luxury goods into Northumberland from the low countries for time out of mind, and taken away wool as well as whisky from the stills up in the hills. In peacetime, no one cares except the King's excise men."

Millie nodded, as she understood, and Lady Kitty put it into words. "Napoleon controls the low countries."

Mr Ogilvy's nod was approving. "Yes, and the excise men would love to get their hands on anything that smuggling ships might be carrying. The military, too, especially spies and information. If the smugglers are hiding Titus, they may lead us to him. Millie, what else have you learned? Anything about where they land? Where they dock the ship? Where the leaders stay when they are not on a run?"

Kitty forced herself to smile as she waved Luke goodbye the following morning. He had woken to make sweet tender love to her, and then announced he would be riding to Berwick-Upon-Tweed to talk to the man in charge of the local volunteer force. "A written message might not convince them," he said.

Kitty understood, but she didn't like it. He refused to take a guard with him, or even one of Rede's footmen. "We need them all to watch the occupants of the dower house and those of the Hall," he insisted. "Especially since we still haven't discovered how Aunt Baldwin got into the village the other day, if she did. The nurses aren't here yet, so we can't watch the woman every moment of the day, which means someone has to patrol the grounds. I won't spread them even thinner by tacking one of them with me. Besides, one companion won't be much use if I am attacked by a large group."

That didn't make Kitty feel any better.

"I'll take a groom," he conceded. "Do not worry, though, Kitty. My safety will be in speed. We will be going too fast to stop, and on the return journey, if I don't bring a troop of volunteers with me, I will bring some more hired guards."

He took the fastest horses in the stable, and, as promised, left the stable yard at a gallop, the groom close behind him. They were soon out of sight.

"He will be back soon," Paul assured her, his own eyes worried. "Perhaps even by nightfall."

"Of course, he will." Kitty reapplied the smile that had slipped as she saw her beloved gallop away into danger. "Come, Paul. Let us go and see what Pierrot is making such a fuss about."

By the time they traced the network of passages from the side door that gave access to the stable yard through to the front hall, their visitor had been shown to the guest parlour, and was sitting at her ease, closely watched by a now quiet but still suspicious Pierrot.

Seeing who it was, Paul remembered an unfinished task, and excused himself.

"I will let you go," Kitty agreed. "However, make sure the lady's carriage is waiting outside in no more than thirty minutes."

Kitty was on her own when she entered the parlour. "Lady Frayne. How good of you to call." In the few days since they met her in the village, the squire's wife had called three times. This would be the fourth. Kitty resigned herself to another interrogation about London Society, peppered with disparaging comparisons about Newcastle, and laced with verbal assaults disguised as innocuous comments.

"Was that Mr Ogilvy I saw riding away?" Lady Frayne asked.

Kitty agreed that it was, and further acknowledged that her husband had business to attend to. The gleam in Lady Frayne's eye looked like satisfaction, but that was ridiculous. How could Lady Frayne benefit from Luke's trip?

"Lady Catherine, I have come for a little chat, and also to extend an invitation," she said. "You must come. Tomorrow, for afternoon tea. I have invited the other notable ladies of the neighbourhood. It is time for you to take your place in our society. Do say you will come."

Kitty hoped that Luke and the soldiers would be back by then. She was certainly not going anywhere in his absence. She said something noncommittal and ordered a tea tray. She then sat, composing herself to endure the lady's questions.

For once, Lady Frayne was more interested in local news. "Was your husband not a friend of the farmer Pattison?"

"Barnaby Pattison," Kitty said.

"Yes. Arrogant man. Does not know his place. The word is that his wife has left him. Taken his daughters and gone away. Has your husband mentioned that at all?"

Kitty shook her head. "He has said nothing to me. Poor Mr Pattison."

Lady Frayne snorted. "You are too kind, calling him mister. He is just a common farmer for all the airs and graces his wife puts on. Of course, she was better born than her husband. A solicitor's daughter from Newcastle. And now she has run off and abandoned him. I daresay he deserved it."

Kitty had had enough. "We can never know what goes on inside another's marriage, Lady Frayne. I can only pity both husband and wife and hope they are able to resolve their differences. Especially for the sake of the little girls. I believe there are two of them?"

"I am not surprised at your sympathy, Lady Catherine," Lady Frayne offered. "After all, you have also married well beneath you. Although, I daresay at your age, the choices were limited, and Mr Ogilvy is a fine figure of a man."

Having weathered six London seasons, Kitty was accustomed to pointed remarks wielded with the skill of a champion fencer. Lady Frayne used words like a hammer, and Kitty had a sudden image of her up against some of the most vicious ladies of the ton, waving a hammer round her head while they poked her from all directions with their rapier wits. She took another sip of tea to disguise her desire to giggle.

When she had herself under control, she agreed that Luke was, indeed, a fine figure of a man. Lady Frayne was definitely in a mood today. She made several more attempts to stir Kitty's wrath. She insulted Kitty's dress: "You are so wise not to dress fashionably for a day at home in the country. Of course, with Sir Thaddeus's position, I must be prepared at a moment's notice to be on display, so I must always be perfectly presented at all times." She smoothed the nearest ruffle with great satisfaction.

She questioned Paul's intelligence. "I see that you have not yet been able to procure a tutor for poor little Lord Baldwin. Of course, his mother was none too bright, and these things can come down in the blood."

That led her to question Luke's motives. "Of course, keeping the poor lad ignorant might be a cunning move on the part of your husband, Lady Catherine. He can continue to manage the boy's wealth even after he has grown."

Lady Frayne really was a nasty besom. Interestingly, in all her gossip and pointed remarks, she made no mention of the local disasters—the fire in the home farm's barn, the collapsing foot bridge that was the quickest access to the village for one of the coastal farms, the unexplained accident that befell the farrier's wife. Those, Kitty thought, were closer to an explanation of Mrs Pattison's departure than any marital disharmony.

The thirty minutes for an afternoon call dragged interminably, and Lady Frayne showed no signs of moving. Kitty rose to her feet at the end of the allotted time, looked pointedly at the clock, and said, "Thank you for your visit. I know you must have much to do. Allow me to show you to your carriage."

For a moment, Kitty thought the woman was going to refuse to move, but she hoisted herself to her feet and allowed herself to be escorted out of the room, across the entry hall, and out the front door, wondering volubly whether her carriage would be ready.

It was. Well done, Paul.

Lady Frayne hesitated at the top of the steps. "I trust you will join us tomorrow afternoon. I have told everyone you will be there."

Which she had no right to do, but if Kitty did not turn up, then Lady Frayne would claim Kitty thought she was too good for them, and all the work she had done to unfreeze the locals would have to be done again.

"I shall send you a note," she temporised.

Paul materialised at her shoulder as the carriage drove away. "What did she want?" he asked.

"To invite me to afternoon tea, or so she said. Paul, have you heard anything about Mrs Pattison and her daughters going away?"

Paul shook his head.

"It was almost the first thing Lady Frayne talked about. Perhaps she wanted to know what I knew?"

Paul shrugged. "I have no idea what goes on in that woman's

mind, if anything. She is not on our side, though, Kitty. I am certain of that."

"She is on Lady Frayne's side," Kitty told him. "I have met her kind before."

Kitty found Millie in the sewing room, mending one of Luke's shirts. When Kitty asked, she knew about the Pattisons. "Had a big argument, right in the middle of the village street. The next thing, she was packing bags for her and her girls, and off they went in the gig. Or so they say in the kitchen. Only…" Her voice trailed off.

Kitty raised her eyebrows. "Only?" she prompted.

After a cautious look at the walls, Millie spoke in just above a whisper. "Three other families had all of their womenfolk run off in the last two days. Wives. Mothers. Sisters. Daughters." She named them.

Kitty stared at her. "Those are the names of the men who have approached Luke in secret, to tell him about Titus's mismanagement and theft," she said, keeping her own voice low. If secret passages ran past this room, any listeners would hear nothing from her.

"They are preparing for a fight," she concluded, "and removing their families from harm's way."

"As long as they plan to fight on our side," Millie said.

CHAPTER 28

Palmer and Millie both counselled against accepting Lady Frayne's invitation. Luke was not back by the following morning, and after some thought, Kitty wrote a letter to the rector's wife, asking her to offer an apology on Kitty's behalf. "The rector's wife may send you on to the doctor's wife," she instructed the groom she was sending with the message. She had enclosed a second letter to the doctor's wife, and had asked the rector's wife to send it on if she had not been invited.

The messenger returned with notes from both ladies. They had not been invited to Lady Frayne's, and neither had anyone they knew.

Kitty showed the responses to Palmer and Paul. It had been a trap. But to what end?

She sat down to write another note, this time to Lady Frayne, saying that she would be unable to attend. Before she had completed it, there was a knock on the door and two of the guard entered with another man between them.

At first sight, Kitty thought it was Titus, whom she had seen in court at Luke's hearing. A second look confirmed that this man was younger and thinner, with none of the tell-tale signs of excess Titus showed.

"Who is this?" Paul asked.

"He won't say." The guard who spoke was one of those assigned to the dower house. "I was coming up the Hall when I saw him. He was in the folly, opening a trap door to a hidden tunnel."

"I just wanted to see Lord Baldwin," the young man protested.

"I am Lord Baldwin," said Paul.

The young man looked taken aback, and then blinked twice. He bowed as well as he could, given he had a guard on each side firmly grasping his upper arm. "My apologies, my lord. I meant Mr Baldwin. Mr Marcus Baldwin." He turned pleading eyes to Kitty. "Please, my lady. I mean no harm. They say in the village that he has been ill. I just want to see him."

"His heart is frail," Kitty told the man. "We do not want anything to upset him. Perhaps you could give me a message."

Palmer was scowling. "We don't know who this scoundrel is, my lady or what his real motives are. I suggest you allow me to take him away and question him."

"I know some of it, I think," Kitty said. "You are George Dixon, Titus Baldwin's valet. Am I correct?"

Dixon nodded, his eyes darting from one guard to another and his shoulders hunching as if he feared that the identification might fetch him a clout.

"You grew up in an orphanage in Newcastle," Kitty continued. "Titus Baldwin hired you for your appearance, since he believed you were probably half-brother or cousin to him."

"Yes, my lady," Dixon agreed, bowing again.

"Truly?" Paul asked. "How did you come to be in an orphanage, then? I thought my father looked after his offspring." He frowned. "Or was Dad an exception?"

Dixon blushed and would not meet Kitty's eyes.

"I suspect Mr Dixon is reluctant to mention his mother's trade in front of me, Paul. Suffice it to say she could not have been certain of the identity of his father at the time she discovered she was with child. Sadly, she died when Mr Dixon was young, and he did not then bear the strong family resemblance that he has today."

"Mr Baldwin could be my father or maybe my uncle, my lady," Dixon pleaded. "He has always been kind to me. I just want to see him."

Kitty examined the valet through narrowed eyes. "I wonder, Mr Dixon, did Titus Baldwin send you?"

Dixon protested. "No, my lady. I swear. Mr Titus—he sent me on an errand. I just wanted to leave. He promised we would go to America. Start again. I thought he'd given up on..." His blush deepened. He fell silent and took a sudden deep interest in his toes.

"On killing me and my half-brother," Paul finished for him.

Dixon turned his head towards Paul. "I don't hold with killing, my lord," he said. "Mr Titus knows that. He sent me away. Told me to meet him in Newcastle. I was heading there but I thought — I wanted to say goodbye to Lord... to Mr Marcus. He was kind to me."

Kitty made a decision. "Paul, go and tell Uncle Baldwin that George Dixon is here. Ask him if he would like to see the man." She then turned to the guard from the dower house. "I take it you were coming to see us when you caught Mr Dixon."

Palmer turned his attention to his guard. "Yes. What are you doing here?"

"Reporting, sir, my lady. Mrs Baldwin, her maid and Mrs Embleton have gone out in the carriage. According to the groom who prepared the carriage, they are going to visit the squire's wife, Lady Frayne. My colleague followed them. "

Kitty exchanged a glance with Palmer. "Perhaps I should go, after all," she said.

"It is a trap, Lady Kitty," the man said.

He was probably right, but still, going to see what they were up to might be useful. "We could learn a lot by tripping the trap," she declared

"It is too dangerous," Paul argued, and Palmer agreed.

"Surely they will not harm me when they know everyone here is aware I am visiting them," Kitty said.

"Don't go, my lady." Dixon shrank a little when the others turned to look at him, but he took a deep breath and set his jaw. "The message I carried? It was to the smugglers. He said it was about his share of the takings, but I think he asked them to help him. He has used them before to frighten those who spoke out against him, and when I said I was coming this way, the Captain said he would see me soon."

"You think they might make a full-on attack?" Palmer asked.

"We are vulnerable, not knowing all the tunnels," Kitty mused. "Dixon, can you show Palmer all the secret rooms and passages you know of that let out in the house or its outbuildings?"

"He cannot be trusted, my lady," Palmer protested. "Titus Baldwin probably sent him."

Dixon protested that Titus had no idea he was even in the area. "I will tell you what I know," he said.

The door opened, and the footman who had been sent with the message to Uncle Baldwin assisted the man himself into the room, then left, closing the door behind him.

Uncle Baldwin sunk into a chair. "Dixon? You're here? Then it is true. Titus escaped. Where is he?"

"I do not know, my lord. Sir, I mean. We split up when we landed in Newcastle. He sent me to the Fox and Hound in Beadnell with a message for the Captain, and I was meant to go back to Newcastle and wait for him, but I came to see you, sir."

Baldwin gave him a distracted smile. "Did you, Dixon? How kind."

At that moment, Millie came hurrying in. "My lady? Oh, Mr Palmer, too. Come quickly."

"You are interrupting a meeting, girl," said Uncle Baldwin, sternly. "Run along, now."

Millie glanced at him and then fixed her eyes on Kitty, standing her ground. "It's Mr Gibson, my lady. He has put something into the soup."

"Rubbish," Uncle Baldwin declared. "Gibson would do nothing of the sort. Here! You!" He pointed at the guard from the dower house. "Get Gibson for me. We will sort this out."

"A moment!" said Palmer. "Mr Baldwin, the rest of us will step into the next room while you speak to your valet. We will leave the door partly open and listen."

"Uncle Baldwin," Kitty said, "If Millie says she saw Gibson put something into the soup, that is what she saw. Ask him what it was."

Uncle Baldwin narrowed his eyes, but when Kitty just regarded him silently, he nodded. "Very well then. Very well. It will be quite innocent. You shall see. A mistake."

The guard went to find Gibson, and the others crowded into the little sitting room that opened into the parlour. Indeed, when the connecting doors were all opened wide, the two rooms flowed into one, which made it easy to leave a folding panel at one end open a couple of inches, so they could hear everything that was said in the other room.

"Sir!" Gibson said. "I thought you were resting."

"I was," Uncle Baldwin told him, "but I heard something disturbing."

"Sir?"

"What did you put into the soup, Gibson?" Uncle Baldwin sounded both stern and confident.

"Sir!" Gibson's shocked exclamation was followed by a patter of denials. "The soup? Nothing! I have not been in the kitchen today, at all, sir."

"But you knew I meant today, and the kitchen." Uncle Baldwin's voice was suddenly weary. "You were seen, Gibson. In the kitchen, adding something to the soup."

"To help you, sir," Gibson insisted. "Mrs Embolton said it would make everyone sleep. Mr Titus is coming, sir. He is going to rescue you. He sent something to make everyone sleep, because he does not want anyone to be hurt."

"Oh, Gibson, Gibson," Uncle Baldwin said. "And you believed what Mrs Embolton said? When did my son ever worry about people being hurt?"

"I don't believe he wants to rescue his father," said Dixon, pushing back the folding panels so he could enter the parlour. "Mr

Titus is furious with his father for supporting Mr Ogilvy and the young lord. He'd rather kill him than rescue him."

Kitty followed Dixon in time to see Uncle Baldwin wince. "We had better go to the kitchen before anyone tries the soup," she said.

She would have led the way, but Palmer apologised as he passed her. "I will go first, my lady," he insisted, though Kitty could not see quite what he intended to protect her from. Such a troop piling down the servants' stairs made quite a noise—all those in the parlour plus another guard who joined them when they passed. Any malefactors would decamp before they could be caught.

Perhaps the sound in the stairwell was less pervasive than she thought, for the cook's assistant turned around, startled, as they hurried into the kitchen, the others stepping in behind them one by one.

In one hand, she held a bowl, and in the other, a ladle.

"Don't taste that soup!" Palmer barked.

The cook's assistant dropped the bowl, which broke, spilling fish soup across the floor.

The cook stood up from her place at the table, putting down her spoon beside another bowl of soup. "Wha' wong wi' a 'oup…" She covered her mouth with both hands, her eyes wide with alarm.

The assistant cast a glance at the mess on the floor, another at Palmer, and a third at the cook, who was dropping back onto her chair. "Ma mou'…" the cook moaned.

"Poison in the soup," Kitty explained.

Pierrot trotted up to sniff at the spilled soup. "Paul," Kitty commanded, "pick up Pierrot, please." She bent over the cook. "You tasted the soup?" she asked.

The cook looked up at her with fear-filled eyes, nodding.

"How much?" Kitty asked.

The cook shook her head. "No mu."

"Just a spoonful, to adjust the seasoning," the cook's assistant assured her.

Kitty wondered what was best to do. "Gibson, have you any idea what was in the bottle Mrs Embolton gave you?" she asked. Milk worked for some poisons. Or perhaps she should administer a purge.

Even as she considered it, the cook paled still further and made a lunge towards the large oak dresser that filled one wall. She reached underneath and pulled out a basin just in time to violently expel the contents of her stomach.

Not a purge, then.

"Send a groom for a doctor," Kitty commanded, and one of the guard set off at a run.

"Fetch me a jug of milk and a glass, and that will need to be cleaned up," Kitty told the cook's assistant, pointing to the mess on the floor. "Millie, help me assist Cook to her room. Paul, find a bucket, and also some water and a cloth so that the poor woman can wash her face."

"I didn't know," Gibson sobbed. "No one was meant to be hurt."

Uncle Baldwin and Palmer exchanged a glance. "Gibson, you must tell Palmer everything you know," Uncle Baldwin said. "Dixon, help Lady Kitty and Miss Price with the cook."

The guard who had gone to the stables burst back into the kitchen. "The grooms are all gone, and most of the horses!" he shouted.

The bitch isn't coming. Emmie Frayne, Mrs Embolton, and his mother had assured him that she would. "Of course, she will, Titus," Emmie insisted. "Lady Kitty has been visiting all over the neighbourhood. Trying to convince our people that she and the gamekeeper's ill-begotten grandson can be trusted." She snorted to express her opinion. "She won't want to miss the opportunity to ingratiate herself with the locals. She is just late, which is very rude."

It doesn't matter, Titus decided. *She will drink the soup with the others, and if she dies, she dies.* The main target had been the remaining guards. The one who had followed the carriage from the dower house had been captured and was tied up in the tunnels, well away from the cell holding Luke.

With the other five poisoned, and either dead or vomiting their guts out, there'd be no one to stop him walking into Ormswood Hall except a sick old man, a Society chit, and a boy.

Captain Relish, curse him, had brought only half a dozen men, and the Scot wasn't with him. Titus had intended to tie off all his loose ends at once, but it couldn't be helped. An adaptable man always had a backup plan. He had already written a letter to the excise men with enough information to hang both leaders and all their crew.

He would send Dixon with it, just before he boarded the boat he intended to take, bound for the Continent, where a certain conquering emperor owed Titus a refuge. Dixon would find him gone when he returned from his errand. If he returned. With any luck, they'd arrest Dixon by mistake for Titus. Even if they didn't, Dixon had committed enough crimes on Titus's orders to be hanged in his own name.

"She is not coming," he said. "It is half an hour past the time." She would have to take her chances with the poison, which was a pity, because he really wanted to make Luke watch while he took the lady in every way he could, and then handed her over to the smugglers. But wait. The soup would not be served yet. There may be another way.

"Where is the groom who brought Luke to me?" he asked.

CHAPTER 29

It wasn't just the grooms. The butler and his footmen were gone, all the parlour maids, and three of the chamber maids. The kitchen maid was there—the cook's assistant had brought her in from the scullery to clean the floor. They and the two Redepenning footmen and the four maids who remained were mystified by their colleagues' disappearance, but Kitty wasn't. Titus was stripping the house, ready for an attack.

Cook was very ill, but neither Kitty nor Palmer wanted to risk someone going for the doctor, only to fall into Titus's hands. She was still conscious, which Kitty took as a good sign, and the numbness in the mouth seemed to be getting no worse, but the vomiting continued.

Kitty ordered a hot drink of lemon cordial, sweetened with honey, and another of just hot water. "Get her to wash her mouth out with hot water when she can, to make her mouth feel better, and sip the lemon," Kitty told the maid she set to watch the patient. "Send for me if she gets worse."

Only the cook had tried the soup, tasting it some ten minutes before Kitty arrived in the kitchen, in order to check and adjust the seasoning. The kitchen servants had been about to sit down to their meal. "We eat early, my lady, so we can concentrate on dinner for upstairs. The rest of the servants have their meal when upstairs has their first course, except those needed to serve the second. They eat after everyone else."

The huge vat of fish soup was to feature in the first of two courses for the family, and would be the centrepiece of the servants' dinner. "Fish soup and bread, my lady, and what we will eat now, I do not know," the cook's assistant explained.

Kitty thought dinner was the least of their worries. "And the guard? When do they eat?" she asked.

Palmer answered her. "My men usually join the servants, my lady. You, there." He addressed the Redepenning footmen. "Who was to serve the family at table today? The butler and who else?"

One of the footmen rattled off some names. "They've all gone, my lady, sir."

Gibson was already pale, but at that, he whitened still further. "They knew, my lord. Mr Baldwin, I mean. They must have known, do you not think, sir? They ran off and left me to…" He ran for the newly cleaned slop bucket that a maid had left outside the door of Cook's room.

They knew enough to believe they could poison the whole household at once, but not enough to realise that the kitchen staff did not eat with the rest of the servants. Mrs Embolton was really a very bad housekeeper.

Gibson made it just in time, voiding his disgust at what he had been made to do. He raised himself from the bucket, accepted the damp cloth Dixon handed him to wipe his mouth, and said, "I was lied to, but I still should not have done it. If Cook dies, I shall never forgive myself."

They were interrupted again, this time by the guard who was patrolling the front of the house. Kitty recognised the groom he hauled in by the scruff of his neck—it was the man who had gone with Luke.

"This fellow has something to tell you, Mr Palmer," the guard said, letting go of the groom so suddenly that he stumbled a couple of steps before he caught his balance.

He ignored Palmer and spoke to Kitty and Uncle Baldwin. "My lady, sir, Mr Ogilvy has been taken."

According to the groom, they had been ambushed on the other side of the village, where the road dipped to cross the river. "I was knocked out, and when I came to, they were gone, and Mr Ogilvy with them. I followed their tracks all the way to the edge of the squire's land. But there were armed men, patrolling the grounds. I couldn't go any further. My lady, sir, we have to rescue him!"

If the man had arrived before the other grooms absconded, Kitty might have believed him… might at least have gone to see for herself whether the squire's estate could be penetrated. But what were the chances that all the grooms except this one had sold out to Titus?

"Show me your head wound," she said.

The groom blinked. "What?" he stammered.

Kitty allowed her eyes to challenge him. "You were knocked out. Show me the bump, or at least a bruise."

The groom's eyes darted in every direction, but he was surrounded. He gulped.

"We don't have time for this," Palmer said. "You. Groom. Right-handed or left?"

When the groom gaped at him, he said. "Your preferred hand, man."

"Right," the groom managed to choke out.

At a nod from Palmer, two of the guards grabbed him. One twisted his left arm up behind his back. The other stretched his right arm out across the kitchen table, forcing his hand flat. Palmer picked a large meat cleaver from the knife rack and stepped up to where the groom could see him.

"What— what are you going to do with that?" The question was croaked.

Palmer smiled, but there was no humour in it. Just a devilish promise. "That is entirely over to you. Jacob. That is your name, is it not? Tell the truth, Jacob, and I will not have to use this. Answer Lady Catherine's questions. For every lie, I will cut off part of your finger. When I have finished with the little finger, 1 will start with the next. You can cope very well without two or three of your fingers. If you don't bleed to death and they don't get infected. Sooner or later, you will tell us exactly what Titus instructed you to do. Save us all time and mess, and make it sooner."

The groom fainted, and a sudden acrid smell accompanied a spreading damp spot on his trousers.

"I believe he is adequately frightened," Paul commented, irreverently.

They brought the man around by the simple method of dragging him into the kitchen courtyard and pouring a bucket of water over his head. When they lugged him back into the kitchen, he admitted that all of the grooms worked for the smugglers, and that he had been told to lead Luke into an ambush.

"They didn't take him to the squire's, Lady Catherine, but I was told to tell you that he was there. Mr Titus said I was to persuade you to come to the estate. He was going to make it look as if the armed guards had left, but they would be waiting to capture you."

"What on earth does Titus want with me?" Kitty wondered.

The groom began to shake his head, but Palmer raised the cleaver and he cringed and said, "He wants to use you to make Mr Ogilvy suffer, my lady. Please, my lady, I've told you everything I know. Make him put down the chopper. I can help, my lady. I'm on your side, now."

"You knew he planned to hurt me, probably assault me in front of my husband," Kitty pointed out. "You were willing to help him to do that. Yet you suggest we should trust you? Uncle Baldwin, are there lockable rooms in the cellars or the tunnels?"

"Yes, there are," Uncle Baldwin agreed. "We shall lock him up, Kitty, and deal with him when this is all over. Show them, Gibson."

The groom began to struggle as the guards pulled him to his feet. "I won't be there for long! They're coming for you, your high and mighty ladyship. Your bastard husband is going to die, and the brat, and you will beg to die by the time we have all finished with you. And you, Mr Baldwin. Your son has a special fate for traitors. You too, Mr Dixon. I'll tell him you were all cosy and comfortable with the enemy."

His voice cut off as he was dragged from the kitchen and one of his guard escorts closed the cellar door.

Luke came around in the dark, his head pounding like a drum, pain radiating from a lump on the back of it and throbbing from numerous other bruises on his body.

He feared he might be blind, since he could see nothing. He hoped he was merely locked in the dark. He cautiously moved each limb, glad to find he was not restrained in any way and that nothing appeared to be broken. That was a pleasant surprise, given the battering he remembered taking when Titus and half a dozen other brutes jumped out on what the groom had described as a short cut.

He'd laid quite a few blows as well as taking them, before someone bashed him over the head and laid him out.

He sat up, feeling around him. He appeared to be on a wooden pallet on the floor. No mattress. No pillow. No blanket. An earth floor, or perhaps a stone one that had not been cleaned in a long time.

He rose to a crouch, paused for a sudden surge of dizziness, then edged his way across the floor, his hands outstretched to encounter any obstacles.

In a few minutes, he had confirmed that he and the pallet were the only objects in the space, and that it was bounded on one side by bars, and in all other directions by uneven walls of rock. In one place, moisture seeped down the wall. If he had something to catch the liquid in, he could soothe his dry throat. After a moment's thought, he took off his neckcloth and spread it over a projection where it would catch the drip.

If he had to guess, he'd wager he was in one of the cave systems that burrowed under the cliffs. He had explored some of them with Barn and a group of others, long long ago, but their elders had warned them off, for the sea caves were used by the smugglers, and the smugglers did not welcome visitors. The detritus on the floor included fragments of shells and dried strands of—by the texture, shape and smell—seaweed.

The realisation was both encouraging and depressing. Encouraging, because it made it likely that his blindness was simply from lack of light this far underground. Depressing, because his chances of surviving a brush with the smugglers was not good, particularly since it seemed they were in league with Titus.

At least they had not yet killed him, which made it likely that someone would sooner or later come to do whatever he had been kept alive for. He needed to be ready to take whatever chance offered itself when that happened. He settled back down on the pallet to wait.

Palmer sent two of the guards to the ramparts of the keep, with instructions to watch for anyone approaching the Hall. Everyone still in the mansion was locked inside the keep. The cook's assistant and one of the maids were upstairs in one of the bedchambers upstairs, tending to the cook. The rest of them gathered on the lower floor of the keep, in a room that looked out over the main carriageway.

The missing books of maps—two volumes--were spread out on the table. One volume was the one Luke remembered, with the hidden ways of the Hall. The other showed the routes to the Grange, the dower house, and the coast. Gibson had produced them, admitting that he had hidden them on instructions from Aileen Baldwin when she first came back to the Hall, because she was worried about Titus using them to open up the old tunnels.

They had all had the chance to examine it, and Palmer had sent another guard to block and watch over the door that was the only access from the secret ways to the dungeon of the keep.

"We do not have enough men," Palmer said. "I beg your pardon, Lady Catherine, my lord. We do not have enough people to defend the whole Hall, but we could hold off an army from the Tower."

They had the book open to the page that showed the floor plans of the ancient keep, and he touched the drawing of the cellar level. "If this is accurate, then the only tunnel that lets into the keep is a single one into the cellars. If we can block that and the doors into the main house, we can wait them out."

"No, we cannot," Kitty objected. "Luke is in their hands. Who knows what Titus will do to him?"

Palmer's eyes were full of pity but his voice was unyielding. "Titus had no reason to keep him alive, Lady Catherine. I am sorry to have to say it, but it is true. Luke instructed me to keep you safe, and that is what I am going to do."

Paul choked down a gasp and Kitty fumbled for his hand without looking away from the head guard. "I will not accept that, Mr Palmer. Titus has a plan. If he wanted to kill Luke, he had no reason not to do so during the ambush." Of course, they only had the groom's word that Luke was captured rather than killed. She shook her head at her own thought, and perhaps Paul saw her despair for he squeezed her hand.

Dixon had been sitting slightly away from the group, slumped over in his chair, but he spoke up suddenly. "I think he is still alive," he said. "Mr Titus hates him. He wants Mr Ogilvy to suffer. I think he will try to capture Lord Baldwin or Lady Catherine so he can force Mr Ogilvy to watch him tort…" he clamped his mouth shut, blushing furiously, his eyes darting wildly around the room.

Torture. Kitty's mind supplied the word Dixon had swallowed. From Paul's wide eyes, he had worked it out, too. Kitty swallowed her own moment of panic and declared, "Well. That is good then. If you are correct, Dixon, we have time to rescue him. We had better do it soon. We have no idea when he might decide to cut his losses."

"We are stuck inside waiting for an attack," Palmer objected, "and we don't know where Mr Ogilvy is being held."

"Let us see if we can work it out." Kitty spread out the other volume, opening it to one of the earlier maps that showed the full cave and tunnel system. From the looks of it, the long-ago builders had taken advantage of natural rifts, caves and tunnels in the limestone, and joined them with man-made excavations.

Under the dower house and stretching under the forest of Ormswood was a tangle of connected caves. One of those must have been Aileen Baldwin's route out of the Hall the day Barn had seen her in the village. Another sat halfway between Ormswood Hall and St George's Grange. Long tunnels, too straight to be completely natural, but with turns and twists that hinted the builders had added to existing holes as they found them, joined these natural underground mazes to Ormswood Hall, the dower house, and the Grange.

Another tunnel took a circuitous route almost to the coast, where it connected to a complex of sea caves.

"There or there," Uncle Baldwin said, putting a finger down on the coastal caves and another on the under croft of the Grange. "He is not locked in one of the cells in our cellar, and the dower house doesn't have any cells. He could be under the Grange or in the smugglers' cells down by the coast.

"Are the cells in the actual sea caves?" Paul asked. "I mean, does the sea come into them? Because I read this story where the villain ties the hero up and leaves him in a sea cave, so if he is killed and can't come back for the hero, then the tide will come in and finish the job for him."

"An unlikely scenario, your lordship," Palmer said dismissively. "I wouldn't worry your head about it. Ridiculous what these writer types think up."

Uncle Baldwin, Gibson and Dixon all spoke at once, in a weird chorus. "It is just the sort of thing my son would do." "Mr Titus would think of it. He has always been one to make plans for all the eventualities he can." "I think I know the book, Lord Baldwin. Mr Titus read it last winter."

Palmer snorted.

Kitty ignored him. "Uncle Baldwin, where would I find an almanac with the tide times?"

"The Tyne Mercury, my dear," he replied. "It gives the tides for

Newcastle. They are a few minutes later this far up the coast." He was rubbing his shoulder, and his jaw was set with pain.

Kitty reached out and touched his hand. It was clammy and cold. "Uncle Baldwin, you are not well. This has all been too much for you. Won't you let Gibson help you to bed?"

"They're coming!" One of the guard lookouts burst into the room already shouting. "Across the fields from the Grange. Around a score of them!"

From the window, they could see men, mounted and on foot, approaching over the lawn.

"We will be safe in here," Uncle Baldwin insisted, but his voice shook.

A plan burst into Kitty's mind as the others around the table exclaimed over the attack and made suggestions for defending the keep. She examined it in her mind while she waited for the initial reaction to simmer down.

When there was a pause, she spoke. "I have an idea." In the past two weeks, she had been included in all of the strategy discussions that Luke had held with Palmer, and had often successfully argued a point. Even so, she was not sure if the head guard would listen to her when Luke was not there to back her view.

He narrowed his eyes as he regarded her. His assessment must have been in her favour for he nodded. "Yes, my lady?"

"It depends upon those out there being most of them," Kitty warned. "But I think that is probable. They will search the house, first, spreading out. But sooner or later, they will find that the door to the keep is locked, and then they will attempt to breech the keep."

"They'll find that hard," Palmer promised. "We will be waiting for them."

"Not if we have already left," Kitty countered.

The other guards made angry or derisive noises. Palmer raised his eyebrows, but said only, "Go on," which silenced his men.

Kitty ignored them, speaking directly to the head guard. "I propose that we split up. Those who are unfit to fight take refuge on the highest level of the tower, with every door between them and the ground floor shut, locked, and barred. The keep is stone. Little in it will burn. Hacking their way through the doors will entertain our invaders while the rest of us go around them. Or under them, I should say."

Palmer nodded, slowly. "Through the tunnel. What if they are waiting for us?"

"That's why we need to go as fast as possible, while they are busy searching the house. If a few of them are already in the hidden ways, we should be able to handle them. I suggest we head back towards the Grange, then divert into the caves and head…"

She examined the relevant map, and put her finger on the house marked with dotted lines in a different colour near the far edge of the maze of natural caves and passages. "Head to the Pattison farm. We gather whatever neighbours are willing to support us, send one of them for the volunteer troops, then come back and attack the attackers."

"It could work," said the man who had made the derisive noise, sounding surprised.

"It will work," Paul insisted.

"We'll do it," Palmer decided. "Lady Kitty, I will leave you in charge of the non-combatants."

"I am coming with you," Kitty told him. "Paul and I both. If the enemy is in the tunnels, you will need every fighter you can have. We are both skilled with knife, sword, gun, and bow."

She held up her hand for silence when Palmer opened his mouth. "Do not bother to remind me that Luke told you to keep us safe. You will keep us safe by getting out of here and getting help, and your best chance of doing that is to have us with you."

Palmer inclined his head. "You are right," he said. He let his gaze roam over the servants. "Who stays and who comes?" he asked.

Uncle Baldwin argued, but in the end accepted that he would be a liability. He, Gibson, and the maids promised to bar the doors as they made their way upstairs, once the two maids who would shut and block the door to the tunnels returned to join them.

Millie insisted on joining the expedition into the tunnels. The

Redepenning footmen volunteered, too, and Dixon wasn't given a choice. Palmer said he'd rather have Titus's valet under his eye.

"But if you acquit yourself well," Kitty told him, "we will speak in your favour."

And Paul added, "You are a member of the family, after all."

Down in the cellars, the man who had been sent to guard the door had moved away the racks that had concealed it. He reported he had heard nothing from the tunnels, though that was not necessarily reassuring. It looked like the rest of the keep's solid doors— two thick layers of oak, the second layer pinned to the first with the grain at right angles. Hard for a sound to penetrate, or an axe.

They organised themselves for a swift exit. Palmer and three of the guard took the lead, with the last bringing up the rear behind Dixon, Kitty, Paul, Millie, and the two footmen.

"Right," Palmer said, nodding to the guard who had removed the bars that held the door shut. The man pressed down the latch and threw his weight into pulling the door open.

A light ahead alerted them to the presence of someone in the tunnel a moment before a shout. Palmer and his men were already in motion, and were onto the two intruders before they could escape.

One was knocked out in the fight. The other babbled protestations of innocence. He worked for the squire, and had been forced to join the smugglers, he insisted. "I don't want to hurt anybody," he sobbed.

The man knocked out was one of the smugglers, sent with the footman to make sure he behaved. "We were meant to get into the cellars and try to open the door to the rest of the house," the footman told them.

One of the guards had quickly and efficiently tied the smuggler's wrists and ankles using a coil of stockinette he had in his belt pack. Palmer set the Grange footman and Dixon to carrying the man and behind them, the maids shut the door, plunging the party into darkness, the lantern Palmer now carried their only light.

Nobody spoke, apart from a sigh of relief when they reached the junction from which another tunnel led, according to the maps, to the tangle of passages and caves under the Grange. It was a fifteen-minute walk, conducted in near darkness and in silence.

The tunnel twisted and turned a couple of times, and sometimes steps led up or down. It widened and narrowed. In places, a stream emerged from a crack in the rock and ran beside them, once even spreading over the path, before vanishing back into the rock again.

At last, the passage they were in opened out into a cavern. Palmer lifted the lantern. Shadows on the walls around them hinted at openings in the rock. To recesses, caves, or other passages? The light did not pierce far enough to be sure.

Kitty recited the directions she had memorised back at the keep. "We take the first passage on the right and keep to the right at the next three forks."

Palmer responded. "Then, at the fourth fork, we take the second passage on the right, and again at the fifth. The first set of stairs on the left will bring us to the Pattison cellar."

Good. That was what Kitty remembered, too. She fell back to walk with Paul and Millie. Palmer led the way around the edge of the cavern, passing three hollows that proved to be shallow caves, and turning into the first passage.

After the fourth fork, Palmer halted suddenly, whispering they should step back. Kitty, who was close behind him again, saw another light ahead. It stopped, then cautiously approached, until Kitty could see the dark shape of a man behind the lantern.

"Who's there?" The stranger made the question a demand.

"Identify yourself," Palmer snapped in return.

Kitty thought she recognised the voice. "Barn Pattison?"

The man lifted the lantern and peered in her direction. "Lady Catherine? Are you…? Who are these men with you? Has Lord Baldwin…?"

"I'm here," Paul acknowledged. "Mr Pattison, these men are on our side. Are you?"

Pattison took a couple of steps forward, the lantern still held high to illuminate the relieved smile on his face. He spoke over his shoulder. "They're safe, lads. They've rescued themselves. Lady

Catherine, we heard that the Hall was under attack and we were coming to see what we could do to help."

"We were on our way to you," Kitty told him. "The Hall is under attack, and Luke has been captured. How many people will stand with us?"

One of the men behind Pattison said, "Let's get upstairs to your place, Barn. I want to see the faces of the people I'm going to trust."

"Couldn't agree more," Palmer grumbled.

CHAPTER 30

Barn's group turned and led the way through the next two turns and up the stairs, which brought them into a cellar and to another flight of steps which emerged in a farmhouse kitchen.

As Kitty's people followed the others, the kitchen filled with wary men, each group eyeing the other with suspicion. "Tea?" Barn asked. "Or ale?"

"Thank you, but we do not have time for that," Kitty told him. "Titus Baldwin and a gang of smugglers have invaded the Hall. Mr Marcus Baldwin and some of our servants are holding out in the Keep, behind locked doors, but eventually Titus will either break in, or give up and move on to taking his revenge on the district."

"What do you want us to do?" said one of the other men with Barn. "We're farmers, not soldiers."

"I want someone to ride for the excise men and the volunteer force at Berwick-Upon-Tweed, and the rest of you to harry the enemy so they are kept busy until the troops can get here," Kitty said. "I have letters for the commander in charge, so you need not fear being ignored."

"It might not be so easy," Barn warned. "Lady Thayne is friends with the wife of the commander in charge. The last man to approach him was arrested for slandering a gentleman."

"I'll go," Paul said. "I'm a baron. That outranks a baronet."

"Will he listen to a boy?" Palmer asked Barn.

"Possibly," Barn thought. "Backed up by her ladyship's letter."

"There's also a letter from Marcus Baldwin," Kitty offered.

"You go with him, Barn," said one of the other farmers. "You're the most prosperous farmer in the district. And you can get the excise officers to listen, in any case."

Barn spoke directly to Kitty. "We've all been afraid to talk to the excise officers since Titus and Sir Thaddeus teamed up with the smugglers. Just a few people had to lose crops or be convicted on false charges or see animals or family members hurt, for us all to do what we were told."

One of the others commented, "We learned not to refuse to offer a horse or a cart or a strong back. We learned to keep our mouths shut."

"But they've taken it as license to terrorise the neighbourhood and take anything they want," a third said.

"We've sent our families away, and we're prepared to lose every-thing else if we can bring them down," Barn declared. "Others won't join us, but we think we've figured out who will help Titus and who will look the other way and pretend they don't see us. Young lord, how good a rider are you?"

"Luke trained me," Paul replied.

Barn nodded. "Good enough. Lady Catherine, it would be best if you came with us."

Kitty thought about that. Palmer would not let her go to rescue Luke on her own. Nor would he—or should he—divert resources from the defeat of Titus and the smugglers.

"We have a prisoner to deal with," she replied. "Palmer, I'll take Dixon and Frayne's footman, and find somewhere I can lock this man up. When we're finished, we'll join you back at the assault on the Hall."

Palmer looked at her, and then at the footman. "You understand that Titus and Frayne have lost." he said.

The footman nodded, his eyes wide. "And a good thing, too," he replied.

"He's my brother-in-law," said one of the farmers. "Henry! You'll not betray the lady, will you?"

Henry shook his head. "I'm your man, my lady," he assured her.

Palmer turned his eyes to Dixon. "I don't trust you. But I do trust Lady Catherine to shoot you if you make a single wrong move."

Dixon rolled his eyes towards Kitty and nodded. "I want to help," he said.

That wasn't the last of the discussion, of course. It was carried through to the stable while Barn selected his two best horses and he and Paul had several sets of willing hands to help bridle and saddle them.

But at last, the group split to go three separate ways. Barn and Paul, their horses' hooves muffled, set off at a slow walk through the least used lanes towards the Great North Road some two miles inland. Once on the road, they'd be able to ride as fast as the dying light of day allowed. They would be at least three hours on the road. If the men in charge at Berwick Castle allowed themselves to be persuaded, help would arrive in about six hours.

Palmer, his men, the other farmers and the footmen from the Hall set off through the fields towards the Grange to check how many men were left in reserve, to neutralise them if they could, and then to go and attack the Hall's invaders from the rear.

Kitty led Millie and her two men away from the village and towards the coast. The smuggler, now gagged since he had regained consciousness with a stream of vituperation—was bound to the back of one of Barn's horses.

"Isn't there somewhere in the village we can leave this brute?" Dixon asked.

"We are going to rescue Mr Luke, aren't we, my lady?" Millie said.

Kitty might as well tell them. If Dixon and Henry were going to let her down, best to know now. "Yes, Millie. I am gambling he is in the cells shown in one of the sea caves, and that he has not more than one or two guards. If he is there, we need to get to him before the tide. If he is not, we can go back to the Grange.

"He might not be guarded," Dixon offered. "The cells have stout bars and locks. Mr Titus might have left Mr Ogilvy on his own, for the tide."

He'd said that before, and Kitty didn't need to hear it again, for her whole being was strained towards reaching Luke before the sea could do so.

"Won't be high tide for a while," Henry offered. "I attended Sir Thaddeus this afternoon on a visit to the docks, and the tide was going out. Reckon it'll be two hours or so before the caves are flooded as high as they go. Won't fill the caves, either. The moon isn't full and there's no storm."

Kitty could feel her body slumping as the tension drained out. She stiffened her spine and kept walking. They still had to find the right cave, subdue any guards, and get Luke out of a locked cell.

There was still enough light to make the twenty-minute walk easy. They covered the ground to the cliffs above the fishing village in silence, seeing no one. And yes, the high tide mark was still a few feet above where waves were breaking on the beach and over the rocks. They were in time, but they would need to hurry. From what Henry said, the cells were completely flooded only in a spring tide, but even now, Luke might be standing in water, and they might have to wade to the rescue.

"You two stay here with the prisoner," she told Dixon and Henry. "Millie and I will scout the area." She adjusted her quiver so she could reach it quickly, took half a dozen arrows, and set one into her small hunting bow.

"I should do that, my lady," Dixon protested. "You are a lady! I can be trusted. I promise."

Kitty thought she probably could trust the man not to betray them, but she wasn't going to risk it. "Stay here," she repeated. "My husband trained me and Millie in woodcraft. We will not be in danger, and will return when we know whether there are guards."

There were. Two men, sitting on a ledge part way up the rock outside of a cave that was awash with each wave. They were passing a bottle between them as they took it in turns to toss a pair of dice.

With all their focus on their game, they didn't see Millie and Kitty creep towards them. Not until Kitty stood, her arrow nocked and her bow drawn. "Hands up," she said.

Both men reached for the guns that lay beside them. Two arrows flew, and both flinched back, dropping the guns into the wave. One gun had an arrow in the stock. The other arrow had glanced off the gun that was its target and struck its holder in the face.

"Millie, collect their guns," Kitty commanded.

Her maid put her own gun down and crept forward, taking care not to get between Kitty and the two smugglers.

"You won't shoot," one of the smugglers ventured. "You're a girl."

"She did shoot, you fool," hissed the other.

"And hit exactly where I aimed," Kitty told them. "The next two arrows will go into your black hearts. That will leave me two spare and another six I can reach and fire in seconds. Don't move. Don't speak. Don't think. Millie, fetch the others."

Millie quickly returned with Dixon, Henry and the bound smuggler, and soon the two who had been guarding the cave were also bound and gagged.

Luke's assumption that he was in a cell in the sea caves was confirmed with the first wash of sea water to surge into the cell, splash onto his boot, and recede. *I am in for an unpleasant few hours, then.*

When he and Barn had explored here long ago as boys, the scold they'd received had included dire warnings about how the sea filled the caves at full tide. He learned later that the water level was deepest near the entrance. Fifty yards back, in the cells, a full-grown man could stand with his head above the waves in all but the highest spring tides. The boys might have had to breathe between wave peaks, but they would not have drowned.

The warning about the tides and the smugglers did not keep them from exploring, but it did cause them to keep an eye on the waters, the ships at anchor, and the donkey trains down from the whisky stills in the hills.

Today was not a spring tide.

In the darkness, he had nothing to do but worry about his wife and his boy, and measure the depth of the water as, minute by minute, wave by wave, it crept higher. First, the water receded between each splash against his boots. A while later, he was standing ankle deep at its lowest level, and the waves struck his calf and splashed up to his knee.

The trough of the wave was at his knee when he saw a light in the direction of the sea. The light, at first shining from beyond the curve of the cave, resolved into a lantern coming towards him.

Luke braced for whatever Titus had in mind for him. In the next moment, his heart soared as the shape behind the candle spoke in a voice he knew better than he knew his own. "I think I see bars."

"Kitty?" Luke called.

The lantern checked in its progress, then its carrier hurried forward. "Luke!"

It was Kitty! He had both hands through the bars reaching for hers before she arrived at the cell. She handed her lantern behind her, briefly illuminating Millie Price's face, and then he clasped both of her hands in his and had his lips on those offered to him between the bars.

"Kitty," he repeated, as the touch of her flooded him with renewed strength.

"Luke, my love. Thank goodness. How can we get you out of here?"

"I'm locked in. Were there men guarding the cave? Did one of them have the key?"

"No keys." Another two figures came into the lamp light, carrying something between them. It was one of them who had spoken. "I can try to pick it if someone has some wire."

The other person interrupted. "Lady Kitty, we can't put this brute down. He'll drown. He'll be out of the water if we carry him further in."

"There are steps about ten paces further on with a cave above," Luke offered. "Can you get him up there?"

"Let me take your place, Mr Dixon." The offer came from Millie. "Henry and I will stash this one away and go back for the others while you open the door and let Mr Ogilvy out."

Kneeling, the man called Dixon had water up to his chest, and had to lift his chin to avoid the highest waves. He inserted two of Kitty's hairpins into the lock and put his ear close to it as he moved them around.

At his request, everyone else remained silent. While he worked, Millie and the man she called Henry passed back out of the cave and returned with a second bound man. They had just reached the cell after depositing that man up the stairs when Dixon gave a sigh of satisfaction, and the cell door swung open.

Luke stepped out and took his wife in his arms. "Are you well? Is Paul?"

Kitty summarised the events of the afternoon. "Paul and your friend Barn Pattison headed north to Berwick to fetch help. Titus and his smuggler friends are besieging the Hall. We crept out through the tunnels while they were breaking into the house, and made our way first to Barn and then here. The other farmers and the guard are attacking the besiegers from the rear."

"Let's go and help," Luke suggested. "Who are these with you?"

Millie was the only one still there. "Henry and Mr Dixon have gone to fetch the last prisoner before he drowns," she said.

Dixon spoke out of the darkness. "The ledge was already under water, but at least he is still breathing."

"Not happy, though," Henry added. "Lady Catherine, it is getting deep out there by the cave mouth."

"Luke, this is George Dixon, former valet to your cousin Titus, and Henry, former footman to the Fraynes, who are in league with Titus."

"Yes, so I discovered," Luke told her. "We can get out through the back of the caves, Henry. Either onto the cliff top or through the tunnels." He led the way up the steps followed by the two women. "Can Titus's valet and Frayne's footman be trusted?" he whispered, while Dixon and Henry were bringing the last smuggler up to safety.

"I think so," Kitty murmured back. "They have been helpful so far."

Luke nodded, thoughtfully. "We'll trust them as far as we can see them, I guess."

She gave him a wry grin. "That's what Millie and I have been doing."

"If we keep going this way," Luke said, as they continued into the cave, "We'll come to the steps up onto the cliff and the tunnel to the Grange."

"If we take the underground route, we'll be going the long way round," Kitty pointed out. "Let us go overland and get to the Hall more quickly. If Paul and Barn made good time, they'll be halfway to Berwick by now. But realistically, we may not see the excise men or the volunteers until lunchtime tomorrow. We should help Palmer."

"Right," Luke said. "Overland it is." He lifted the lantern, and there before them was a wooden staircase leading up flight after flight into the gloom above.

Luke waved the others on ahead, handing the lantern to Millie who led the way. He could not wait a moment longer to kiss his wife, to revel in the feel of her body against his. "I thought I would never hold you again," he murmured.

"I wasn't going to let that happen," replied his redoubtable wife, before melting into his kiss.

CHAPTER 31

The besiegers were besieged. Palmer and those with him had
Titus's attackers pinned down in the new wing. "They were
searching the house," he explained to Luke," and it was easy to pick
off those who were alone in other parts of the house and to herd
larger groups in the right direction. I wanted them where they
would have no access to the hidden passages or the tunnels."

Even though several of the villagers and men from the farms
had joined their side, they were spread thin, keeping watch on the
external walls of the new wing as well as the inside doors that joined
it to the rest of the house on all three levels. Palmer had beaten back
two attempts to break free, "But if they have the sense to sacrifice a
few footmen in a feint, they could get out another way while we are
containing the first group," he acknowledged.

"What of our own people in the keep?" Kitty asked.

"They are still barricaded upstairs in the keep," Palmer said.
"Gibson and I thought it best for those who can't fight to stay out of
reach. We don't want the villains to have any hostages." Gibson had
reported that Cook had recovered consciousness and was spitting
mad at him, and even more so at Mrs Embolton and Mrs Baldwin,
who were presumably behind the poisoning.

Uncle Baldwin was asleep, and Gibson hoped he would not wake again until the whole crisis was over.

Luke turned to practicalities. "Have your men been fed, Palmer?"

"No time," Palmer answered. "They could do with something to eat. Something to drink, too."

Luke turned to Kitty and she rose to the occasion. "A cup of tea or failing that, small beer. As to food, Millie and I will see what we can find in the pantry. Henry and Dixon, you can come with us to help us serve those on watch."

"Can those two men be trusted?" Palmer asked, as she led the way into the house by the nearest door.

Luke returned Kitty's answer. "They've been helpful so far, and Kitty and Millie can handle them if they think to betray us. Let's do the rounds of our sentinels."

They moved from post to post, chatting for a few minutes with each pair of sentries, taking care to remain in the shadows so they did not present a target. The windows of the new wing were dark, but a number of them were open and any one of them might have a man with a rifle behind. Those who were not trained to be cautious had received a quick lesson when several of them were shot at.

"One minor flesh wound, not much more than a scratch," Palmer reported. "The other shots missed. They're either not marksmen, or they have old weapons that are not accurate beyond fifty yards. Still, the men are not about to give them target practice and find out!"

Inside, where their people guarded the doors between the new wing and the rest of the house, they met up with Kitty and Henry carrying bread, cheese and ale to the guards. "Millie and Dixon are going around outside," Kitty said as she passed Luke his portion.

A clatter of feet on the stairs preceded Millie, with Dixon at her elbow. "A troop of horses coming from inland," she reported. "At least thirty, by their torches, says the maid on watch on the tower."

"Reinforcements for them or for us?" Palmer wondered. "Our people could not have reached Berwick yet. Watch for an attempt at a breakout," he commanded. He and Luke took off at a run towards the servants stairs to the attics, followed by Kitty.

From an attic window, they could see the road from the highway to the west, and a column of approaching torches that flicked in and out of view, now one part of the column, now another, as they went over hills or out from behind trees. They were not more than half a mile away, and approaching rapidly.

"This is earlier than I would have looked for the troops from Berwick," Luke commented. "I find it hard to believe the smugglers could muster such a crowd, though. Or ride in such disciplined ranks."

A crash from below followed by several shots had them running for the stairs again, Luke doing his best to keep Kitty behind him. On the ground floor, the hall outside the double doors to the new wing were in chaos, with wounded men from both sides still fighting. Luke shot a man who was taking aim at Millie, who was crouched defensively over the body of Dixon.

The arrival of new combatants turned the tide, and soon they had three prisoners, one seriously injured. On their own side, all three of the defenders of this door were wounded, one of them a tenant farmer who had taken a stab to the chest that was likely to be lethal. Dixon had been knocked out by a bullet that creased his skull. Another wound in his side was probably more serious.

"He threw himself in front of me," Millie told Kitty and Luke, a catch in her words as she fought back a sob.

"They broke out in strength," Palmer's man told his commander. "They went that way." He pointed down the passage on the other side of the hall. At a nod from Palmer, a guardsman hurried after them.

"Bastards abandoned us," one of the attackers complained. "Leave the wounded, that mad bastard Titus Baldwin said, and the captain did it. Told us we'd all break out together, all stick together. Bastard."

The guard came back to say the enemy had gone into the tunnels. "We need to organise a pursuit, pull our people in to defend the Hall if those approaching are enemies, and check the new wing in case my cousin has left any nasty surprises," Luke summarised.

"I'll make sure the wounded are cared for," Kitty assured him.

It had all fallen apart, but Titus had a plan for that, too. When a watchman first noticed the approaching troops, he'd had a moment's triumph, thinking the Scot had sent people to subdue Titus's treacherous tenants and neighbours. But the captain had soon disabused him.

"We don't have that many men," he said. "Besides. Look at those torches. Those men are riding in column. Those are trained troops, and far more of them than we can handle."

"We run," Titus said, crisply. A gentleman played the hand he was dealt. He led the assault that saw them overrun those guarding the exit closest to the hidden door he wanted, and was first into the hidden ways. Within a minute, they were down into the cellars and through them into the caves below.

They headed for the Grange, where they separated, only Titus, his butler and two of his grooms climbing the steps up to the Grange cellars and into the house. The smugglers and the rest of the locals ran for the coast.

"Good luck," Titus wished them. "If you have time, whip down to the cells and shoot my cousin for me, would you?" Titus should have done it himself. The tide wouldn't be high enough to kill the bastard. Unless he was still unconscious, of course. Titus could hope for that.

He doubted his allies would escape. The troops were on horseback, and would be waiting for them at the other end of the tunnel. Titus hoped they wouldn't tell the authorities where to look for Luke. If the bastard didn't drown, he could starve to death.

Emmie Frayne had seen the troops, too, and she and Mother were already at the stables, chivvying the Frayne grooms who were putting the horses into the traces as fast as they could.

"Into the carriage, Mother, Emmie," he ordered. The men would go faster without the women nagging them.

"Where is Thaddeus?" Emmie demanded. The silly cow had always thought she was in charge, just because he tupped her. He had tolerated her delusions because she kept Frayne under his control, but she no longer had that benefit. If he took her with him, she would have to learn that her place was no different to that of any other woman.

"Dead," he told her, baldly. Probably dead. He'd been shot in the stomach and was no longer able to fight. Not that he'd been much use before he was downed. The men he was with took him into the new wing with them, but Titus hadn't allowed him to be a nuisance. He had just ordered him dumped on a bed, and sent the men back to watching the windows.

The women were still standing there, staring at him. "Get in the carriage. Now!"

"Titus!" his mother scolded. "The woman has just lost her husband."

"Get in, or stay here," Titus told them both. They jumped at his tone and clambered aboard. Good. The Hall's butler, at a nod from Titus, climbed in too. The ladies could make what they liked of that.

He spoke to the milling group of grooms and footmen, waiting for direction. "The rest of you, grab horses and follow. Once the troops have combined forces with the people at the Hall, they'll be after us."

He climbed up onto the driver's seat, shouldering aside the man who was preparing to take up the reins. "I'll do it," he said. "You take a gun and watch for pursuit."

Those holding the team stepped away, and Titus shook the reins and cracked the whip over the horses' heads. They took off out of the stable yard at a gallop.

Which way? They couldn't take the road inland. There was nothing to say another troop wasn't right behind the other. North or south on the coast road? Berwick, where the excise and military were quartered, blocked the way north. He had a berth on a ship there, but he also had one on a ship at Newcastle. Double insurance in case the smugglers failed him. South, then.

He reached the end of the carriage way and took the corner onto the road south without slowing, the carriage lurching a bit as it settled back on its wheels after the fast turn.

Moments later they passed the side road to the Hall and shortly after that, they raced through the village. Over the rattles and groans of the carriage and the clatter of his team, he could hear hooves behind him.

"Who follows?" he shouted.

"Our men," yelled back the man he'd set to watch the pursuit. Good. With luck, the troops would pursue the smugglers and leave him to get away clear and free, at least for the moment. Perhaps for good if he let them have the occupants of the carriage. He could just walk off when they got to the wharf. Leave them searching for him while he got away.

He needed another plan. He wouldn't go to the ship, he decided. Dixon knew the name of the one where the berth was waiting, for Dixon had bought the tickets. And the traitor had gone over to the other side. Titus had seen him with the enemy, carrying food and a beaker of some beverage to a guard post. He'd stepped into the light. The only reason he wasn't lying dead, the treacherous scum, was that the men in the new wing had been told to conserve their ammunition, and by the time Titus had grabbed a gun, the woman with Dixon had dragged him out of range and into the shadows.

No. Titus would abandon the carriage and buy a horse. Or steal one. That would be wiser. Harder to trace. How far to the next place that might have a boat large enough to take him to the continent? Perhaps he could hide out at Tynemouth and get a fishing boat to take him out to one of the ships as it sailed from Newcastle.

The shout from his man interrupted his reverie as the carriage raced up the hill towards the top of the cliffs. "Troops!"

Titus risked a quick glance backwards. His grooms were peeling off in a frantic effort to evade capture by leaping hedgerows into the fields, but the troops were ignoring them to thunder ever closer behind him.

He reached the top of the climb, and the hedgerow on the coast side dwindled to nothing. Ahead, the road dipped again to a small bay, then rose on the other side, vague in the moonlight except for the torches of another column of horses coming towards him down that slope.

Hell. He did not doubt for one minute that they were coming for him. His father had always told him his sins would catch up with him. He gave a bark of harsh laughter. *Damned it would be, then.*

He wrenched on the reins, driving the horses straight across the short rough ground between them and the cliff top. They fought him, of course, but the ground was slippery with dew and they could not get purchase on the slope. In a moment, they were over, and the carriage after them, the horses' screams echoed by those of the females. Or was one of those screams that of the butler?

Time slowed as they all drifted downwards. He had what seemed like minutes to worry the fall would not kill him. But the rocks disclosed by a retreating wave removed that concern.

Titus would have death at a time of his own choosing, and company on his final journey. That would have to be victory enough.

CHAPTER 32

Luke pursued Titus and the smugglers, leaving Palmer and Kitty to greet their rescuers and bring order to the chaos at the Hall. Dixon said his employer planned to go to Newcastle-Upon-Tyne. "He has passage on the Ariadne, sir," he explained. "But he might not risk taking it. Still, he will want the money I collected for him. I left it with the innkeeper at the Drunken Nanny, and sent him a letter, care of Lady Frayne, to say it was there."

The block in the tunnel to the dower house worked to Luke's advantage. The villains had gone underground, so they must have headed to the Grange. He and the two guards with him borrowed horses from the farmers who had come to help, and rode overland to the Frayne's manor, arriving on the edge of the wood just in time to see the carriage explode out of the stable yard, bounce down the short carriage way, and take the corner onto the road on two wheels, only narrowly missing the gate post.

Titus was driving. His hat had blown off, and he was standing, his legs spread and an unholy grin on his face.

Titus was heading south, so Dixon was probably right. "Let's see how much speed we can get out of these beasts," Luke said to the guards. He led the way across field and hedgerow, keeping an eye on the carriage to make sure it continued in the expected direction.

Various other horsemen had followed the carriage out of the stable yard and were still with it, until one of them looked back, shouted to his mates, and jumped the hedgerow to race off across the fields.

A troop of horsemen, their torches marking their passage, were gaining on the carriage.

The road dropped to a cove where it joined the coast road. Titus turned south. Luke set off on the diagonal, crossing the fields to get ahead of his cousin's carriage. The troops stayed on the road.

And there! Coming towards the carriage on the road from the south! More torches in neat ordered lines. More troops? Where did they come from?

Titus must have seen them, too. Before Lucius knew what Titus was about, his cousin drove the horses straight over the cliff.

Luke jumped the hedgerow and ditch to the road, and threw himself off his horse. A little way from where Titus's carriage had gone over, he flung himself down on his belly to crawl to the edge.

It was too dark to see much—just vague shapes in monochrome. Black lumps and shifting patterns of white. Rocks with waves breaking over them. The carriage and the poor horses must be broken among the rocks. Surely nothing could have survived that fall?

"Mr Ogilvy?" said one of the guards.

He pushing himself backward away from the edge and stood to find that the troop of soldiers who had followed from the Hall had arrived behind him and were holding him and his two companions at gun point.

"Titus Baldwin?" the officer in charge asked.

"Lucius Ogilvy," Luke answered. "I am the guardian of Lord Baldwin who, I take it, brought you here to the Hall." He pointed down and behind him. "Titus Baldwin was driving the carriage."

"I can't take your word for that, can I?" argued the officer. "This Baldwin is a slippery customer, by all accounts." He looked beyond Luke and Luke turned to see the other troop of soldiers riding up.

This was a much larger group, and their uniform was gaudier. Scarlet, with green facings and gilt buttons. "What are the Tinsel Dons doing here?" the officer with Luke muttered.

To his surprise, Luke recognised the man in civilian clothing riding beside the commander of the troop. "Mr Tolliver!" he exclaimed. The gentleman was one of those who had questioned him and Paul about the French spies. He had never explained his interest or his authority.

Rede knew him, though. He was an irregular connection of the Haverford family, to whom Rede was connected by marriage, and the head of a shadowy Crown agency that concerned itself with defending the United Kingdom from traitors and spies. He was a spymaster, in other words.

The spymaster touched two fingers to his hat in greeting. "Mr Ogilvy," he replied. He nodded towards the clifftop. "Your cousin?"

"Dead, I assume." Luke shrugged. "I could not see the details."

"We shall set people to watch," Tolliver said. "Colonel Clennel, may I present Mr Lucius Ogilvy of Ormswood Hall? Mr Ogilvy, Colonel Clennel." He beckoned to another civilian, who rode a few paces forward. "And this is Supervisor Wilson from Customs and Excise. Colonel Clennel and his men have been good enough to lend their support to the suppression of the smugglers who have been trading secrets across the channel." He turned his gaze on the officer of the other troop. "But I take it we have arrived after the fact. You are, sir?"

The officer drew himself to attention, and managed to address both Tolliver and Clennel, without committing himself to deciding who was in charge. "Lieutenant Bacon of the Loyal Berwick Volunteers, sir. My colonel is chasing the smugglers, sir, and I was sent to pursue Mr Baldwin. Sir."

"I will lend you some people to watch the clifftops and the coves on both sides until we can assess the crash by daylight," Clennel told Bacon. "If anyone has survived the crash and tries to leave the area, detain them and bring them to me in the morning. At the Hall, I take it?" He addressed his question to Tolliver, but Luke answered it. "You and your men are welcome to the hospitality of the Hall, sir, though we have just fought a pitched battle with the smugglers and Titus's bullies. You will need to take us as you find us."

"The volunteer force from Berwick was already on its way," Paul reported to Kitty, when she commented on the speed with which he had returned. "We met them just out of Belford. Barn figured they must be out on exercises, and he stopped them to tell them we needed them."

"And they agreed to come and help," Kitty commented, to assure him she was listening, though in truth most of her attention was on the chaos that was slowly being restored to order by the mixed group of servants, villagers and soldiers under her direction and Barn's.

"They were already coming," Paul explained. "The excise men got a tip-off from someone called Jock. This Jock is a well-known smuggler, the commander told me, but his partners have been carrying information and spies for the French, and Jock wasn't happy about it. He said he has brothers and cousins in the field against Napoleon, and he wasn't going to help the French to kill them."

The excise men had gone off with Luke and most of the brigade of volunteers, pursuing the smugglers and Titus. Kitty had to stay calm, had to keep working, had to set an example for all of those who were looking to her for leadership. But inside, her heart was yearning for Luke, and her mind kept fracturing as her thoughts skittered away from the demands of the situation before her to fret after the man she loved.

Her ears didn't register the sound outside until Paul said, "Horses. A lot of them." He gave the blankets he was carrying to a passing villager. "Take these to the doctor's wife. Come on, Kitty. It might be Luke!"

Luke was just dismounting in the forecourt, and he approached her with a civilian and a couple of officers. Behind them, many soldiers dismounted and began to lead the horses towards the nearby field. Some were in the dark blue of the volunteer troop from Berwick. Most were in scarlet, with green lapels.

"Is all well here?" Luke asked. The words were practical, but his hand reached for hers and his eyes said all that he would not speak in public.

At his touch, the cold core of fear that had haunted her warmed and dissolved. She clutched him as her one anchor in an uncertain word, but managed to retain her dignity and his by resisting the urge to cast herself onto his shoulder and weep with relief. "We are making sense of it," she replied.

"I have brought guests with me, my lady," he said, his eyes apologetic. "Allow me to present Colonel Clennel of the Newcastle volunteers, Mr Tolliver, who represents the Crown, Lieutenant Bacon of the Berwick volunteers, and Supervisor Wilson from Custom and Excise. Gentlemen, my wife, Lady Catherine Ogilvy, and this young gentleman is Lord Baldwin, my ward."

Kitty had seen the civilian in the company of the Duchess of Haverford. His real name was Fitzgrenford, and the Marquis of Aldridge called him Uncle Tolly. She met his gaze as she offered him greetings, and his slight smile said he knew she recognised him, and was pleased she accepted the name he was using in this company.

"We can camp with our men," the Newcastle colonel assured her. "Mr Ogilvy has offered the use of the nearby field."

"Not at all," Kitty assured him, her mind feverishly planning which bedchambers to open and which maids to allocate to making beds. "Come inside, gentlemen, and have a drink and something to eat while your rooms are being prepared."

She saw them to the drawing room and left them to Luke and Paul while she gave Millie instructions to pass on to the maids. Barn approached. "I think we have done what we can tonight, Lady Catherine," he said. "I've told our helpers to go down to the kitchen for a bite to eat and then find their beds. Was that Luke I saw coming in with some fancy soldiers?"

"Luke and a volunteer force from Newcastle," she told him. "Come and meet them, Barn."

Luke introduced him as, "One of our most prominent local farmers and the organiser of the opposition to Titus and the smugglers." He poured his friend a brandy.

Even Paul had a finger's depth in a glass. "Kitty," he said. "Luke says that Titus is probably dead. He drove his carriage off the cliffs and into the sea."

Kitty turned to Luke, who confirmed the story, and also explained the timely arrival of the Newcastle contingent. "Mr Tolliver got a message from an agent to say that Titus was conspiring with the smugglers to attack the Hall."

"Apparently," Paul told her, "Titus was selling secrets to the French, sending them over the channel with the smugglers. Mr Tolliver has been investigating him for some time. He arranged Titus's escape and you will never guess who his agent is!"

Kitty hadn't until that moment, but several pieces fell into place. "Dixon," she declared, and Paul's face fell. "I didn't know," she assured him, "but it makes sense."

"A good lad," Mr Tolliver said. "He intended to leave his master when he knew the villain was pumping Mr Baldwin senior for information and selling it to the French, but we persuaded him to stay on and work for us. How is Mr Baldwin? Mr Ogilvy tells me he was unwell."

At that moment, Gibson came into the room. The usually contained and immaculately presented manservant was dishevelled and distressed, tears running down his face as he hurried to Kitty and grabbed her hands. "Oh, my lady, my lady. It is my master. He is…"

He turned to Luke. "Sir, he heard you had arrived home and insisted on coming to ask you about Master Titus. He was hurrying, sir. I said I would come and fetch you. He didn't want to wait." Tears were streaming down the man's face.

"He has had another attack?" Luke asked.

"Dead, sir. My lady. My master is dead."

Three days later, Luke and Paul stood at the gravesides as the Baldwins were laid to rest: father, mother and son. They had attended the Fraynes funeral, too, immediately before. Sir Thaddeus had died of his injuries. Lady Frayne's body had been found with Mrs Baldwin's and that of the Hall's butler, still in the carriage. They had probably died on impact, but if not, the carriage would have been fully flooded at high time.

The wreckage had also included the poor horses. Titus's body had been found a few hundred yards away, badly battered not just by the fall but by being tossed repeatedly against rocks by the waves. The carriage's driver was rescued from the cliffs. He had jumped to precarious safety as the carriage fell. He was now in prison, protesting his innocence, along with at least a score of smugglers and others from the Hall, the Grange or the village.

Tolliver had searched Titus's study and that of Sir Thaddeus, finding ample evidence of their involvement in theft, smuggling, and corruption of justice, as well as spying. He had left for London yesterday, and the troops of volunteers had ridden off—one to the north and one to the south—leaving only a handful of soldiers and a couple of excise men.

They had been burying local people all day yesterday; a dozen of them, some leaving wives and children. Luke, Kitty, and Paul had agreed they would pay for all the funerals and help all of the families no matter what side the men had chosen to support.

The bodies of several smugglers had been taken to Newcastle, and would be given a pauper's burial if nobody claimed them.

Luke threw a handful of dirt on each coffin in turn, and Paul did the same. They were the only mourners, though even that was an exaggeration. Paul was there for Luke. Luke mourned his uncle, but he couldn't honestly say he felt the loss of his aunt. As for Titus —the young man he had loved had never existed. He mourned the loss of the fictional character that Titus had created, nothing more.

Paul was standing over a small grave that had, until a few days ago, been marked by a gravestone with his name on it. Luke had ordered the stone removed, and had commissioned a new one with the name of the poor drowned baby whose mother had come to claim his body so long ago, and had been paid to go away and leave the baby to be buried as the little baron.

Luke put an arm over Paul's shoulders. "He will have his own name again," he said.

Paul quirked one corner of his mouth. "It just feels strange. That's all. It was my grave for nine years, and yet here I am."

"Here we all are, and those who conspired against us are gone," Luke pointed out. "Let's go home."

They had walked down from the Hall, and as they strolled back through the village, Luke noted the change since their first visit. Was it only days ago? It felt like months!

They were greeted by smiles. A few people called out good wishes or comments on the weather. A woman, her hastily dyed dress marking her as one of the recent widows, hurried up to ask Luke to pass on her thanks to Lady Kitty for the basket of food sent down from the Hall.

They walked beyond the gate into the woods and passed several farms, where the same shouted greetings prevailed. "Everyone seems much happier now," Paul observed, and he was right. The pall that had hung over the neighbourhood had lifted.

They passed the Pattison's place. Barn's wife and daughters had returned, and the Pattison family were joining Luke and his family for dinner tonight. Barn was out in his fields with some of his farm workers, cutting the spring barley. It looked as if it was going to be a good crop. Luke idly wondered how much of the barley would be malted for whisky.

Kitty was just coming out of the stable courtyard as they approached the front of Ormswood Hall, Millie at her shoulder. She changed direction when she saw Luke and Paul, and Luke hastened his steps.

"Our horses have arrived," she said when she was still ten paces away. They had been brought up by slow stages from Essex, taking fifteen days to make the journey in order to keep the horses in as good a condition as possible.

"Come and see," Kitty invited. She tucked her arm into his as they turned in that direction. Millie and Paul hurried ahead, but Luke was happy to take his time.

He had the woman he loved on his arm and life was good. Yes, he still had a lot of problems to untangle, and he and Kitty had agreed to loan Paul's estate some of the money that Kitty had brought into their marriage to help it to recover faster.

But not two months ago, he had been living in a gamekeeper's cottage in West Gloucestershire, trying to raise his brother as a gentleman, always nervous about being discovered.

Now, Paul was baron as he should be, and living in the home of his ancestors. Their enemies were gone. The smugglers' reign of terror had been ended. The neighbourhood was at last inclined to like them. He had a good friend living on his doorstep.

He had Kitty, and she had him. "You were right, you know," he said.

She looked up through her lashes, her smirk provocative. "About what, specifically?"

"About marrying. About us coming to Ormswood together. I did much better with you as my partner than I would have alone."

"Of course," his wife said. "Just as I do much better with you."

They were passing under the stone archway that led to the stable yard, and temporarily out of sight from both sides. Luke took Kitty into his arms and kissed her until they were both breathless.

"Partners, now and always," he said.

"Facing whatever comes together," said Kitty. She added, with a twinkle, "And winning."

"As long as I am with you, my love," Luke told her, "I have already won."

EPILOGUE

T wo agile ponies galloped down the field to where Kitty was picking blackberries with her daughter Anne and Millie's daughter Kate, while Luke was crouched at the edge of the stream, patiently teaching their son Julian to tickle trout.

Julian turned indignantly on the riders when they skidded to a halt a few feet from the stream and leapt to the ground. "You've scared the fish," he told his older brother, Steve.

"Never mind that," Steve said. "Uncle Paul is here!"

Julian's interest in the trout evaporated, and Anne dropped her bucket to rush to her brother. "He's here?"

Luke spoke sternly over the excited buzz of chatter. "Next time, Stephen and Mark, approach more quietly. You didn't lose us a catch, as it happens, but you could have. You both owe Julian an apology."

Mark Dixon, who was as good natured as his father, apologised immediately. "I am sorry, Juju."

"Yes, sorry." Steve waved off the apology. "But we were excited. Uncle Paul, Dad!"

Luke was clearly attempting to keep his stern mien but his eyes, as they met Kitty's, were dancing. Her husband was as excited to see his former ward as the children.

"If Julian accepts your apologies, young gentlemen, then you are forgiven, and we shall go to meet our traveller."

"Kate," Kitty said. "Leave those berries for Anne to pick up. She spilled them. Anne?"

Drooping a little, but mainly for effect, Anne returned to the spilled bucket, but it took no more than a moment for her and Kate to refill it, and they were soon on their way back across the field, the boys leading the ponies with Kate on Steve's horse and Anne on Mark's.

They left the ponies with a groom, the boys being released from the duty of seeing to their care on the promise of mucking out the stalls later.

Paul was coming out of the manor as they crossed the garden. Every time she saw him, Kitty had to adjust her thinking. At twenty-five, he was much the age Luke had been when he first came to Longford. He looked a lot like him, too. Perhaps an inch taller, and his hair a fraction darker, but the build and the eyes were the same.

She, though only a girl of thirteen, had thought Luke the handsomest man she had ever seen. Paul had been attracting female attention since before he went away to university, although, to be fair, while he flirted as easily as he breathed, he never allowed anyone to doubt that it was all light-hearted fun.

He stopped on the terrace to wait for them. "Kitty, how do you manage to look younger and more beautiful every time I see you? Anne, you are even lovelier than your Mama. And Kate, what a pretty picture! A beautiful girl on a charming pony."

"Flatterer," Kitty teased him, offering her cheek for his kiss. "Do those lines work for you?"

Paul winked, and offered his hand to Luke and then to Julian. "I have already greeted these two scoundrels," he confided, with a casual wave towards Mark and Steve. "Whereupon they immediately took off on their beasts to tell you I was here and spoil the surprise." He scowled, but his grin took the edge off it, and the boys only grinned back.

"We are surprised," Kitty assured him, "and enormously pleased. You are, of course, welcome any time, Paul."

"But what am I doing here?" Paul finished, though Luke doubted that Kitty had been going to say that. "Is it not reason enough that my family have abandoned me at Ormswood Hall for the joys of Horncroft Manor?" He attempted to pout, but the act failed to convince, for that grin kept breaking through.

"Something has you looking like the cat that got the cream," Luke observed.

The grin broadened, but Paul shot his eyes to the children and shook his head slightly.

"Children," said Kitty. "Take the berries to Cook, please, and then wash and change. You may then, with his permission, take your uncle captive for an hour before you return to your lessons. Luke, I shall go and change likewise, and you shall take Paul to your study. I'll have them bring in ale and sandwiches."

"Will you come with us for a minute?" Paul asked, as the children hurried on their way. "There is something I want to tell you both."

Kitty put her hand on the arm Paul offered, and allowed him to escort her to Luke's study, where he made a ceremony of conducting her to a chair. He was stalling. Kitty and Luke exchanged another laughing glance, and made a silent agreement to let him take his time.

He asked about the children, and about Millie and George, who had remained Kitty's maid and Luke's valet even after their marriage, but who were more friends than servants.

They answered his questions and asked after the servants and neighbours at Ormswood Hall. It had been two years since they had moved permanently to Luke's estate in the Tyne Valley, but they still had many ties to Ormswood.

"Do you remember," Paul said, in an uncanny echo of Kitty's thoughts, "when you told me you had decided to move permanently to Horncroft Manor?"

"Of course," she replied.

"You said it was time to leave Ormswood Hall to me and its eventual mistress," Paul continued. "Well, Kitty, I've chosen her."

Whatever Kitty had expected, that wasn't it. "You have chosen a bride, Paul?"

Paul turned to Luke. "I have found my partner, Luke. You told me to wait until I found the woman who would be my friend, my ally, my lover. Who would stand beside me come what may. Who would make me stronger and better, not just because she loves me, but because she thinks and acts with me and we are more than twice as powerful together than either of us apart. You told me you have that with Kitty. Lorna is my Kitty."

Kitty swallowed the lump in her throat. "I am so happy for you, Paul. And when do we get to meet this paragon?"

Paul hesitated and looked at his hands. "Right now? She is upstairs. I shall go and get her."

Luke and Kitty stared at one another as Paul left the room.

"Upstairs?" Kitty asked.

"Are they married, do you think?" asked Luke.

Kitty shook her head. "I do not know. But I do know that Paul is your son, or as good as. He is level headed, intelligent, reliable and a good judge of character. If this Lorna is his chosen mate, then she is our sister, Luke." She stepped into her husband's arms, and tucked her head under his chest.

"We will face whatever comes together, my love." His breath blew across the top of her hair. "As Paul just reminded me, we are partners, allies, friends, lovers."

A noise outside hinted at the approach of the younger couple. Luke dropped his arms and Kitty turned to face the door with him at her side.

They entered, surrounded by children. The young lady on Paul's arm was holding Anne's hand, and Millie and George were bringing up the rear.

"I've taken the liberty of ordering champagne, Luke," George said. "I believe we have something to celebrate?"

Paul, beaming, presented Lorna to Kitty, and Luke to Lorna. "My wife," he said, with great pride. The butler arrived with the champagne and even the children had a little, even if just a thimbleful.

"Married?" Luke asked again, and Paul reddened slightly.

"Married," he confirmed. "Let me explain, and I will tell you at the outset that it was quite an adventure!"

THE END

Readers, I had no idea that Paul was going to use the epilogue to surprise Kitty and Luke with his new bride. Which means I now have to write the story! I have the elements of it, and I know it begins on the drovers' roads that cross from the borders in the northwest of Northumberland, when Paul comes across a broken-down carriage misled by the word "road", an eloping couple who are becoming disenchanted with one another, and the reluctant bride's poor relation cousin. There may be a bit of illegal whisky involved. Follow my blog or subscribe to my newsletter and be among the first to know when it is available.

AUTHOR'S NOTE

MAGISTRATES COURTS

There's a bit of a fashion for Bow Street runners in Regency romance. I thought I'd have one myself, come to arrest my hero on a false charge of murder. Except when I looked into it, I found out they weren't necessarily from Bow Street, and they weren't called runners.

Bow Street Magistrate's Court was the prototype, of course. Henry Fielding and his brother established the runners. (They preferred to be called Principal Officers, since they thought 'runners' made them sound like servants.)

The model was successful, and in 1792, more than forty years after Fielding started his experiment, the government passed the Middlesex Justices Act. This established seven more police offices. Each had three paid magistrates and up to six paid officers or constables.

So, in Westminster, there were Bow Street, Great Marlborough Street, and Queen's Square. I picked Great Marlborough Street, which was closest to the townhouse where my hero was staying.

Police offices in the rest of London were Worship Street in Shore-ditch, Lambeth Street in Whitechapel, Union Hall in Southwark, and also Shadwell and Hatton Garden. In 1798, the Thames Police Office (the river police) was opened in Wapping. There had been a couple of changes by the time of my story, in 1813, but good to know!

My hero's powerful friends paid for him to have a private room instead of being in the police cells, where he countered two attempts to murder him. Corruption was a significant issue with some police offices, so a bribe to look the other way was not unlikely. He appeared before the three magistrates in a preliminary hearing a few days after he was arrested, and the case was dismissed when the person he was meant to have murdered stood up in court, alive and well. Other cases heard that day might have received an immediate judgement and penalty for a minor crime, or been bound over to appear at a full court hearing before a judge and possibly a jury.

They were different times, but already shifting in a direction that is more familiar to us today.

By the way, when the Great Marlborough police office closed in 1839, as the Metropolitan Police took over all policing duties, the building continued in service as a Magistrate's Court. A case against John Lennon of Beatles fame for exhibiting sexually explicit material was heard in this court in the 1970s. It is now a boutique hotel, and the courtroom itself is an Asian Fusion restaurant.

NORTHUMBERLAND, WHISKY AND SMUGGLERS

The Flavour of Our Deeds is partially set in Northumbria.

I wanted my hero and heroine far away from their natural allies, faced on all sides by enemies and uncertain who to trust. Learning a bit about Northumbria introduced all sorts of new plot elements.

For example, did you know that the Coquet Dale area of Northumbria was a whisky distilling area (whisky is the Irish, Scots and, as it happens, English borderlands spelling of what the US call whiskey). Coquet Dale, in what is now the Northumberland National Park, was full of illegal stills that exported their product not just south into the rest of Northumbria, west into Cumbria, and further afield in the United Kingdom, but also by ship to the Lowlands. The distillers were supported and protected by the locals.

The smugglers carried whisky and wool overseas and brought back genever (Dutch gin) and luxury goods from the continent. They had havens in fishing villages like Boulmer, on which I have based my own fictional fishing village, close to the shore. I've removed a few aristocratic families—in my story, the Earls of Grey and their home, Howick Hall, is not mentioned, and nor is Alnwick Castle, or the Duke of Northumberland whose residence the castle was. The sea caves are real, and were used by the smugglers. The excise men did, indeed, have a base at Berwick-Upon-Tweed, and another at Newcastle, and were too few in number to make much of a dent in the trade.

I would have loved to set the story closer to the Roman wall, but I needed limestone for a good caving system that could be improved by enthusiastic tunnellers. A vast maze of caves was once discovered under Alnwick Moor, and has now been lost again, but caving experts believe there may be many more tunnels and caves than those shallow hollows known to our modern cavers. I've invented some, putting it in limestone country to make it plausible.

I'd also have loved to include the Holy Island of Lindisfarne. Maybe the plot elves can find a way to take Paul and Lorna there.

MILITIA AND VOLUNTEERS

When including a soldier or a military unit in a Regency romance, an author has to ask who was in the area at the time, and what sort of military unit was it. At the time, the regular army was heavily committed overseas, in Portugal and Spain, in India, in the Americas—though, depending on the year, there were regiments who were not on active duty, or who were on home defence duty. The two other options were the militia and the volunteers. Think of the militia as a sort of army reserve, and the volunteers as the home guard. Not quite, but sort of.

The regular army and the militia had long been a feature of

Britain. The army was relatively small before the Napoleonic threat —just 45,000 men, two thirds of whom were stationed abroad. They had recruiting issues, and the rank and file were notoriously those who had few other choices—the poor, the unskilled, those who didn't fit in.

The militia in Georgian Britain, by contrast, were part-time soldiers serving one month a year (that is, one week a quarter) in peacetime. There had been a militia since 871, so they were an older establishment than the army itself. By the mid-18th century, every county had to supply, and pay for, a certain number of militia men. They were chosen by ballot, though they had the option to pay someone else to serve in their place. They had to serve for four years and did one week's training four times a year. They served in their home county, and could be called out to deal with an emergency.

With the rising threat from France, the government first passed a law to increase the militia by a further 60,000 men. The innovators didn't provide any money, so the spaces were filled by those who could afford to pay for their own uniforms and weapons. In other words, the upper and middle classes. Then, after a major military defeat in 1797, the government called for each county to find out how many men were within their borders, and how many would volunteer to defend Britain.

They were stunned by the response. By 1803, 380,000 men had volunteered. The officers tended to be from the upper classes, and the ranks from the lower middle class. Volunteers were exempt from military service and from taxes. They committed themselves to local defence in case of invasion or insurrection, but otherwise remained civilians.

The volunteer forces proved to be a problem. The State couldn't afford to outfit and train them, and the small local volunteer forces operated outside of military rule, and often refused to serve outside of their own area. There were also manpower problems in the other military units, since men would rather be volunteers than militia, and militia than regular army.

The government went down the compulsory service line, and between 1806 and 1815, most volunteer units were disbanded. In many cases their members were taken into militia units. However, this was not the last time Britain raised volunteer forces to its defence.

REGENCY BOOKS BY JUDE KNIGHT

A TWIST UPON A REGENCY TALE

Fairy tales (loosely) reinterpreted as Regency romances, but with magical elements transformed into natural happenings and the role of hero and heroine reversed.

Lady Beast's Bridegroom (Book 1 in *A Twist Upon a Regency Tale*)

Is the love of Beauty and his Lady Beast strong enough to overcome prejudice, hatred, and rejection?

The Talons of a Lyon (Part of the Lyon's Den Connected World)

Lance promised Mrs Dove Lyon he would take Lady Frogmore from Pond Street into High Society. Her nasty relatives are determined he will fail.

PUBLISHED APRIL 2023

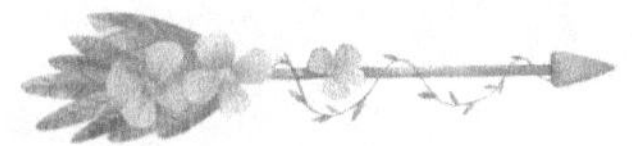

One Perfect Dance (Book 2 in *A Twist Upon a Regency Tale*)

For sixteen years, Ash has owed Regina a dance. His step-brothers will do anything to keep him from the ball.

PUBLISHED MAY 2023

Snowy and the Seven Doves (Book 3 in *A Twist Upon a Regency Tale*)

The hero raised in a brothel. The heroine born to wealth and title. The villain who wants to destroy the first and own the second.

PUBLISHED AUGUST 2023

ALSO IN THIS SERIES AND *PERCHANCE TO DREAM* (NOVEMBER 2023)

THE GOLDEN REDEPENNINGS SERIES

True love is rare and elusive, but they won't settle for less

Candle's Christmas Chair (A novella in *The Golden Redepennings* series)

They are separated by social standing and malicious lies. He has until Christmas to convince her to give their love another chance.

Gingerbread Bride (A novella in *The Golden Redepennings* series)

Mary runs from an unwanted marriage and finds adventure, danger and her girlhood hero, coming once more to her rescue.

To Claim the Long-Lost Lover: The Diamond and the Doctor (Book 3 in The Return of the Mountain King series)

The beauty known as the Winderfield Diamond hides a ruinous secret. Society's newest viscount holds the key.

To Tame the Wild Rake: The Saint and the Sinner (Book 4 in The Return of the Mountain King series)

The whole world knows Aldridge is a wicked sinner. The ton has labelled Charlotte a saint for her virtue and good works. Appearances can be deceptive.

Paradise Triptych (A collection in The Return of the Mountain King series)

Long ago, when they were young, James and Eleanor were deeply in love. But their families tore them apart and they went on to marry other people. This set of two novellas and a set of memoirs tells their story.

LION'S ZOO

New series to be published from June 2023, about officers from an elite cadre of exploring officers returning to England and find love and danger.

Chaos Come Again, PUBLICATION IN JUNE 2023

Grasp the Thorn, PUBLICATION IN JULY 2023

OTHER NOVELS

A Baron for Becky

She was a fallen woman. How could the men who loved her help set her back on her feet?

Revealed in Mist

As spy and enquiry agent, Prue and David worked to uncover secrets, while hiding a few of their own.

House of Thorns

His rose thief bride comes with a scandal that threatens to tear them apart.

OTHER NOVELLAS

The Husband Gamble [This novella]

When the pawn becomes Queen, she and the opposing King will both win the game of love.

Lord Calne's Christmas Ruby

One wealthy merchant's heiress with an aversion to fortune hunters. One an impoverished earl with a twisted hand. Combine and stir with one villainous rector.

A Suitable Husband

A chef from the slums, however talented, is no fit mate for the cousin of a duke, however distant. But Cedrica can dream.

The Beast Next Door (A novella in the Bluestocking Belles collection *Valentines from Bath*)

In all the assemblies and parties, no-one Charis met could ever match the beast next door.

A Dream Come True (A novella in the Bluestocking Belles collection Storm & Shelter)

The tempest that batters Barnaby Somerville's village is the latest but not the least of his challenges. He does not expect the storm that will batter his heart.

Lord Cuckoo Comes Home (A novella in the Bluestocking Belles collection *Desperate Daughters*)

Two people who have never fitted in just might be a perfect fit.

LUNCH-LENGTH READS: STORY COLLECTIONS

Hand-Turned Tales and Lost in the Tale

A double handful of short stories and novellas, free from most eretailers. Try the range of Jude's imagination one bite at a time, in a lunch-length read.

If Mistletoe Could Tell Tales

A repackaging of six published Christmas stories: four novellas and two novelettes. Because nothing enhances the magic of Christmas like the magic of love.

Hearts in the Land of Ferns

Five stories all set in New Zealand: two historical and three contemporary suspense. All That Glisters has been published in Hand-Turned Tales. The other four have all been published in multi-author collections, but never before in a collection of Jude Knight stories.

Chasing the Tale and Chasing the Tale: Volume 11

Short stories just long enough for a lunch or coffee break. In volume 1: Nine Regency plus one colonial New Zealand and one medieval Scotland. In volume 2: mostly Regency, with one Victorian New Zealand. Multiple tropes, catastrophes and barriers on the way to a happy ending.